TROUBLE IN PRIOR'S FORD

TROUBLE IN PRIOR'S FORD

Eve Houston

SPHERE

First published in Great Britain as a paperback original in 2010 by Sphere
Reprinted 2010, 2011

A CIP catalogue record for this book
is available from the British Library.

ISBN 978-0-7515-4207-3

Typeset in Bembo by Palimpsest Book Production Limited,
Grangemouth, Stirlingshire
Printed and bound in Great Britain by
Clays Ltd, St Ives plc

Sphere
An imprint of
Little, Brown Book Group
100 Victoria Embankment
London EC4Y 0DY

An Hachette UK Company
www.hachette.co.uk

www.littlebrown.co.uk

This book is for
ALASTAIR
a special son

Acknowledgements

Sometimes I feel as though a writer is like someone who works in a gold mine, continually trying to seek out those precious little nuggets of experience and knowledge locked in other people's brains.

I shamelessly use everyone I come across, and this time my thanks and eternal gratitude go to the following good and patient friends:

Rachel Picard, for being a friend, for being French and for taking the time to help me to work out the French sentences I needed for this book. And for not laughing at me as you did it.

Pat Anslow of the West Kilbride Initiative for teaching me about wormeries and for being so enthusiastic and caring about worms that I ended up loving the little creatures myself.

I also want to acknowledge a yellow-headed wee laddie called Oor Wullie – Scotland's Peter Pan. Oor Wullie (aka Our Willie to non-Scots) is seventy-three years old, having been created in 1936 by R D Low, then editor of D C Thomson & Co, the Dundee-based Scottish publishing house, but to his millions of fans all over the world Willie is still aged about ten; a mischievous wee scamp dressed in jersey and dungarees (overalls), sitting on his upturned bucket as he dreams up his next venture.

Oor Wullie appears regularly in D C Thomson's *Sunday Post* newspaper, and has his own Christmas annual every other year, taking turn with another popular and loved D C Thomson creation, the Broon (Brown) family.

If you haven't met Oor Wullie you haven't lived.

Main Characters

Fliss and Hector Ralston-Kerr – Hector is the Laird of Prior's Ford and lives with his wife Fliss and their son Lewis in ramshackle Linn Hall

Genevieve (Ginny) Whitelaw – Is helping to restore the old kitchen garden at Lin Hall

The Fishers – Joe and Gracie Fisher are the landlord and landlady of the local pub, the Neurotic Cuckoo. They live on the premises with their widowed daughter **Alison Greenlees** and her young son **Jamie**

Jenny and Andrew Forsyth – Live in the private housing estate, River Walk, with their young son, **Calum** and Jenny's teenage, rebellious step-daughter by a previous marriage, **Maggie Cameron**

Helen and Duncan Campbell – Helen records the village news for a local newspaper and is also, secretly, the newspaper's agony aunt columnist. Duncan is the gardener at the Linn

Hall, the 'big house'. They have four children: **Gregor**, **Gemma**, **Lachlan** and **Irene**

Clarissa Ramsay – Lives in Willow Cottage. A retired teacher who is rebuilding her life after discovering that her late husband betryaed her with her best friend

Sam Brennan – Lives in Rowan Cottage and runs the local Village Store with his partner, **Marcy Copleton**. They have a somewhat stormy relationship

The Reverend Naomi Hennessey – The local Church of Scotland minister, part Jamaican, part English. Lives in the manse with her Jamaican godson, **Ethan**

The McNairs of Tarbethill Farm – **Bert** and **Jess McNair** are struggling to keep the family farm going with the help of their two sons: **Victor**, who cares more about money than the land and **Ewan**, whose deep love is shared between the farm and the local publican's daughter, **Alison Greenlees**

Alastair Marshall – An artist, lives in a small farm cottage on the outskirts of the village. Although **Clarissa Ramsay** is some twenty years his senior, Alastair has strong feelings for her

The McDonalds – **Jinty** and **Tom McDonald** live with their large family on the village's council housing estate. Jinty is a willing helper at Linn House, and also cleans the village hall and the school, while **Tom** is keen on gambling and frequenting the Neurotic Cuckoo

Molly Ewing – Lewis Ralston-Kerr's girlfriend, and mother of his baby daughter, **Rowena Chloe**. Molly looks forward to being Lady of the Manor one day, but in the meantime, her love of travelling worries **Lewis**. The prospect of Molly as Lady of the Manor worries Lewis's mother, **Fliss**

TROUBLE IN
PRIOR'S FORD

1

'I'm taking you to the pub for a drink,' Clarissa Ramsay said as she and Alastair Marshall left the village hall. 'You deserve it for courage above and beyond the call of duty.'

'I only saw to the slides. You were the one who had to give the talk.'

'I didn't mean just that, I meant you having to judge the rock-cake competition as well. I didn't realise we would be expected to judge things,' said Clarissa, who had had to deal with the home-made jam competition.

'The rock-cakes were good . . . well, most of them. It was the dirty looks I got from the people who didn't win that unnerved me. You were great,' Alastair said admiringly as they turned into Adam Crescent and began to skirt the half-moon village green. 'As cool as a cucumber, even at question time.'

'Being a school teacher trained me for every eventuality, including dealing with parents. To be honest, I quite enjoyed myself, but I'm sure you were bored to tears, ploughing through all those letters I sent while I was away, then having to listen to it all over again while we sorted out the photographs for the talk . . . and, again, this afternoon.'

'I've enjoyed every minute of it.' He had, more than she realised. Clarissa had been brought to Prior's Ford by her domineering husband when he retired; he had died suddenly a mere seven months later. Alastair, an artist, had come across her one wet day, sitting on a stile in the middle of a field, rain-soaked, wretched, and with no idea of what to do next with her life.

When he took her to his shabby farm cottage on the fringe of the village he hadn't realised at the time that it was to be one of the most important days of his life. Although Clarissa was in her fifties and Alastair in his mid-thirties, they had become firm friends. With Alastair's encouragement, Clarissa had regained her confidence to the extent that she had rented out her cottage for a year and gone off to travel the world, an adventure that resulted in being asked to give a talk about her experiences to the Prior's Ford Women's Institute.

It was mid-April. Easter was behind them but the schools were still on holiday. A group of teenagers loitered by the war memorial on the green, and as Clarissa and Alastair neared the pub a couple detached themselves from the group and came towards them.

'Hi,' Alastair said amiably as they passed. The dark-haired girl mumbled a 'Hello,' back, while the youth with her, his head covered with dyed-blonde spiky hair and with three hoops through the lobe of one ear, shot them a swift sidelong glance that seemed to Clarissa to take in an incredible amount of detail in a single second.

'Who's that pretty girl?' she asked when the youngsters were out of earshot. 'I've seen her around the village a few times since I got back.'

2

'That's Maggie Cameron, Jenny Forsyth's stepdaughter. Apparently Jenny acquired her as part of a brief marriage before she and Andrew met. Her first husband died and Maggie was raised by his parents, but her grandfather's suffering from ill health, so she's come to stay with the Forsyths. The lad's not local but I've seen them together a few times. Must be her boyfriend.' Alastair, tall and lanky, reached out a long arm and pushed the pub door open, holding it in place while he eased back to let her pass. 'After you, ma'am.'

Jemima Puddleduck skimmed over the bridge and in no time at all was bowling into Prior's Ford. Ginny Whitelaw heaved an enormous sigh of contentment and slowed Jemima down so she could look her fill.

The village had not changed in the seven months or so since she had last seen it. The sunshine on this mid-April day gave the well-cared-for houses and shops a scrubbed-fresh look. The primary school, the community hall, the village store, butcher's shop and church were all as she remembered.

Ginny drove past the green before easing the steering wheel to the right. Jemima, obliging as ever, turned into Adam Crescent. The first house at this end of the crescent was Willow Cottage, where Ginny and her mother had stayed the year before. 'Hello, you,' she said affectionately to the house, neat and tidy behind its little front garden, as she passed.

At the centre of the crescent a young woman swept the pavement before the village pub, a long freshly whitewashed building. 'Hi, Alison,' Ginny called through the open passenger window as she stopped the caravanette. 'Remember me?'

Alison Greenlees stooped to the window. 'Hello, Ginny – working at Linn Hall again this summer?'

3

'I am indeed; back to see how the kitchen garden's been getting on without me.' Ginny climbed out of the cara-vanette and walked round the bonnet to lean against the passenger door, glancing up at the painted sign above the pub's open door. The Neurotic Cuckoo, it proclaimed, beneath a painting of a bird that might or might not be a cuckoo, but certainly seemed to be troubled. 'Good old Cuckoo,' she said affectionately, 'I'll be in for a pint tonight.'

'You're welcome to have one now,' Alison offered. 'Mum's gone to the Women's Institute meeting, Dad's taken Jamie fishing and Alastair's having a drink in the bar with Mrs Ramsay – the lady who rented her cottage to your mother last year.'

'Are there many fish in the river?'

'I said fishing, not actually catching. Jamie's got his own wee net and he just likes splashing around with it. Coming inside?'

'Thanks, but I'd like to get settled in first.' Ginny studied the other girl, noting the healthy colour and sparkling eyes in a face that had been thin and pale last year. 'You look well. In fact, as a gardener, I'd say you're positively blooming.'

Alison's parents, Joe and Gracie Fisher, had become the landlord and landlady of the Neurotic Cuckoo almost fifteen months earlier, following the death of Alison's husband. A barman in the Fishers' Glasgow pub, he had been murdered by a group of drunken youths he had evicted earlier. When Ginny first arrived in the village Alison had been thin and withdrawn, but over the winter she had gained much-needed weight, her brown hair, in a page-boy that almost reached her shoulders, was glossy and the once down-turned mouth now smiled easily.

'I'm not a pale city girl any more. The country air suits me.'

'It certainly does. So . . . how's Ewan?' Ginny asked with a lift of the eyebrows.

'He's fine.' Alison's tone was carefully casual, but her colour heightened slightly.

'Will I see you both in the drama club's show this summer?'

'I'm in it, but Ewan's too busy now he's got his new wormery to see to as well as working hard on the farm. The wormery's coming along well.'

'That's good. I'll have to go and see it some time. Still walking out together, are you?'

'I wouldn't call it that. He's busy there and I'm busy here.'

'So you don't see much of each other these days?'

'Well – Jamie likes being taken to the farm and Mrs McNair's very kind to him,' Alison said evasively. 'It's good to see you back again, Ginny.'

'It's good to *be* back,' Ginny said warmly. 'I'll be in tonight for that drink.' Then, as she settled into the driving seat and switched on the engine, she said, 'You might have stopped blushing by then.'

'I used to be quite intimidated by Alexandra,' Clarissa was saying in the lounge bar. 'She was at university when I first met her, but even then she was so cool and confident, but when I called in on her on my way back home from my travels, I felt she was much more human.' She fixed Alastair with the sort of gaze she must once have used to wrest the truth from reluctant pupils. 'I can't help wondering if you had anything to do with that.'

'Me? Good Lord, no . . . How could I?' He tried hard to meet her eyes, but found it difficult. 'I scarcely know the woman.'

'She mentioned you quite frequently, as it happens. I don't know how you managed to break through her protective shell, but she likes you.'

'She scares me,' Alastair said firmly. It wasn't entirely a lie. The first time he encountered Clarissa's stepdaughter and stepson at the dinner party where Clarissa announced her intention to set off to see the world, cool efficient Alexandra had terrified him. But while her stepmother was away she had paid an unexpected visit to the village and Alastair had found himself helping her, as he had helped Clarissa. It was a surprise to find that even a cold beauty like Alexandra Ramsay could fall in love with the wrong man – in this case, a married man – and get hurt. But he had given his word to keep her secret, and Alastair never broke his word as Clarissa knew.

'It's so good to be back again,' she said, letting him off the hook. 'I can't believe that when Keith died I almost went back down south. Going off on my own to see the world made me realise where my home really is – right here, with genuine friends.'

'I'm glad to hear it,' he said lightly, knowing she had no idea how much he meant the words. During her absence he had hungered for her letters, tearing them open when they arrived, devouring the contents, looking again and again at the enclosed photographs showing the real Clarissa emerging from the dull-coloured chrysalis that had been her marriage to a man who, he suspected from comments made by Alexandra, had not been faithful to her.

She had left Prior's Ford a quiet, middle-aged ex-teacher, dressed conventionally, with brown hair worn in a tidy knot at the nape of her neck. She had returned looking at least ten years younger, her hair cut in a soft feathery style, skin glowing and eyes sparkling; a woman not afraid to wear bright colours and modern styles.

The problem facing Alastair Marshall now was that she had left the village as a good friend, and had returned as more than that.

And given the difference in their ages, he doubted if he would ever be able to tell her of his true feelings.

2

Jemima Puddleduck passed between identical gatehouses originally built for the head gardener and head groom and swept up the long driveway leading to Linn Hall.

'Wow,' Ginny said as she saw the unexpected activity at the front of the building. Two vans were parked on the great gravel sweep, and the honey-coloured stone walls were covered by scaffolding. Several men were busy working on the three tiers of windows.

She continued following the drive to the rear of the house, where she raised her eyebrows at the smart people-carrier parked on the flagged courtyard. She couldn't see Lewis Ralston-Kerr wasting a penny of the money his impoverished parents had been gifted on a big car. Then, as she brought Jemima to a standstill by the stables, she spotted his shabby little car lurking behind the strange one.

Once out of the caravanette she couldn't resist taking a quick peek at the kitchen garden before announcing her arrival. The year before, she had rescued the large walled area from obscurity and gone some way to restoring it to its former glory. It had been her special project and she longed to see how well it had come through the winter. She had almost reached the gate when she heard an odd mixture of heavy breathing and scratching behind her. Before she could turn to investigate something banged against the backs of her thighs, and then she was on the ground, slightly winded and being smothered in some sort of woolly blanket while her face was washed by a warm flannel.

'Muffin!' a voice yelled. 'Get off, you daft mutt!'

The blanket and flannel suddenly retreated and Ginny was free to roll over on to her back and blink up at Lewis Ralston-Kerr.

'Sorry, Ginny, he's just— Muffin, stop it, I said! Too friendly. Here . . .' He hauled her to her feet.

'What is it?' Ginny asked of the large creature gambolling round the two of them. 'And what did you call it?'

'Muffin. Silly, I know, but Mrs Paterson – the old lady who owned him – apparently thought he looked like a little toasted muffin when she got him as a puppy.'

'So it's a dog?' Ginny brushed herself down. 'He looks more like a Shetland pony having a bad-hair day, or perhaps a great pile of unravelled double-knitting wool that's taken on a life of its own.'

'Now that you mention it, Mrs Paterson was never seen without knitting in her hands, even in church. Perhaps she knitted him herself. She died, poor old soul, and nobody was willing to take Muffin in. So, as this is the perfect place for a large dog, we offered. I like the wheels,' Lewis said.

'Meet Jemima Puddleduck. She's more useful than the little car I bought last year.' Ginny patted the caravanette affectionately. 'Third hand, so I got her for a reasonable price. She's been well looked after, so everything's working.

And it means that I can be completely independent. Right now she's packed with plants for the kitchen garden.'

'Good. I'm glad you're going to see it through another year.'

'Things look busy at the front of the house.'

'Stage two,' Lewis said happily. 'All the windows are being dealt with now. It's costing more than we budgeted for because they've got to be restored rather than replaced, but once the roof and windows are sorted we'll be in a position to apply for a loan to start on the interior. Come on in and say hello.'

Ginny eyed the people-carrier. 'You've got visitors.'

'It's Molly and her parents and sister – and Rowena Chloe, of course. They're all going on holiday for a couple of weeks and we're looking after the baby while they're away.'

'Oh.' As Lewis led her towards the house Ginny felt her excitement at returning to Prior's Ford begin to evaporate at the news that his red-headed girlfriend and mother of his daughter was on the other side of the kitchen door.

'Ginny's arrived,' Lewis announced, leading her into the large kitchen.

While Jinty McDonald, who lived in the village and helped out at Linn Hall, poured tea for the newcomer from a large battered metal teapot, Fliss Ralston-Kerr, Lewis's mother, began to introduce her visitors to each other, but was interrupted by the plump red-haired woman sitting opposite Ginny.

'No need to be so elaborate about it, Fliss pet, we're all family here. I'm Val, dear,' she told Ginny, 'Molly's mum, and this,' she laid a possessive hand on the arm of the burly man by her side, 'is my husband, Tony. You know Molly, don't you?'

10

'Hello, Ginny.' Molly Ewing still wore her glowing red hair in two long plaits and looked too young to be a mother. 'How are things?'

'OK. You?'

'Great!'

'And that's our other daughter, Stella,' Val prattled on, indicating the bored-looking teenager reading a book at the end of the table.

'Hi,' Stella said briefly before returning to her book. She had none of her sister's or her mother's lush roundness, and her hair was more auburn than Molly's, though they had the same green eyes.

'And this,' Lewis said proudly, lifting the baby from Molly's lap, 'is Rowena Chloe. Isn't she gorgeous? Just like her mother.'

As he dropped a kiss on her soft red curls the baby reached out to pat his face with the hand that held a half-chewed crust. It fell to the ground and a loud gulp told that Muffin had claimed it. Rowena's round little face puckered up and she let out a protesting wail as she reached down to the dog.

'Never mind, pet, I'll get you another,' Jinty cooed, setting a mug of tea before Ginny.

'Isn't this a grand place?' Val Ewing rattled on. 'I remember when our Molly worked here that summer, she said in her letters that it was the grandest place she had ever seen. Like a palace.'

'A tumbledown palace,' Fliss Ralston-Kerr said ruefully.

'But that's all behind you, isn't it, now that you've got all that money given to you to do it up. It's going to be lovely once it's finished. We can't believe that one day our Molly's going to live here, mistress of Linn Hall, can we, Tony? It's like a fairytale!' Val beamed round the table.

11

Someone was missing, Ginny realised. Mr Ralston-Kerr was probably hiding in the large pantry used by the family as a living room, since the usual family rooms were too chilly, even in summer. A shy man, he must feel quite intimidated by the Ewings, who seemed — Molly and her parents at least — to have taken over the place.

'Molly said you're Meredith Whitelaw's daughter. Is that right?' Val asked and, when Ginny nodded, went on, 'That must be lovely. *Bridlington Close* on the telly hasn't been the same since she left. What's she doing now?'

'Filming a television series.' After her character in a television soap had been killed off the year before, Meredith Whitelaw, in search of somewhere to sulk, had rented Willow Cottage in Prior's Ford. Ginny had accompanied her, out of pity for her humiliated mother rather than affection. During her time in the village, Meredith had played havoc with the local drama group before being offered a role in a costume drama for television and departing as suddenly as she had arrived.

'When can we see her in her new play?' Jinty held out a fresh crust to Rowena Chloe, who snatched at it. 'We're all looking forward to it.'

'Quite soon, I think. They've almost finished filming.'

'Is she starring?'

'I believe so.' Over the winter Ginny had been working as a gardener for the local council in Leeds while her mother had been filming in London. On the few occasions when they met, Meredith had been vague about her work, claiming that talking too much about the character she was playing could spoil the essential concentration needed before the cameras. Since Ginny was as interested in television dramas as her mother was in gardening, she had not asked any questions.

'It was lovely having a celebrity living in the village,' Jinty told Val. 'She's a very nice lady. She helped Mr Pearce with the drama club, and she gave acting lessons to my eldest girl, Steph. Steph wants to be an actress. Did you know,' she turned to Ginny, 'that your mum's told her to get in touch if she decides to go to drama school and needs a good reference? Steph'll be finishing with school in July.'

'No, I didn't. She must have been impressed.' Ginny meant it; it wasn't like her mother to hold out a helping hand unless she thought it would eventually be worth her while.

'A really lovely lady.' Jinty nodded.

'Well, I just wish she was still here,' Val enthused. 'I'd love to meet a real live television actress.'

Ginny was no longer listening; she was watching Lewis, noticing how comfortable he seemed to be with the baby in his arms. She envied Molly for having found him.

Maggie Cameron took her new boyfriend's hand as they reached the bus stop. He pulled his fingers free at once, but as the bus taking him home to Kirkcudbright came into view he turned her to face him and gave her a long, lingering kiss, sticking his tongue into her mouth and holding her close by clamping both hands on her bottom. She didn't care for that sort of kiss, but pretended that she did. She still couldn't believe that Ryan, seventeen years old, in the year above her at school, and handsome too with his fair hair and piercing blue eyes, had chosen her from all the girls who fancied him. She was so lucky but at the same time terrified of letting him down and being dumped.

'See ya,' he said, breaking away as the bus arrived. He leapt up the steps, one shoulder nudging aside a woman who had just alighted.

'See ya,' Maggie called after him.

'They've got no manners these days, young people,' she heard the woman complain to her friend as they walked away. Maggie shrugged and grinned. They could say what they liked – what did she care?

The past fifteen months hadn't been kind to her. An orphan raised by her grandparents until her grandfather's ill-health made it impossible for her to stay, she had been moved from Dundee to Prior's Ford to live with her step-mother, Jenny Forsyth. Jenny's apparent desperation for a sweet, loving daughter had alienated Maggie, who retaliated by being as difficult as she could. It was like living on a battlefield and, deep down, she had been wretched until Ryan had come into her life. For the first time since arriving in Prior's Ford, Maggie Cameron was happy.

But she had a lot to learn. She quite liked Alastair Marshall, an artist who lived in an old farm cottage outside the village, and there was nothing wrong with Mrs Ramsay even though she had been a teacher. She had said hello to them earlier without thinking, and then had to endure merciless teasing from Ryan for behaving like 'a nice little girlie'.

Ryan was so cool, and she was so nerdy! As she headed down River Lane to the smart housing estate where she now lived, she vowed to herself that she would work hard to become the sort of girl Ryan wanted her to be.

'Is that you, Maggie?' Jenny Forsyth called when she heard the front door open.

'Yeah.'

'Cup of tea? I was just thinking of putting the kettle on.'

'No.'

Jenny went to the kitchen door as Maggie began to climb the stairs. 'I'm making a risotto for tonight. OK?'

'Fine.'

'Had a nice afternoon?'

'OK. Ryan came over.'

'That's nice. You should have invited him for dinner. We'd like to meet him.'

Without answering, Maggie continued on up the stairs and went into her room, closing the door loudly behind her. This was her sanctuary, and nobody else was allowed in. Here, in her own space, she could be herself.

'You should have invited him for dinner. We'd like to meet him.' She imitated her stepmother's anxious-to-please voice, and then shared a laugh with her reflection in the mirror.

Her Ryan coming here for dinner and meeting that lot downstairs?

As if!

3

The kitchen at Linn Hall seemed unusually quiet when the Ewings had left. Jinty made a fresh pot of tea and Ginny washed and dried the mugs. Fliss, flustered by the hugs and kisses she had been subjected to from Molly and both her parents, subdued her hair, which was never really tidy, with agitated little pats. Hector, who had been dragged from the pantry like a whelk from its cosy shell to bid farewell to the guests, collapsed into his usual chair with a sigh of relief.

'Molly and her parents are very . . . demonstrative, aren't they?' Fliss said weakly.

'You get folk like that. Not my sort of thing. Tea, Mr Ralston-Kerr?' Jinty asked, and filled his mug when he nodded. Then, as Lewis came back from seeing the Ewings on their way, Rowena Chloe in his arms, 'Tea, Lewis?'

'Why not?' He tucked the baby into the old-fashioned high chair retrieved from one of the lumber rooms and sat down beside Ginny. 'She's wonderful, isn't she?' he said proudly. 'Not a fuss, not a tear when they all drove away and left her.'

'She's lovely,' Ginny said honestly. Rowena Chloe *was* lovely. In fact, thought Ginny, who had never been interested in small children before, she was adorable.

'I'll put some milky tea into her beaker, shall I, so she can feel as if she's one of the crowd.'

'Thank you, Jinty. Thank you for everything,' Fliss said warmly. 'I feel bad about the Ewings thinking she's going to be with us all the time when she's not.'

Jinty lived in a council house in the village with her husband, Tom, a man with two hobbies: gambling and enjoying a drink in the local pub with his mates. He was more successful at the second than the first, and as both took up a considerable percentage of his wages as a joiner, Jinty, who adored her handsome husband and had seven children to feed and clothe, cheerfully took on any job on offer, be it working behind the counter in one of the village shops, cleaning the primary school and village hall, or helping Fliss at Linn Hall, especially between Easter and autumn, when young backpackers descended on the hall to help keep the gardens under some form of control.

Faced with the prospect of having to look after a ten-month-old baby for two weeks, Fliss and her husband had panicked, but Jinty, as always, had come to the rescue, offering to take Rowena Chloe home with her each day after work.

'Oh, nonsense, Mrs F, it'll be a pleasure, and what they don't know won't hurt them,' she said now. 'The boys have brought the old cot down from the loft, and the girls can't wait to look after her. She'll have a grand time with us, won't you, my pet? And since she can't talk yet, her mum and her gran won't know a thing about it.'

'How long are they away for?' Ginny asked.

'Two weeks. Val, Tony and Stella are off to Lanzarote and Molly's meeting up with a girlfriend and backpacking in

Portugal. Then they're all coming back here together to collect Rowena Chloe.'

How on earth Molly could just go off like that and leave such a sweet little girl, not to mention the chance to spend two weeks with Lewis, was beyond Ginny.

'You'll be wanting a bed in the gatehouse,' Fliss was saying. 'The bedding's ready and Jinty and I will take it down the drive today.'

'No need, Mum, she's gone all independent.' Lewis pointed out of a window, and his mother and Jinty went to have a look.

'A van? Oh, my dear, you'd be more comfortable in the gatehouse.'

'It's a caravanette, Mrs Ralston-Kerr, complete with a little kitchen and three bunk beds and even a toilet and shower.'

'Well, I still think you should use the bathroom in the house and have your meals with us.'

'Thanks, I will. That'll save having to empty tanks and carry water. I see work's started on the windows.'

'It's all quite exciting. We had a good winter, didn't we, Hector?' Fliss said happily. 'Now the roof's been fixed and the rain's not coming in any more, that horrible damp feeling's left the place. And we've been assured that once the windows are done we won't have any draughts. It's like a miracle!'

'Are you coping with all the workmen being around?'

'We're fine,' Jinty said. 'They're no more bother than the backpackers in the summer. The men bring packed lunches and if it rains they eat in their vans. No bother at all. Off you go now, Ginny, I know you're dying to see that kitchen garden of yours.'

'Where's Duncan?' Ginny asked as she and Lewis rinsed their empty mugs in the huge stone sink. Duncan Campbell was the Ralston-Kerrs' gardener. A local man, he lived on the council-house estate with his wife, Helen, who wrote local items for the weekly *Dumfries News,* and their four children.

'He took one look at the Ewings and headed back to the garden with his tea. You know what Duncan's like.'

Ginny did. Though good at his job, Duncan was a morose man who didn't care for a lot of company, especially company that consisted of noisy strangers.

'On my way in I noticed some caravans in the field opposite the farm lane,' she said as she and Lewis left the kitchen. 'There weren't any last year, as I recall.'

'It's a new business idea of Victor McNair's. You know that Ewan had persuaded his dad to let him have one of their fields to set up a wormery?'

'Oh, yes . . . I saw Alison on my way here, and she said it's coming along well. I'll have to have a look at it.'

'He's really started something; the school's set up its own small wormery now. Anyway, Victor insisted on getting a field of his own since Ewan has one. He's a good few years older than me, but I remember when we all played together as kids Victor was competitive; never satisfied until he won other boys' marbles or conkers, or got to decide what we should play at. And now he's engaged to a Kirkcudbright girl he's keen to make his fortune. He's planning to turn the field into a caravan park and in the meantime he's allowed some small vans to use the site for Easter. Come and see what Duncan and I have done with the stables,' Lewis urged her, and Ginny followed him obediently, though she was itching to see the kitchen garden.

The stables, which had housed the family's horses and carriages in the days when the Ralston-Kerr family had been wealthy, had been used for storage for decades until fortune smiled on the current family. Eighteen months earlier, the villagers had been split into two camps when interest was shown in the derelict slate quarry owned by the Ralston-Kerrs. Glen Mason, then landlord of the Neurotic Cuckoo, headed the committee opposed to the re-opening. There was an even greater shock in store for the village when Glen and his wife Libby were revealed as multi-millionaire Lottery winners who had changed their names and settled on Prior's Ford as the quiet little backwater they had sought. Local anger had forced them to leave, but in compensation for their deceit they donated £100,000 to build a children's playground at the quarry, no longer threatened with re-opening, and £200,000 towards much-needed renovation work at Linn Hall. To his delight, Lewis had been allocated £50,000 of the money to spend on tidying up the neglected gardens so he could open them to the public. He also wanted to set up a shop in the stables where he would sell home-grown fruit, vegetables and flowers.

When Duncan and Ginny began to help him clear the stables the previous summer Ginny had pointed out that a lot of the items scornfully dismissed as 'junk' by Duncan were worth selling or using to give the shop atmosphere.

She stopped just inside the door, staring. 'Goodness, what a difference!' The cobwebby coach house, once packed with discarded items, had been cleared and cleaned, the cobwebs gone, the flagged floor swept, the stone walls whitewashed, shelves put up and a wooden counter installed, Some of the items retrieved from the former clutter decorated the other walls: two cart wheels, cleaned and painted, jelly pans and copper pots burnished until they glowed, horse brasses, carriage lamps and harnesses.

Lewis grinned, delighted at Ginny's reaction. 'It was your suggestion that we use some of the junk to give the place an authentic look, and you were right. Duncan and I worked on it over the winter. The money we spent on it came from the stuff we didn't want. You were right again when you said it was worth something; I called in an auctioneer and we couldn't believe the money he raised by selling it. Look,' he led her round the large empty area, pointing out framed photographs on the walls, 'when Mrs Ramsay's step-daughter did an inventory for us while she was in the village last year she found all these old pictures of the stables and the horses and carriages as they used to be. I had them enlarged and framed. And we've whitewashed the area where the horses used to be stabled to use as a store.'

'When do you plan to open the shop?'

'I reckon we could do it in June or July – in a small way at first. There are things still in store in the house we can sell here and Duncan took a lot of cuttings last autumn and brought them on in the polytunnel. We collected seeds as well so we could sell them, and I'm hoping you'll be able to give me some veg from the kitchen garden.'

'Well, then, let's go and see what's on offer,' said Ginny, hurrying to the door.

Lewis let out a piercing whistle as he and Ginny went into the large kitchen garden. An untidy mop of fiery red hair appeared from behind some healthy-looking rhubarb plants at the far end, rising up into the air as Jimmy McDonald, one of Jinty's sons, got to his feet, his long skinny body unfolding in sections. His over-large T-shirt in red and white horizontal stripes gave Ginny the illusion that she was watching a deckchair being opened out.

His freckled face split in a wide grin as he came loping down the path towards them, wiping his hands on the sides of faded blue jeans.

'Ginny! You're back!'

'I am, and is it possible you've managed to grow another three inches?' She looked up at him as he came to a halt before her.

'Mebbe.' He looked down at his jeans, which stopped halfway down his calves. His bare feet were clad in ancient shabby trainers. 'What d'you think?' He waved his hand at the raised, weed-free vegetable beds.

'It looks great, Jimmy. You've been working hard since I was last here.' Jimmy, who had inherited his love of gardening from his maternal grandfather, once head gardener at Linn Hall, had spent the previous summer helping Ginny turn the neglected wasteland within the old stone walls into a kitchen garden again. His long face, already flushed by the sun, took on even more colour and he tugged so hard at the hem of the T-shirt it was almost pulled from one bony shoulder.

'Och, it wasnae difficult. Not after all the work you'd put in on it.'

'I've brought some seedlings; come and help me fetch them, then we'll have a look at the polytunnel. I hope you're going to be able to help me again this year?' Ginny asked as the three of them left the garden.

'Aye, of course. Is this yours?' Jimmy asked as he spotted the caravanette.

'My pride and joy. Meet Jemima Puddleduck.'

'Cool!' Jimmy leapt into the interior as soon as the side door was opened, easing his way round stacks of carefully packed boxes. 'It's just like Doctor Who's Tardis, this – little from the outside and big inside.'

'It's a handsome wee rig,' Lewis agreed, poking his head in at the door. 'Well done, our Ginny. I'll have to crack on. Catch you later.' He went off, Muffin at his heels.

'You've even got a door that lets you go from here to the cab without having to go outside! What did it cost?'

'More than you could afford, even with the money you earn from gardening.'

'I'm goin' to get one of these as soon as I'm old enough.'

'You'll have to wait until you get your driving licence before you can take to the road,' Ginny pointed out, surveying the boxes.

'I'm not bothered about that. I like Prior's Ford and I want to stay here. I'd keep a van like this in our back garden so I could sleep in it by myself instead of having to share, and have somewhere to go when I get fed up with all the noise in our house. And if anyone wanted to come into it they'd have to knock on the door and ask. It would be all mine,' the boy said wistfully, 'somewhere to keep all my own things safe.'

Ginny was taken aback. An only child, she had always had her own room and Jimmy's description of living with a large family in a small house, brief as it was, suddenly made her realise how pampered she had been.

'I'm sure you'll get your own caravanette one of these days,' she said gently, then, picking a box up, 'Hey, back to business. You get out and I'll pass the boxes to you, then we'll move them to the garden.

'What's been happening in Prior's Ford, then?' she asked once they were opening the boxes.

'Did ye hear about the peregrine falcons?'

'No.'

'There's a pair nestin' in the old quarry, and it was me that discovered them,' Jimmy bragged, holding out his thin arms so Ginny could pile shallow wooden seed boxes on to them. Despite having a prodigious appetite he was as thin as a broomstick, but stronger than he looked. 'I saw a

23

picture of a bird on the front of one of the magazines in the store and I said to Marcy Copleton that I'd seen birds like that at the quarry. So she told Mr Kavanagh that runs the Prior's Ford Progress Committee and he told the Scottish Natural Heritage, and they came to have a look. They're rare birds, d'you know that?'

'Yes, I do.'

'Marcy and Mr Kavanagh kept it a secret at first, but now everyone knows and it's bringing folk to the village who like birds. They're called twitchers,' Jimmy explained importantly. 'And that'll be good for Prior's Ford. There's a hide been built where folk can watch the birds without botherin' them. Mr Kavanagh took me there when the parent birds arrived last month and started buildin' their nest. He's got ace binoculars – it was as if I could touch the birds. They're bonny.' And then, as Ginny picked up the last two boxes and led the way back into the garden. 'And a new play area's been put up at the quarry, too. My sister Heather was on the committee that helped decide what it should look like. Climbin' frames and ropes and that sort of thing.'

'Is it a good idea to have a play area in a quarry where there are rare birds?'

'It's cool,' Jimmy assured her. 'The birds are at the far end of the quarry and they nest really high up where nob'dy can get at them. We've all played there for years and we've often seen the birds. We didnae know they were rare, though. The playground was put up at the start of this year, before the birds moved back in.'

'Sounds good.' Ginny balanced her boxes on one arm and used her free hand to open the door to the polytunnel she had persuaded Lewis to buy the year before. Stepping inside, she relished the smell of moist warm earth, greenery and trapped sunshine.

4

'Toilets an' showers an' cables for electricity. I've never heard such nonsense,' Victor McNair raved.

Although it was mid-April, the sky had darkened an hour earlier, then unleashed a torrent of rain. It was still pouring, and Victor, hatless and in his best clothes, had been soaked on the short walk from his car to the farm door.

'It's the way of the world now, son. Everythin' needs planning permission. Go upstairs and change intae your workin' clothes, then I'll hang your good suit up tae dry.'

Victor shook his head and water droplets fell from his dark brown hair. Unlike his younger brother, Ewan, he liked to keep his hair as well-groomed as possible, and now when he smoothed it back by ramming impatient fingers through it, it fell into place neatly. 'Accordin' tae the snooty jobsworth I saw, I'd need tae be a millionaire tae get that field the way the council wants. Ye'd think I was buildin' a luxury hotel! An' there's no way I'll get a bank loan on the pittance I'm paid for workin' here!'

Jess continued with her ironing while he paced the

25

flagged floor, still dressed for the business meeting he had just had with the planning department. She knew nothing of financial affairs, other than how to make a small amount of housekeeping money stretch like elastic. It was best, she decided, to let her firstborn work through his anger. She didn't often see Victor wearing anything other than working clothes; looking at him now, tall, lean and handsome in his dark blue striped suit, white shirt and light blue tie, she suddenly knew why Jeanette Askew, a town girl, had fallen for him.

'Those blasted politicians and councillors sittin' in their plush offices don't know what real life's like at all,' he raged on. 'My only hope's a big win on the Lottery, and that's no' likely, seein' that I cannae even afford tae put a pound a week on it.' He went on bitterly, 'Surely we should have the right tae do what we want with our own land?'

'Ye'd think so, but the folk in power say different and that's all there is to it. Could Jeanette's father not help you with the cost?' Jess suggested. 'Ye said he owns two garages, so surely he's got a sight more money than we have. And after all, it's for her future as well as yours.'

'But I want tae do it on my own. I want tae show him that I'm not just a farmer.'

'Here you, there's nothin' wrong with bein' a farmer! It's an honourable trade, good enough for your father and his before him and his before him!' Jess bristled, slamming the iron down on the board.

'Sorry . . . sorry!' Victor held his hands up, palms out, in surrender. 'I didnae mean it the way it came out. I just meant that with the farm no' offerin' me and Ewan much of a future I need tae show Jeanette's dad that . . .'

His voice tailed off as the outer door was thrown open so hard that it crashed against the wall before starting to swing back again. For the second time, Bert McNair's fist met it and, as it thudded against the wall once more, he stormed into the kitchen. Old Saul, startled from sleep, scrabbled on his belly to hide behind an armchair while a sickly lamb being kept in a box near the fire's warmth gave a nervous bleat.

'So there ye are,' Bert snapped at his eldest son. 'And what are ye doin', dressed up like a dog's dinner in the middle o' a workin' day?'

'I'd a meetin' tae go tae, about plannin' permission for the field.'

'A meetin' was it? An' what about my permission?'

'Would ye have given it?'

'Ye're d—' Even in his anger, Bert knew better than to swear in his wife's presence. 'Ye're right,' he said between his teeth. 'Well, I hope yer blasted *meetin'* was worth yer while, because it almost cost us five hundred pounds!'

'What are ye talkin' about?'

Bert thrust his chin forward. 'I'm talkin' about the money we'll get for Ruby's calf. You knew that Ewan and me were goin' tae spend the afternoon in the top field with the sheep tae make sure the lambs were all right. You knew that Ruby was due tae calf any minute and she needed tae be taken intae shelter. You said ye'd keep an eye on her. But where were ye when she dropped her calf and it almost died out in the rain? At a *meetin'*!'

Colour flooded Victor's face. 'I wasnae away for long . . . I was just goin' out tae have a look at the cow.'

'Dressed like that? Standin' here chattin' tae yer mother like a visitor while Ewan and me were fightin' tae save the calf? Lucky for it, and for you, that we found it in time. Ye're a disgrace!'

Victor's face hardened and his fists clenched. 'I had tae

go tae the council offices tae see about this plannin' permission, and I didnae tell ye about the meetin' because I knew ye'd not let me go and it was important tae me. I'm sorry I forgot about the calf, Da, but I'll not have you or anyone else call me a disgrace.'

Bert's fists bunched, and for a moment Jess thought her son and her husband were going to go for each other.

'Stop that! Stop it this minute if ye don't want me tae set about ye with this iron!' They hesitated, turning to face her. 'Victor, get upstairs and intae yer work clothes,' she ordered, and he stormed from the room. 'He's a grown man, Bert. Ye can't treat him like a bairn.'

'Then he shouldnae behave like one. Put down that iron, Jess, I've no wish tae get my lug burned. Ye've always spoiled him,' he went on as she put the iron on the board.

'I have not!'

'I've tae get back tae the calf,' Bert said, and once again the door was thrown back against the wall before being slammed shut.

On her own, Jess returned to her ironing. She and Bert had been married for almost ten years before Victor arrived, ten years in which she had suffered several miscarriages and buried two stillborn babies. Carrying him to full time had been as close to a miracle as she had ever come, and perhaps she had spoiled him without realising it. It was as though his birth had brought her good fortune, because there had been no more miscarriages or stillbirths.

Alice, the next baby, now lived in the Lake District with her farmer husband and their three children; her future was secure, but it was a different matter for her brothers.

Jess wished she and Bert had been able to buy up other farms for their sons to inherit, but even if they had, farming wasn't what Victor wanted; it never had been. Jess had always hoped he would settle down to it eventually, but her hopes were dashed when he fell for Jeanette, a town girl used to living in a nice house, wearing nice clothes and having money to spend. Jeanette would never make a farmer's wife. At least, not unless the farm was much larger and much more profitable than Tarbethill.

The smell of scorched cloth distracted her from what might have been and hurled her into the present. With a muffled yelp she snatched up the iron and peered anxiously at the damage. One of Bert's work shirts now sported an iron-shaped brand. Fortunately, it was on the tail, so no harm done.

As she gave a sigh of relief Victor thundered down the stairs and through the kitchen, closing the outer door with a slam that sent poor old Saul, who had returned to his place in front of the range, back behind the armchair. Jess went to comfort him, grabbing the arm of the chair and grunting slightly as she bent stiff knees.

'Pay no heed, son,' she assured the trembling dog. 'It's just a storm in a teacup. It's over.'

But in her heart of hearts, she felt the estrangement between Bert and Victor was only just beginning.

'I'm pleased for her, really I am, but I wish she would let us meet this new boyfriend. I've suggested more than once she should bring him to the house, but she always looks at me as though she'd sooner take him to an abattoir.'

'She's a teenager, Jenny,' Ingrid McKenzie said comfortably, 'and this is her first boyfriend. She wants to keep him to herself right now, but once the novelty wears off she'll be keen to let you meet him.'

'Did that happen with Freya?'

They were in the Gift Horse, Ingrid's craft shop, getting it ready for its summer opening.

'She's brought one or two boys back from school, but there may have been more her father and I knew nothing about. You're worrying too much.'

'Probably, but I can't help it. It would be different if we'd raised Maggie ourselves, but becoming the mother of a teenage girl when you haven't seen her since she was a two-year-old's so difficult!'

Maggie was Jenny's stepdaughter by an early, ill-fated marriage to Neil Cameron, a man who had made Jenny so miserable she had run away from him before their first anniversary. For years she had agonised over the way she had deserted little Maggie, then a chance meeting with Malcolm Cameron, her former brother-in-law, revealed that Neil had been killed in an accident, and Maggie, now a teenager, was living with his parents. When his father had a heart attack, Malcolm had turned to Jenny for help. His mother had her hands full nursing her frail husband, and Malcolm's wife, Liz, suffered from multiple sclerosis. Maggie, then fourteen years old, would have to go into care unless Jenny was willing to take her. To Jenny, it had been the answer to years of prayer. Ignoring those who warned her that it would not be easy, she brought Maggie to Prior's Ford, only to discover that the girl blamed her for deserting her as a child. The eighteen months since had been quite a battle.

'I'd just like to know what the boy's like,' she said, as she began to unpack the box she had brought to the shop. 'Things like, is he sensible and dependable?'

'That,' Ingrid said dryly, 'is unlikely at his age. But perhaps one of the reasons why Maggie doesn't want you to meet him is that she is afraid you might ask him that question.'

'Of course I wouldn't!'

'But you would think it, and young people are very good at reading minds. We Scandinavians have a healthier outlook on relationships than the British,' Ingrid said in her precise, almost perfect English. 'I was encouraged to have boyfriends so I could gather the necessary experience to know when the right one came along. As, of course, Peter is and always will be,' she added fondly. Ingrid was married to Peter McKenzie, a college lecturer who adored her and their two daughters. 'Maggie's a nice girl at heart,' she went on, 'and I think she needs to know you trust her. What's that you've got?'

Jenny, who like Ingrid was deeply interested in crafts, was carefully removing a series of tiny, brightly dressed dolls from the box.

'John – Maggie's grandfather – has found it difficult to give up his beloved pipe, so his wife decided to throw it out to be on the safe side. But when Maggie was staying with them last week she asked if she could have the pipe. She says the smell of it reminds her of him, and she brought back a box of pipe-cleaners as well. She was going to put them in the bin, but I started playing around with them and some scraps of cloth, and this is what I came up with. What do you think?'

She laid the little figures along the counter in a row. 'Of course, they can't take much handling, but I thought they might do for dolls' houses or even little bedroom ornaments.'

'They're lovely.' Ingrid picked one up and balanced its plasticine feet in the palm of her hand. 'I love her little bag and umbrella.'

'That's supposed to be Mary Poppins. And these are the pirates of the Caribbean.'

31

'Of course. Do you have any more of these pipe cleaners?'

'Lots. John always had a good supply. I don't even know if smokers still use them or if something better's been invented.'

'Then make some more figures. I think we could sell them,' Ingrid said. Jenny's mobile phone rang. She dug it out of her bag.

'Hello? Oh, hello, love, how did you get on?' She listened for some time, and then, her voice suddenly flat, 'But didn't he say what was wrong? Yes, but . . . Oh, all right. When are you likely to get an appointment? Oh. Well, we'll just have to wait. No, of course I'm not worried, why would I be worried? I know you're not. Yes, see you this evening.'

'Problems?' Ingrid asked as her friend switched the phone off.

'Andrew's had this tummy trouble for absolutely ages, but you know what men are, they insist on thinking if they ignore something it'll go away. I finally got him to make an appointment with the doctor this afternoon, and he's going to be referred to a hospital in Edinburgh for tests. The doctor didn't say why.'

'That's because he doesn't know. General practitioners have a vast amount of knowledge about a vast number of medical problems, Jenny, but they can't possibly solve every one. That's why they refer their patients to specialists.'

'Yes, I know, and you're right.' Jenny summoned up a smile. 'It's just that it's taken me so long to persuade Andrew to see a doctor, and I suppose I was hoping he would come home with a bottle of pills and a name for whatever's ailing him.'

'He will, all in good time. They need to find out the true situation before they know which pills to prescribe.' Ingrid stroked the other woman's arm. 'It will be all right, Jenny.'

'Yes, of course it will. Andrew's as fit as a fiddle; that's why I'm so anxious to get whatever it is dealt with quickly. Anyway, I'd better get home. You really want more of those wee pipe-cleaner dolls?'

'Why not? They're something different, and if we put them into pretty little boxes they could sell quite well. Worth a try,' Ingrid said.

5

Clarissa Ramsay had spent a deliciously lazy winter filling albums with the photographs taken during the previous year's travels, writing letters to the many new friends she had made on her journey, putting her cosy little cottage to rights, and reading her way through several boxes of books she had brought with her to Prior's Ford. It was lovely, after her long trip, to spend time on her own, eating what and when she pleased. At least once every week she invited Alastair over for lunch or dinner.

'You,' she had said to him one miserably cold January evening when snow was melting into slush outside and the two of them prepared dinner together in her kitchen, 'are my hold on reality.'

'I don't think anyone's ever told me that before.'

'But you really are. I've never been entirely on my own before; there were my parents, and my colleagues and pupils, and then Keith, and when he died you came along and saved me. Then,' she rattled on, too intent on what she was doing to see the look he gave her, 'there were so many

34

people in so many countries last year. But since getting back home I've been on my own for the first time ever, and it's been bliss. I went away to find myself, but I think that really happened after I came back to Prior's Ford. Those days and nights pottering about the house, reading, writing, thinking; when I felt like company I only had to go across to the shops or into town or to the Cuckoo for coffee or lunch. But it's your visits every week that have kept me from turning into a total couch potato. The things we talk about, the way you make me laugh, the way you make me feel . . . alive.' She stopped suddenly, then smiled at him. 'Listen to me, raving on. I just wanted to say thank you for being such a good friend.'

'It's not all one-sided, you know.'

'I've gained a friend, while you've gained a second mother.'

'Don't talk nonsense,' he said sharply, then reddened as she stared at him. 'Sorry, but I hate to hear you say something like that. Age has nothing to do with friendship, nothing at all!'

'I suppose not. Could you fetch the colander down from that cupboard for me?' Clarissa asked, and then began to talk about her plans for the following day.

As winter gave way to spring she organised her garden with Jimmy McDonald's help, and explored the countryside in her small car. Occasionally she thought she should do something more positive with her life, such as taking up a new hobby or learning a new skill, or perhaps trying to find some voluntary work, but the days continued to drift past without any decisions being made. There was plenty of time, she told herself as she drove through beautiful villages, stopping in lay-bys to look over lush fields, some cultivated, others grazed by contented cattle, sheep or horses, to the farmhouses surrounded by barns and outhouses, or half hidden among trees.

She was leaning over a gate one April day, watching some bullocks, exhilarated by the joy of being alive, race each other across a field, when she heard a car slow down and stop behind her own. Turning, she saw Naomi Hennessey's little yellow Citroën. The engine was switched off, the driver's door opened, and Naomi suddenly popped out, for all the world like an exotically feathered chick emerging from an egg.

'Hello! Can I join you or are ruminating on your own?'

'Please do.'

The minister bent low in order to duck back into the car and when she joined Clarissa she was carrying a Thermos flask and a plastic cup.

'I often stop here for a drink when I'm in this part of my parish.' She unscrewed the top of the flask and handed it and the cup to Clarissa. 'Hold these. It's a lovely spot, isn't it, looking down into the valley? I hope sugar's all right?'

'Yes, fine,' Clarissa lied. The coffee was hot and strong, and not too sweet. Naomi put the flask down on a handy flat stone, and the two women leaned on the gate, shoulders touching, drinking their coffee in silence, until Clarissa said, 'I was just thinking, when you came along, how good it is to be single again. Does that sound terrible?'

'Not at all.'

'You never got to know Keith, did you?'

'Sadly, no. I saw him around the village, but we never spoke, other than a polite word as we passed each other. I don't think he approved of me, being a woman minister and dark-skinned and a lover of colourful clothes.' Today

36

she was wearing an orange top with green lightning zig-zagging all over it, and a long dark blue skirt. On anyone else it would have looked dreadful, but on Naomi it looked good.

'I suspect he didn't like independent women in general. His first marriage ended because his wife insisted on working when their children were teenagers. And as soon as we became engaged he persuaded me to take early retirement. He was my headmaster and he thought it inappropriate' – she used Keith's word, rolling it off her tongue as he had – 'for us to work in the same school when we were in a relationship. He liked to be head of the house as well as the school. He used to call me his little sparrow. It sounded affectionate at first, but then it struck me that sparrows are quite drab little birds.'

'I like sparrows,' Naomi said thoughtfully, 'and you're not in the least drab. That hairstyle suits you, and drab people don't go off on a year's travels on their own.'

'I had to do that, it was the only way to get to know myself again. I was independent and happy with my life before I married Keith,' Clarissa said. 'I don't know why I did it. I suppose it was because he was used to getting his own way, and since he was my boss I felt I should go along with his wishes. Only this time it wasn't a change to the school curriculum, it was a change in my life.' She hesitated before saying quietly, 'Not long after he died I found letters – love letters – to Keith from my best friend.'

'Ah.'

'I fell apart and if Alastair hadn't found me sitting on a stile in the rain goodness knows what might have happened. I felt . . . betrayed, ashamed, angry. Keith had always presented himself as an honest, upright man. And then I felt guilty about being angry.'

37

'No need for guilt. He was the sinner, not you.'

'Being angry with someone who's dead seemed so wrong.'

'Just because a person's no longer here doesn't make their sins or their virtues go away. We treasure the virtues of people we knew, and as for the things they did wrong – well, we have to face them, work our way through whatever we feel about them, and then fold them up like towels, put them away and get on with our own lives.' Naomi drank the last of her coffee. 'And try not to commit any sins that might make others suffer when *we've* gone. Talking of going, I have two more calls to make before I go home. To start on the dinner. Ethan's always starving when he gets home.' A few years earlier, Naomi had fostered her cousin's son, Ethan Baptiste, bringing him from Jamaica to Scotland. Like Naomi, Ethan had a Jamaican mother; Naomi's father was English while Ethan's was French.

As Clarissa returned her empty coffee cup Naomi touched her wrist. 'The past is past, Clarissa. You've created a good future for yourself; make the most of it.'

When the little Citroën had rounded a corner and disappeared, Clarissa leaned on the gate again, feeling greatly comforted as she always did after talking with the minister.

Naomi was right when she said that Clarissa had created her own future. She had learned to drive, something Keith had always discouraged, and had gone out into the world on her own, something she might never have done if Keith had not betrayed her. She had recovered her lost independence, found true friends, and now lived in one of the most beautiful, restful parts of Britain. She knew without a doubt that she was her own woman, and nobody would ever again be able to deceive her. And she was happier than she had ever been.

'When I'm ready to do something new with my life,

I'll do it,' she told a bullock who had ventured near and stood blinking his large dark eyes at her, 'and if I want to just keep on drifting like a dandelion seed on the wind, I shall do that!'

And she returned to the car to do some more exploring.

The key was stiff in the door, which creaked when Ewan McNair managed to unlock it and began to push it open. Jess, following him into the gloomy cottage interior, banged hard on the door frame with the stout stick she had brought from the farm, making him jump.

'Mam, what did ye have tae do that for?'

'Rats.'

'There's no rats in here.'

'Don't you be so sure,' Jess said. 'Those pests get in every- where. There's bound to be someone in the village with a Jack Russell terrier you could borrow. Jack Russells are bred to hunt rats.'

She followed her son through the door on the left, stamping hard on the flagged kitchen floor as he began to ease the wooden shutters from the windows. Daylight fought its way through the dirty but intact panes to illuminate the living room.

'Still wind an' weather tight. They built tae last in the old days,' Ewan said proudly.

'It's no' bad at all, I'll give you that, seein' as it's been over five years since it was last lived in,' Jess conceded. Five years since Bert had had to pay off their last farmhand. 'This is where your dad and me lived when we were first wed. Victor was born here, then your granddad died not long before Alice came along, and we moved intae the farmhouse proper.'

Jess peered into the stone sink, where a large spider

39

scuttled around. With one deft movement she scooped the creature up, clamping one hand over the other to keep it from escaping. 'Open the back door, Ewan.'

He managed it after a brief struggle, and Jess released the spider and watched it scuttle off into the undergrowth. Like the garden at the front, the small back patch was a jungle of grass, nettles and brambles, and the hedge had been allowed to grow thick and tall. Beyond it, the Tarbethill dairy herd, smaller than it had ever been before, grazed on lush green grass.

When the boys were growing up the herd had been much larger, every cow born on Tarbethill land, but in 2001 they had lost all their cattle and sheep to the country-wide epidemic of the dreaded foot and mouth disease. The cruellest part of the disease was that all animals on an affected farm, even those who were fit and well, had to be slaughtered. Killing off animals he had raised from birth had taken its toll on Bert McNair. He had built up the new herd carefully, but it wasn't the same. Nothing would ever be the same for Bert, Jess thought, with an ache at her heart as she followed Ewan up the narrow staircase leading from the living room. When she caught up with him he was peering from the bathroom window.

'It's strange how different places you know look from different windows,' he said. The farm cottage was halfway up the lane between Tarbethill farmhouse and the main road, set back behind a four-foot hedge that had been kept trimmed, though the small garden behind it had gone wild.

'So, what d'you think, Mam?'

Jess wrinkled her nose at the brown painted walls, wood halfway up from the floor, then plaster to the ceiling. The sink and lavatory bowl were stained, the overhead cistern ancient, with a rusty chain hanging from it, and the bath was thick with dust. 'This'd need a lot of work. D'ye really think it's worth it?'

'It's a good sound cottage and I know lads in the village who'd be willin' tae lend a hand for the price of a drink or two at the Cuckoo. It could earn its keep as a holiday cottage; town folk'd pay tae live in a place like this for a fortnight at a time. And there's plenty of people wealthy enough tae change bathrooms when they buy a house, whether they need changin' or not. Cam Gordon says he's seen lovely bathrooms an' kitchens thrown on to skips, an' nob'dy minds if the workmen help themselves. He could get all sorts of stuff for the cost of the transport.' Cam Gordon, a local man, was a joiner.

'Mmmm.' Bert and his father had put in the bathroom, formerly a tiny third bedroom, just after Victor's birth. At the time, Jess had been as proud as Punch to have a real bathroom. It was sad to see the state it was in now. She went into one of the two bedrooms and Ewan followed, catching her arm and swinging her round so he could gaze into her face. 'Mam, try thinkin' of the way the place'd look once it was done up, instead of seein' it the way it is now,' he coaxed her.

Jess peered round the room where Victor had been born. It had been over thirty years before, but she could clearly recall her fear of the unknown ordeal before her, and the pain; then had come the joy of holding her firstborn in her arms, his crumpled face as yet unwashed, his skin mottled, his damp dark hair slick against his round skull and his eyes screwed shut while his mouth gaped open, protesting loudly at being ousted from the comfortable, snug billet that had been his for nine months and was his no longer.

41

She remembered, too, the cosy room, the sprigged curtains at the grime-free window, the sun on the cream-painted walls, and the patchwork quilt, a wedding gift made by her own mother. She and Bert had been happy in this cottage.

'I'm goin' tae do it, Mam,' Ewan said. 'It'll be worthwhile, you'll see.'

Jess had always loved his enthusiasm, which never faltered, even in the face of his father's and brother's scepticism. Now, she felt herself caught up in it.

'It might make a nice wee home for you and Alison one of these days.'

'Don't be daft,' he protested, a crimson flood riding up his weather-browned neck and into his face. 'I'm talkin' about a holiday home that'll make money for us all. This place wouldnae be good enough for Alison an' wee Jamie.'

'Alison might not agree with you about that. You could do an awful lot worse than her, Ewan.' To Jess's mind, Alison Greenlees was the perfect daughter-in-law, and she was certain that Ewan was helplessly in love with the girl.

'And she could do a lot better. I cannae afford a wife, let alone a bairn, you know that.'

Jess said nothing, but she knew what he meant. The farm was making less money than ever before. Half their fields had been let out to other farmers in need of extra grazing land; even if Victor, who disliked farming, let Tarbethill go to his young brother, who loved it with a passion, Ewan would find it difficult to support himself, let alone a wife and family.

Nowadays, love wasn't enough. It needed financial support to flourish.

'I'm goin' tae ask Victor tae help me with the cottage,' Ewan said as he and his mother walked back to the farmhouse. 'It'd be good tae have the two of us workin' on

42

somethin' together . . . somethin' for the good of the farm. We don't see much of each other these days.' He sounded wistful, and Jess realised he missed the camaraderie he had once shared with his brother. There had been a time when Victor was protective of Ewan, patiently teaching him childhood games and introducing him to the mysteries of football. But grown to manhood, they had turned in different directions: Ewan concentrating on the farm, Victor hungry for more than Tarbethill had to offer.

'I don't know about that, son,' she said gently. 'He's all taken up with seein' Jeanette and plannin' tae turn that field into a caravan park.'

'I know, but it's still worth the try,' Ewan said.

6

'Have one.'

'I don't smoke.'

'Don't?' Ryan lifted one eyebrow in a sophisticated gesture that Maggie had been practising in front of her bedroom mirror. 'Or won't?'

'What d'you mean?'

He heaved a sigh, then said, 'I *mean*, have you ever tried?'

'Of course. Didn't like it.'

'It's an acquired taste.' He took two cigarettes from the pack, which he dropped back into his pocket, and put them both between his lips. Then he took out a lighter and lit them both before offering her one. 'Go on,' he insisted, and this time it was more of a command than an offer. 'It's only tobacco . . . I'm not pushing you onto the strong stuff.'

Maggie slipped the white cylinder between slightly trembling lips, desperately trying to remember how friends who smoked went about it. She pursed her lips and breathed in, then went into a coughing fit, only just managing to rescue the cigarette before it shot out of her mouth like a rocket. Ryan roared with laughter.

'You're a character, d'you know that? Fifteen and never smoked before,' he mocked. 'Never been kissed either, till I came along.'

'I was!'

'Yeah, right. Playing postman's knock at a birthday party? You've got a lot to learn. Suck it in properly – into your lungs,' he said, and laughed as she started to cough again. 'Keep trying; you'll learn.' He put his arm about her. They were sitting on a stile between two fields in the late April sunshine.

At her third attempt Maggie only took the smoke into her mouth, then held it there for a few seconds before breathing out, so he wouldn't realise she was cheating. That made smoking much easier. She leaned against Ryan's shoulder, happy to be alone with him in this nice quiet place. A wood pigeon called from a small copse not far away, and smoke rose into the clear air from a farm cottage chimney several fields away. It was great to be there, with her boyfriend, and nobody else around.

'It's a right dump here,' he said just then. 'It must drive you mad, livin' in that borin' village.'

'Yeah, it does. Can't wait to get finished with school and out of this place,' she said swiftly.

'Me too. If it wasn't for my dad goin' on at me about gettin' qualifications I'd be off round the world by now. But he's right,' Ryan said, surprising her.

'Your dad's right?'

'Well, not about most things, but I suppose he's right about me gettin' on at school and goin' to college or university. It's the best way to get a good job an' make good money. There's no way I want to be like him and my mum, stuck in dead-end jobs and a dead-end house with dead-end lives. I'm goin' to find a job that gets me travellin'.'

'Sounds good,' Maggie said. It did. Her and Ryan, travelling anywhere they wanted to go, doing whatever they wanted to do, and not having to worry about money. Or about parents and step-parents.

Ryan was right; the best way to gain freedom was to do as well as she could at school and at college, if she had to, then get a good job.

She quite liked school, always had done. It shouldn't be too hard.

'Ye're daft, man!' Victor McNair said as he brought his car to a stop outside the old cottage. 'Look at the place – it's fit for nothin'. We'd be better tearin' it down and buildin' a decent house on the site.'

'But it's got character,' Ewan protested. 'Folk would pay good money tae holiday in a wee cottage like this.'

Victor got out of the car, and by the time Ewan did the same his brother was leaning his folded arms on the car's roof, staring over at the cottage.

'Oh aye, it's got character, and it's got rats an' beetles an' spiders as well. Who'd want tae live in a dump like that?'

'It's still sound enough. A good clean out and some decoratin' and bits of furniture would make a world of difference. And we could get the garden put tae rights in no time, you and me. It wouldnae take long with the two of us workin' on it,' Ewan coaxed him.

'I've got enough tae do with gettin' plannin' permission for that field. Ye've no idea how difficult that is. An' Jeanette's father's asked me tae help out at the garage at weekends over the summer. He's payin' decent money.'

'Oh, right. Well, that'll help to keep us goin',' Ewan acknowledged.

'I'm no' doin' it for the farm.' Victor gave his brother a hard, blue-eyed stare. 'I'm doin' it for me and Jeanette. It costs money tae get married, y'know. Where are we goin' tae live, for a start? An' don't suggest this cottage, for Jeanette's expectin' a lot better.'

'It costs money tae keep a farm going. That's what the wormery's about. We can sell the compost they make, an' sell worms tae fishermen.'

'An' how long is it goin' tae be before it starts tae make decent money?'

'A while,' Ewan admitted, flushing, 'but I want tae get this place fit tae let tae holiday-makers as well. Dad needs all the help we can give him, Victor.'

Victor made a disgusted sound deep in his throat, then turned his head to one side and spat. 'The farm's sinkin', Ewan, have ye no' noticed that yet? Even if we worked our hearts out you an' me arenae goin' tae make enough o' a difference. We'd be better callin' it Titanic instead o' Tarbethill.'

'That's nonsense! We *can* make a difference if we work together.'

'Ye'll be tellin' me next ye still believe in Santa Claus,' Victor jeered.

'Let's just have a look at the cottage.' Ewan led the way, swallowing back his anger. He wanted Victor's cooperation, and losing his temper wasn't going to do it.

It was a case of a glass half-full and half empty at the same time, he realised five minutes later. When he looked at the cottage's sturdy walls and neat windows he was able to visualise the snug home it had once been and could, with some tender loving care, be again. Victor merely saw a building too old to bother about.

47

'I'm tellin' ye,' Ewan said doggedly as he led the way upstairs, 'townsfolk would enjoy spendin' a few weeks here in the summer. There's the village down the road, and they could buy eggs from Mam, and maybe some of her home bakin', and perhaps we could do wee tours round the place as well.'

'Ye could be right,' Victor agreed. 'We could turn it intae a sort of Disneyland, eh? Dress the cows up as characters from films an' maybe hold barn dances in the evenin's in a real barn.' He walked into one of the bedrooms and went to the window, rubbing a clear spot in the glass as he spoke. 'Get real, Ewan! If ye're that fond of this place, why not do it up for that lass o' yours? You could paint the walls white and grow roses round the door and all over the garden an' live happily ever after.'

'Don't be daft!'

'I'll stop if you stop,' Victor said sarcastically. 'It's time you started to live in the real world. Time you realised that this farm— good God!'

'What is it?' Ewan joined his brother at the window.

'Damned cheek! Look at that!'

'What?' Ewan anxiously scanned the field by the house, but could see nothing out of the ordinary.

'There!' Victor pointed a shaking finger. 'My field! There's vans movin' intae it!'

'Holidaymakers?' Ewan joined his brother. From the upper window he could see that there was indeed a convoy of assorted vehicles moving in through the gate.

'Holidaymakers be damned, it's travellers movin' on tae my land without so much as a by-your-leave!' Victor spun round so swiftly that he sent Ewan reeling against the wall, and charged towards the door.

'Victor, wait . . . Take it easy!'

But Victor was already pounding down the stairs, and by

the time Ewan got to the landing the cottage door had been thrown back on its hinges and Victor was outside. Ewan reached the door in time to hear the car starting up.

'Victor, wait for me!' He lunged for the gate as the car took off, its wheels churning up a dust cloud in its wake.

'Idiot!' Ewan thumped a fist on the gate post, then started to run down the lane in the wake of the car. Normally driven carefully along the rutted lane, it now hurtled down it at speed, rocking dangerously from side to side as the wheels bounced in and out of holes. Victor had always been hot-headed, and heaven only knew what would happen if he tried to evict the trespassers single-handed.

By the time Ewan reached the end of the lane Victor was out of his car and in the field, arguing with a grey-haired man and a blonde woman, both well built. A small group of adults, children and dogs were gathered around the three.

'My land,' Victor was saying angrily when Ewan arrived at his side. 'And who gave you permission tae come ontae it?'

'It doesn't look as if you're doing much with it at the moment,' the blonde woman observed, glancing round at the uneven field with its clumps of trees and bushes.

'That's where you're wrong. I'm turnin' it intae a caravan park.'

'And isn't that just what we're lookin' for?' the man said, and the group behind him nodded.

'A *caravan* park where the folk *pay* tae park their *caravans!*' Victor stabbed a rigid finger at the collection of vehicles, consisting of two transit vans, one enclosed and one open, two caravans that looked as though they had seen a lot of travelling, two buses – one a single-decker and one a double-decker – and a small lorry with a trailer.

'But they'd be paying for fancy things like showers and toilets, son, and they're not in place yet,' the woman pointed out. 'We're used to managing without them when we're on the road. Holidaymakers aren't.'

The travellers, Ewan noticed, all seemed to be calm and reasonable, as though sure of their rights, while Victor, red-faced and angry, spluttered over his words as he snapped back at her, 'That's why I don't want you lot here! How can I get the field tae rights with a bunch o' Irish tinkers livin' on it, messin' up the area?'

The spokesman made a sudden move forward, then halted as the woman laid a hand on his arm. 'You're taking a lot for granted, son,' she said. 'My man here's from Southern Ireland, right enough, but the rest of us are from Cumbria. And we're travellers, not tinkers. There's a difference. And you shouldn't go accusing folk of making a mess of your land until you've got proof. Has your planning permission been granted?'

'It's nearly there,' Victor lied.

'There you are, then; there'll be no harm in letting us stay for a week or so while you're waitin' for the council to get themselves sorted out, eh?' the man said. 'They take a while, do councils,' he went on almost sympathetically, and his companions nodded as one.

'As far as rent goes, we're all willing to work our way,' the woman offered. She glanced across at the noticeboard in the lane. 'Tarbethill Farm. Would that be yours? Well then,' she went on as Ewan nodded, 'those of us hale enough'll be willing to help you out with farm work, and no doubt there's folk in the village looking for a gardener or a painter. My brother here's a fine painter and decorator, aren't you, Rog?'

A handsome man with silver glittering among his thick dark hair nodded. 'One of the best,' he confirmed.

'Wait a minute,' Victor's voice rose to something near a squeak, 'ye're not stayin', so ye can forget about lookin' for work. I'm goin' straight tae the council tae report ye.'

50

The older man stuck his thumbs in his belt. 'The thing is, lad, they'll give us four weeks' notice and we're not plannin' on stayin' that long. We'll be out of your hair by the time they come to evict us, so you might as well leave us in peace for now. It'll save you a lot of trouble in the end.'

'And what sort of state will you leave this place in?' Victor wanted to know. 'Travellers cannae be trusted tae respect other folks' land.'

A young man with long curly flame-red hair pushed forward, chin jutting and fists clenched by his sides. 'I've had enough o' this. Who are you to be miscallin' folk without stoppin' to find out if you're right or wrong?'

Ewan grabbed his brother's arm just as the spokesman did the same to the other man.

'Calm down now, Jay, some folk can't help being preju-diced,' he said in a reasonable, almost kind voice.

Ewan, half a step behind Victor, saw the back of his brother's neck, already red, deepen in colour.

Just then a girl stepped out of the single-decker bus. 'What's going on?' she called, and then, coming towards them, 'Jay, are you causing trouble?'

'Nobody's causin' trouble,' said the man who was detaining Jay. 'We're just sortin' out a few ground rules with these lads who own the field.'

The girl's left hand supported a sling holding a small baby, its round head with a cap of red-gold fluff resting securely on the swell of her creamy bosom. Smiling, she held the other hand out to Victor.

'How d'you do? I'm Petra, Mr . . . ?'

'Victor.' Thrown off balance, he dragged his cap off then took her hand. 'Victor McNair.'

'Victor owns the farm across the road there,' the woman said.

'M–my father owns it.'

'I hope you'll explain to him that we're not staying long, and we're very grateful to him, and to you, for letting us use your field for a week or two. How d'you do?' Petra turned her attention to Ewan, who suddenly realised his mouth was hanging open.

'Ewan McNair.' He felt colour rush to his face at the touch of her soft, cool hand.

'Ewan.' It sounded like music on her lips. 'My parents,' she indicated the middle-aged couple Victor had been arguing with, 'Jean and Ruben Parr, and my gran and granddad' – an almost identical couple, both lean and wiry with tanned skins and short white hair, nodded at the McNairs – 'and this is my brother, Harry, my half-brother really, and his wife Lydia and their three rascals, Nathan, Debra and Leo, and this is my Uncle Rog, who's very good at anything you need doing. And this,' she beamed at the red-headed man who had almost come to blows with Victor, 'is my husband, Jay. And last but not least . . .' one hand stroked the tiny head against her breast, 'is Aisha.'

Suddenly Victor and Ewan were caught up in a flurry of hand-shaking, even from the three children.

'Come on in for a cup of tea, the two of you,' Petra suggested when the two groups had finally extricated themselves.

'We've work to do,' Victor said sharply. 'Come on, Ewan.'

'We'll be meeting again,' Petra called as the two of them left the field.

7

'Damned tinks!' Victor swore as the brothers drove back up the lane.

'They don't behave like tinkers,' Ewan said. 'I've never known tinkers tae introduce themselves an' shake hands. Anyway, you heard them saying they weren't tinks.'

'Hearin' isnae believin'. Damned lying tinks!'

'There's no harm in givin' them a chance.'

'Oh yes? Wait until they're well settled in an' the rest o' their clan's arrived an' they've got squatters' rights on my land?'

'Ye're gettin' a bit ahead of yerself, Victor,' Ewan said, receiving a snarl in reply. 'They don't even look like real travellers.'

'Folk like us get ontae buses at bus stops and get off them at bus stops. Folk that *live* in buses are tinks.' Victor drew the car to a stop in the farmyard, sending his mother's hens into a noisy panic. 'Get out. I'm goin' off tae Kirkcudbright tae see what I can dae about gettin' that lot off my land.'

'What about the cottage?'

'For God's— D'you no' think I've got enough tae dae without that?'

'I'll maybe ask the travellers tae give me a hand, eh?' Ewan asked as he got out of the car. 'They said they'd be lookin' for work, didn't they?'

'You dare and I'll no' answer for the consequences,' Victor growled, slamming the car into gear and taking off.

Ewan grinned as he watched his brother go. Sometimes, it was so easy to get a rise out of Victor. That girl with the baby had taken the wind right out of his sails, shaking hands and inviting them in for tea as though they were the best of friends. Victor had almost skulked out of his own field, head hanging in confusion and embarrassment.

But what a girl! Tall, shapely and beautiful, with that mass of golden curly hair cascading over her shoulders and almost halfway down her back. Her mouth full and red, her eyes green as the deep sea, slanted at the outer corners and fringed by thick fair lashes. She was a goddess, or perhaps a warrior queen. There had been a warrior queen, a long time ago, in Britain's history, but he couldn't for the life of him recall her name.

'Mam,' he said when he went into the kitchen, 'd'you mind that warrior queen who fought the Romans long ago? The one with the chariot?'

Jess was scraping carrots at the sink. 'Boudicca,' she said promptly. Once dinned into her head, nothing was ever forgotten.

'That's the one.'

'What about her?'

'I think I just met her.'

'Where?' Jess selected another carrot from the pile on the draining board.

'In Victor's field.'

'Oh aye? Your dad's been lookin' for you and Victor. He's found a break in the fence in the cows' field. Ye'd better get up there now,' Jess said.

The travellers' arrival caused a stir in the village. Some people, like Victor and his father, reckoned that travellers, be they New Age, as this group appeared to be or descended from generations of folk who preferred to roam the country rather than settle within communities, spelled trouble. Others were in the wait and see category, willing to give the newcomers a chance. And there were those who were secretly amused at Victor's predicament. Although Bert, Jess and Ewan were well liked, Victor was another matter.

'A bit of a bully at school,' Cam Gordon recalled over a pint in the Neurotic Cuckoo. 'Always wanted his own way when we played games, and he'd try to get it by hook or by crook.'

'There's no great harm in those folk, as far as I can see,' Joe Fisher said. 'They're civil enough when they come in here. Don't drink all that much, and there's no hassle when it comes to paying. A family group, and they've told me they're not stayin' long. I reckon they'll be gone by the time Victor's got the go-ahead to start work on his caravan park.'

'That lass is a looker, isn't she?' Cam said enthusiastically.

'So's her husband, so think on,' Gracie Fisher warned him, 'and they've got a lovely wee bairn, too.'

As soon as she heard about the new arrivals Lynn Stacy, who had been appointed Head Teacher of Prior's Ford Primary School at the start of term the previous August, called at the camp where she received a warm welcome and an invitation into one of the caravans for a cup of tea. She looked about with open interest.

'I haven't been in a caravan for years,' she told her host and hostess, who had introduced themselves as Ruben and Jean Parr. 'They're so compact, aren't they?'

'An exercise in design,' Ruben nodded. 'Not an inch of space wasted. Folks who design houses could learn a lot from looking round caravans.'

'D'you live in this one all year round?'

'No, we're summer travellers. We like our comfort come the winter.' Jean poured tea into mugs. 'This is a bonny part of the world; we've not been here for years, and the wee ones are looking forward to exploring the place. Sugar and milk? Help yourself.'

'Thanks. When I was a child my grandparents had an old gypsy caravan. They kept it in a field in Troon, in Ayrshire, right by the Clyde. We had wonderful holidays there,' Lynn said almost wistfully, then brought herself back to the present, and her real reason for visiting the field.

'It was the children I came about. They're school age, aren't they?'

'Nathan's nine, Debra's seven and Leo's five. And then there's wee Aisha, but she's only three months.'

'The school year's still running, and the three older children would be welcome to attend our primary school while you're here,' Lynn said carefully.

'That's very considerate of you, Miss Stacy, but Lydia, their mother, home-tutors them. She's a teacher herself,' Ruben explained. 'Would you like to meet her? They live in the double-decker. They've been out most of the day with the children, but I think they're back now.'

'I would indeed. Are you sure you have everything you need here? In the way of washing and . . . so on.'

56

'Don't you worry about that,' Ruben assured her. 'The vans all have showers, and we've got our portable chemical toilet set up among the trees, out of sight. We dig ditches to carry away the water, and anything else is buried deep, then the turf's put back in place before we leave. You'll be hard put to tell that we've ever been here.'

'More tea?' His wife topped up the half-empty mug. 'Have another biscuit, they're from the local shop. When you've finished, I'll take you over to meet Lydia and the children.'

With summer visitors coming to the village earlier than usual in the hope of catching sight of the falcons, Ingrid and Jenny had opened the Gift Horse in April. The move proved to be wise, for there was a steady stream of customers browsing, buying, or even just having a cup of coffee at the two tables set outside on good days. Because of the peregrine falcons, Ingrid had bought in several books on birds and persuaded Alastair Marshall to try his hand at some small paintings of the peregrines, which were selling well.

Lynn looked in for a coffee and a chat when she returned from visiting the travellers.

'They're very well organised, and I really don't think they're the type to leave litter and destruction. As for the children . . . their mother teaches them herself, and they're well ahead of some of our local youngsters.' Her face broke into a broad grin. 'She gave me some of their work to read, and one of them had written, "Politically correct people are the pimples on Britain's backside."'

'Oh dear!' Ingrid was shocked. 'Did you disapprove?'

'Of course not; it's perfectly true, and very well put for a seven-year-old. And her writing was well above the standard for her age, too. It's amazing the way they've turned that old bus into a really nice comfortable home. It's got a shelf of guide books on this area; apparently their parents use travelling as a way of teaching the children about the UK. And they get to meet all sorts of people into the bargain.'

Helen had also dropped in for coffee, as she often did. 'D'you think they might give me an interview for the local paper?' she asked hopefully.

'It would be worth asking. Lydia's agreed to bring the children along to the school next Thursday morning to talk to our children about life as travellers. You're welcome to come along.'

'Thanks, I will.'

'So you think it would be safe for us to let our children play with them?' Ingrid enquired.

'I think it would be downright beneficial. Their manners are immaculate.'

'Then I shall tell Ella to go along and introduce herself. She's looking for people to play five-a-side football during the summer holidays.' Ingrid's younger daughter was eleven years old, and obsessed by football.

'Unfortunately they won't be here in the summer. They're going on to Stirling in about three weeks.'

'I'll send her along in any case. It would be good for her to meet children with good manners.'

Lynn, Helen and Jenny exchanged glances. Both Ingrid's daughters, even tomboy Ella, were the best-behaved youngsters in the village. Helen never grew tired of telling the story of eighteen-month-old Ella saying, 'Pad'n,' every time she hiccuped.

'Oh, isn't that sweet! Where did you get it?' Lynn's attention was suddenly caught by the little Mary Poppins figure that Jenny had brought to the Gift Horse.

'Me,' she admitted. 'They're only made of pipe-cleaner and plasticine, no use for playing with. All right for dolls' houses, though.'

'I love them.' Lynn put Mary Poppins down and picked up another figure. 'I have to have this little scarecrow . . . Oh, you've got more scarecrows. Would it be greedy to buy them all for the children? I could tell them all about the history of scarecrows, and we could perhaps have a drawing competition.'

'Of course you can have them all.' Ingrid found a box and began to pack the small figures into it carefully, while Lynn paid Jenny.

'D'you remember the Worzel Gummidge stories?'

'I remember the television series,' Jenny said, and then explained, as Ingrid looked puzzled, 'he was a scarecrow who befriended two children; there were a lot of books about him and his scarecrow friends.'

'I adored those books. I still have them in a box somewhere. So imaginative! I think I'll dig them out to read to the children. You don't see so many scarecrows in the fields nowadays, do you? Perhaps the children could make one – they'd enjoy that!'

'I liked the Worzel Gummidge books too,' put in Muriel Jacobsen, looking up from a book she was studying. 'I'm sure they would love to hear some of the stories.'

'I agree. Television programmes for children can be very educational, but they still love being read to, I find. Thank you so much.' Lynn picked up the box and, as she headed for the door, said, 'Now I'm off to find those books. It's high time they were rescued from their box and put onto shelves.'

'We were blessed the day she was appointed headmistress,' Jenny said as the door closed behind Lynn. 'I'm sure

Miss Terrell was a very good teacher, but Calum's come on really well since Lynn took over.'

'Miss Terrell was a good disciplinarian,' Ingrid said. 'We don't have enough discipline in our schools these days.'

'They don't have any, but Miss Terrell scared the children into behaving, while Lynn achieves the same results through affection.'

'Have you noticed,' Muriel brought a book to the counter, 'that you refer to the current headmistress by her first name, and the last headmistress by her title?'

'I hadn't, actually. What *was* Miss Terrell's first name, Ingrid?'

'I have not got the faintest idea. She wasn't the sort of woman one addressed in such a familiar way. Very much old school.'

'Most parents went in fear of Miss Terrell, including me,' Jenny explained to Muriel, a middle-aged widow and a comparative newcomer to the village. 'Lynn Stacy's a breath of fresh air to parents and children alike, and I hope she stays with us for a long time.'

'In that case, so do I. I'll have this, please.' Muriel handed the book over. 'I've always felt I should learn more about birds and now that we have such special guests nesting in the old quarry, I might even decide to invest in a pair of binoculars.'

The door opened to admit Lynn Stacy, pink-cheeked with excitement. 'I've just had an idea. I could write a little play about scarecrows for the children to perform as part of the summer concert. Nothing too long, just twenty minutes or so with music. I'm sure I could think of some lyrics they could put to well-known music. What d'you think?'

'It sounds like an excellent idea to me,' Ingrid said, while Helen added, 'The kids would enjoy it.'

'Good. I'll get started on it right away!'

'Miss Terrell,' Jenny said as the door closed behind the teacher for the second time, 'would never have thought of anything like that.'

Within their first week the travellers had become part of village life. The men put up a poster in the village store offering their services as gardeners, decorators and general handymen, complete with a mobile phone number. With spring now well under way, there was no shortage of people looking for someone to help with gardens or paint fences or even have their homes redecorated.

Lydia Parr's visit to the school with her three children turned out to be a roaring success. All four, even the youngest child, happily answered questions about their travelling life, and the talk ended up as more of a party when the local children and the newcomers started to teach each other songs.

After the event Helen hurried to the Gift Horse to report to her friends. 'They're amazingly well informed about their own country, and really interesting to listen to. The children have all become firm friends, and Lydia says the family would be happy to give me an interview about their lives on the road, but she asked me to wait until they were due to move on because she wants her children to see as much of this area as they can.'

Cissie Kavanagh was wandering around the Gift Horse shelves. 'Do you think she'd speak to the Women's Institute? We've got a free afternoon next week.'

'I'm sure she would,' Helen said, and on the following week all four women from the camp – Jean Parr, her mother-in-law, Mags, Lydia and Petra, for once without the baby in a sling – were welcomed to the Institute meeting where they were so successful they were invited to attend the regular meetings during their stay in the village.

'They were so entertaining,' said Jess, who had managed to find time to attend the meeting. 'Funny and interesting. A real breath of fresh air. Not one person fell asleep this afternoon, not even Ivy McGowan, and she's known for it.'

'For pity's sake, Mum, they're only travellers,' Victor snapped. 'Trouble! I don't know why the village is makin' such a fuss about them.'

'Some travellers are trouble, I grant ye, but not this lot. They're as decent and as clean as the rest of us.' Jess gathered in the empty soup plates and took them to the sink, then donned oven gloves in order to carry a huge casserole dish to the table. 'Ewan, fetch the potatoes, will ye, son?'

'Clean they may be, but I don't know about decent,' Victor grumbled. 'They're trespassin' on my field!'

'They're not doin' any harm or any damage,' Ewan pointed out.

'It shouldn't be allowed. An' welcomin' them tae the school an' the Institute meetin's doesnae help!'

'Naomi was at the meetin' and she's invited them to the church service on Sunday.' Jess took the lid off the casserole.

'I'll no' be there, then,' Victor grunted.

'You will be, same as usual!' Jess gave her firstborn her most severe glare. Although the fragrant cloud of steam billowing from the piping hot stew had turned her glasses into opaque discs the set of her lips and the tone of her voice was enough. Jess had raised her offspring to be regular churchgoers with absences only permitted when farm work kept them at home. The only person she had never managed to impose the rule on was Bert.

Ewan passed the potatoes round, keeping out of the argument. Although her sons were full grown Jess was still known, if sufficiently riled, to set about them with the broom. If she had known about Victor's attempts to get some of the young men in the village to drive the travellers from the field, goodness only knew what she would have done – sent him to his room without his dinner, Ewan thought, suppressing a smile at the idea.

Fortunately, nobody had volunteered to help evict the visitors. 'They seem decent enough to me,' Cam had said, while the others had voted to wait and see.

8

The school visit cemented a firm friendship between the village youngsters. Lydia's three quickly found their way to the playground in the old quarry, while the local children were made welcome at the camp and returned home filled with envy.

'Can we not buy an old bus and live in it, and travel all over?' Gregor Campbell asked his mother wistfully once he had run her to ground, working at the makeshift desk in her bedroom.

'Why would we want to leave this nice house and Prior's Ford?' Helen, who wrote a weekly report on local news for the *Dumfries News,* was hurrying to meet her deadline and could have done without the interruption.

'We could travel about and see interesting places, like Nathan and Debra do. Their mum and dad took them to Dundrennan Abbey yesterday and Nathan said it was great.'

'They went in the bus?'

'No, they have a van.'

'We haven't got a van or a car.'

'But if we lived in a bus we could go in that. They're going to write down all the things they found out about the abbey in their school lesson. They don't have to go to school cos their mum teaches them. Why can't you teach us? It would be great.'

'Because I'm not a teacher and you're going to the Academy next term to learn things I don't even know about. Gregor, why don't you go downstairs and get yourself a biscuit? And get one for the others as well,' Helen added as she heard Gemma, Lachlan and Irene thundering up the stairs, talking over each other shrilly. 'Keep them quiet for five minutes, will you? I've almost finished what I'm doing.'

Victor was still in the black mood he had fallen into when the travellers took over his field. He scarcely spoke to his parents or his brother, and rushed off at every chance he got to be with his fiancée and her family.

Even so, Ewan made one last stab at asking for help with the old cottage, broaching the subject when they were cutting back an overgrown hedge.

'I told ye, I've got better things tae do!'

'We need tae keep Tarbethill goin'. We could rent the cottage out tae holidaymakers in the summer, and maybe even tae students and folk like that in the winter. I've been offered a bathroom suite someone's replacin'.'

'Get real, Ewan. The only way Tarbethill's goin' tae make a profit's if the land's sold off tae builders.'

'That's not goin' tae happen.'

'Not in Dad's lifetime, I know that.'

'Nor in mine.'

Victor had taken his gloves off, and a curling strand of bramble snagged his hand; he tried to pull free and yelped

65

as long sharp thorns dug in. Finally managing to extricate himself, he sucked hard at a bleeding wound then spat into the grass.

'You're livin' in cloud cuckoo land if you think this place is still goin' tae be here in three years, let alone the rest of yer life. Anyway, I'm busy helpin' Jeanette's father in my spare time. That's more worthwhile than your tumbledown cottage.'

'At least,' Ewan said in exasperation, 'I'm tryin' tae help Mum and Dad. The money from your caravan park won't be goin' tae the farm, will it? Even though you're usin' one of our fields.'

'Dad gave the field tae me and I need the money tae give Jeanette a decent life. I don't want her tae have tae work her fingers tae the bone an' worry about money the way Mam does. It's not what she's used tae. I'm goin' tae make some-thin' o' mysel',' Victor said. 'We'll find out who does best, your worms and old cottage or my caravan park. Jeanette and me'll be celebratin' our silver weddin' while you're still tryin' tae save up for an engagement ring for that lass o' yours.'

Ewan said nothing because he had a terrible feeling his brother could well be right.

'Almost there.'

'Good,' Ginny grunted as she floundered up the steep, narrow, overgrown and rock-strewn path behind Lewis.

'Here, take my hand.' He reached out and hauled her up a particularly difficult stretch of overgrown path. 'I bet you're sorry you insisted on trying to trace the water course now.'

'Not a bit of it,' she gasped as she reached his side. 'Look up there, at that tumble of rocks and bushes. '*That's* what's blocking the water flow.'

'Careful,' Lewis warned her but now she had almost reached her goal there was no holding Ginny. With new found energy she launched herself up the final steep bank, clutching at bushes and hauling herself on until she was standing above him.

'Yes, that's what's happened,' she called down. 'The water course has been neglected, and stones have been carried down this far and then formed a dam. Then bushes have grown between and round them and the roots have held the stones fast. There's some flat land here, and it's really marshy, because the river's blocked.'

'It was never broad enough to be a river. More of a burn.'

'A what?'

'A stream,' Lewis said. 'We call them burns.'

'Why?'

'I don't know.' He looked at his watch. 'I have to get back to the house. Molly and her folks'll be here soon to collect Rowena Chloe.'

'OK.' Ginny turned to go back down, then squealed as one foot skidded on a patch of waterlogged grass. Both legs flew up in the air and she landed on her backside with a force that drove the breath from her lungs. She began to slide with ever increasing speed towards Lewis, who stepped to one side and then caught her by the hand as she reached him and hauled her to her feet.

'Ow!' She rubbed her soaking rear. 'That hurt! And you howling with laughter doesn't help!'

'You're supposed to use a sledge,' he spluttered.

'I forgot it.' Ginny moved cautiously and then said, 'No bones broken, but every one of 'em's jarred.'

'Are you going to manage back down the hill?'

'I'll have to.'

'Take my arm and watch where you put your feet. I think

67

the original stream was diverted to feed the lake in the garden,' Lewis went on as the two of them lurched carefully downhill together. 'It probably found its old bed again when it got blocked.'

'You'll have to start by clearing the lake itself, then working back from there towards the blockage. Then make sure the water course beyond's clear before you remove the dam itself. Once that's gone, everything should be straightforward. It's going to be a big job, but well worth it.'

'It could be, but not this year, Ginny. If we're going to open the grounds to the public this year *and* get the shop started, even in a small way, Duncan and I need all the help we can get. So far, we've seen fewer summer workers than usual.'

He and Duncan depended on the help they got each summer from young people backpacking round the country, willing to take on work in the grounds or, sometimes, the house in exchange for bed and board.

'But you and Jimmy have done such a good job with the kitchen garden you might be able to make it your special project next year,' Lewis went on.

'You want me to come back?'

'We'd all miss you if you didn't. Is it too much to ask?' Lewis said anxiously. 'You've probably got better things to do than keep coming back here every summer.'

'Not really . . . no plans for next year at any rate.'

'Good. So it's Operation Lake in 2007, then?'

'I'm all for that,' Ginny said happily as she limped back to the hall.

They arrived to find the Ewings' people-carrier parked outside the kitchen door.

'They're here!' Lewis's face lit up and he headed for the door while Ginny hung back.

'I'd better go and give Jimmy a hand.'

'Don't you want a coffee after all that exercise?'

'I'll get one later,' Ginny said, and hurried off to the kitchen garden. It was Saturday morning and Jimmy was working in the polytunnel.

'Everything's lookin' good,' he announced when Ginny arrived.

'Glad to hear it. Come on,' she said, still filled with excitement over the prospect of bringing the lake and its stone grotto back to its former glory, 'we're going exploring.'

When Lewis went into the kitchen, Rowena Chloe was sitting on Val Ewing's knee, playing with a squeaky duck while Tony Ewing looked on adoringly. As before, Stella was immersed in a book at the far end of the table. There was no sign of Molly.

'Our Molly's still travelling,' Tony said as he saw Lewis glance round the table.

'Little minx that she is,' Val said fondly. 'Isn't your mum a minx, Weena? She was supposed to meet us in Dover when we came off the ferry from France, but instead she phoned to say she's met up with some group and she's staying in England for a bit longer. She's had itchy feet since she was a tot, hasn't she, Tony? Disappeared one day when she was only six, and a policeman found her on her way to the station because she wanted to go on a train.'

'When's she coming back?' Lewis wanted to know.

'Going by past experience, when she's good and ready, or when she runs out of money,' Molly's father said amiably.

'As I was saying when you came in, Lewis, we've got a bit of a problem. Tony and me are both back at work on Monday and Stella's got school.'

'And exams,' Stella put in without lifting her eyes from her book.

'And exams,' her mother agreed. 'We can't keep her off school to look after Weena.'

'Wouldn't if I could,' Stella muttered.

'So we're in a bit of a pickle till Molly gets home. We were wondering, Fliss – Lewis – if she could stay on here for a few more days.'

'Of course she can,' Lewis said while his mother was still searching for a polite refusal. 'We'd love to have her for a bit longer.'

'She's no trouble at all, is she, Mrs F?' Jinty chimed in, nodding reassuringly at Fliss. 'We've managed beautifully, and she's a dear little girl.'

'Isn't she just,' Val said warmly, and the rubber duck quacked in loud agreement as Rowena Chloe sank her little white teeth into its beak.

The Prior's Ford Progress Committee filled Naomi Hennessey's small study. Naomi had gathered up the piles of papers and books that usually balanced precariously on her desk and chairs and had deposited them in a corner of the floor to make way for Robert and Helen, industriously recording the minutes. Lachie Wilkins and Muriel Jacobson were on the low sofa, both wondering how they were going to clamber out when the time came, while Naomi herself occupied a folding garden chair and Pete McDermott perched on a piano stool. Overhead, on the music centre in Ethan's room, the mercifully dim voices of a pop group chanted a repetitive phrase.

'Sorry about that,' Naomi had said when the meeting convened. 'He's promised to keep it down. I can never understand why today's pop singers have to keep saying the same thing non-stop. I always wonder if they've forgotten what comes next, poor things.'

Robert Kavanagh was coming to the end of his report on the interest being shown in the peregrine falcons. 'People from all over are already making use of the hide to watch the birds come and go. And Joe Fisher's a happy man, with his guest rooms booked up for the next few months.'

'The new playground at the quarry isn't bothering the birds?' Pete McDermott wanted to know.

'Not at all, they're happy in their own area. We were wondering if we could mount a webcam so people could see the birds on the nest, but I don't think that's going to be possible.'

'The playground's a success,' Naomi put in. 'The young-sters seem to be enjoying it. It made sense to let them choose the equipment they wanted.'

'So everyone's happy – that's good. Any problems regarding our temporary visitors?'

'Victor McNair's in a right lather about them, but since he can't start work on the caravan park until he gets the plans through, it makes no real difference to him,' Lachie said. 'And we seem to have hit lucky with this lot – no mess, no trouble. Remember 2000?'

Heads nodded. A large collection of travellers had camped for a full summer in a field near the quarry, and there had been a lot of petty problems: vegetables going missing from fields and gardens, quarrelling among the children and some damage to the area.

Robert glanced at his watch. 'Is there any other business before we close the meeting?'

'Now that we've got the playground organised, is there much point in going on with these meetings?' Pete asked. 'We started as a protest group against the quarry and won our argument, then we became the Progress Committee in order to make sure the playground was built, but what happens next?'

'I feel we should keep going, for the sake of the community,' said Robert, who was enjoying his position as chairman. 'If people want something done they can come to us for support. We're the village voice in a way.'

'But things have quietened down now. It just seems daft to have monthly meetings with nothing to discuss.'

'There's still some money left from the donation Glenn Mason made for the playground. We need to make sure it's looked after until such time as it's needed by the villagers,' Robert pointed out.

'There is one thing,' Muriel ventured from the depths of the sofa. 'I was in the Gift Horse the other week when Miss Stacy came up with the idea of writing a little musical about scarecrows as part of the end of term concert.'

'That's right.' Lachie nodded. 'She's definitely going to do it. My two are well taken with the idea, they've been telling us all about it.'

'Well, I just wondered,' Muriel pressed on, 'how you would feel about a Prior's Ford Scarecrow Festival? Quite a few villages have them now, and they seem to be popular.'

'It would certainly help to bring tourists in,' Robert said thoughtfully.

'And the children would love it,' Naomi added. 'It gets my vote. We could get Alastair to design posters, and have competitions for the best exhibits – start with a parade, perhaps.'

'The children could parade in the outfits they'll wear for the school concert and maybe sing one or two of the songs,' Muriel suggested.

'I'm up for it,' Lachie said.

'I can get information about it into the *News*,' Helen offered. 'When would be the best time to hold it?'

'We'd have to get as much publicity as possible to bring outsiders in. This is mid-May . . . say we allow a good three weeks to get the posters designed and printed . . .'

'. . . and put up, and obviously we need to give folk time to make their scarecrows . . .'

'. . . it would be grand if there could be an exhibit in every garden and in the shop windows and . . .'

'. . . hang on, how do you make scarecrows?'

Robert slapped a hand on the desk top and the babble of voices died away. 'If we're going to do this, we have to do it properly,' he said sternly. 'First question is whether or not we're going to suggest a Scarecrow Festival. And the second thing,' he went on as heads nodded vigorously all round the room, 'is when. The Linn Hall Garden Day's always held round about the middle of August, so if the community wants it, I think we should plan the festival for July, starting with the parade that Naomi suggested. All in favour?'

Every hand went up, and Naomi got to her feet. 'Good. Muriel, come and give me a hand with the tea. We've all earned it.'

9

Rowena Chloe was thoroughly enjoying her stay in Prior's Ford. Linn Hall's large kitchen had been a more interesting crawling area than the small rooms in the Ewings' modern home, and Muffin had become her best friend, suffering her passionate hugs stoically, with only the occasional whimper of protest if she pulled at his coat too hard. She had discovered that the sturdy old wooden chairs round the table made perfect climbing frames for a girl who was learning to stand on her own two feet.

Whenever possible Lewis took her with him, tucked into a baby sling provided by Jinty, when working in the grounds but, wherever she was, there was always someone to keep an eye on her. All the backpackers made a fuss of her, as did the men working on the windows. And she was a firm favourite with the McDonald family who she stayed with at night.

'The girls are besotted with her,' Jinty had told Fliss. 'Heather and Faith are trying to coax me into having another baby. As if I haven't got enough to cope with. Mind you, having the wee one around's made me feel quite broody, not that I'd let on to them about that.'

At the moment the baby was working her way happily round a chair, using little shuffling sideways steps, while Ginny, at the table, was trying to sketch a rough map of the route the water would take from the hill, once the dam had been removed, to the lake. She became so intent on her work that when Muffin gave an anxious little bark she said absently without taking her eyes from the paper, 'Let go of Muffin, Rowena, there's a good girl.'

A few seconds later she was startled as two small fists suddenly gripped the edge of her sweater. She turned to see Rowena Chloe, her face wreathed in smiles, rocking slowly backwards on her heels, heading for the floor and taking the sweater with her, while Muffin did his best to avoid the fall by nuzzling his snout into the baby's back.

'Oops!' Ginny only just managed to throw an arm round the child before she reached the point of no return. An icy chill ran down her back as she realised how close Rowena Chloe had come to banging the back of her little red head on the flagged floor.

Fliss Ralston-Kerr was at a Women's Institute meeting in the village, and Jinty had taken a mug of coffee to the pantry, where no doubt she had stopped to chat with the laird. 'Keep an eye on the bairn,' she had said, and Ginny had nodded, then become engrossed in the map before her. So engrossed, she realised, she had ignored the dog's attempt to alert her. Goodness knows what might have happened . . .

Then it occurred to her that the first she knew of the baby's arrival was the two-fisted grip on the hem of the sweater rather than the hand–over–hand upward climb from the floor that the adults at Linn Hall had become used to.

'What . . . how did you get here?' She glanced at a chair three feet away. 'Did you *walk*?'

Rowena Chloe chuckled, then babbled out a stream of baby talk.

'Come here, trouble.' Ginny carried her over to the chair and stood her carefully against it, then backed off a little and knelt down, holding out her arms. 'Come on, Rowena, come to Ginny.'

Rowena Chloe hesitated, eyeing the space between them. She frowned, gave a thoughtful clucking noise, then put one foot in front of the other.

'Good girl – come on, then!' Ginny leaned forward, ready to catch her if necessary. Rowena took three wavering steps then lunged forward. Ginny caught her just as Lewis came in.

'She walked! From that chair . . . I saw her do it!'

'Really?' He dropped to his knees. 'Who's daddy's clever girl?'

Rowena Chloe gave a coy giggle and buried her face in his shoulder as Jinty came out of the pantry.

'Jinty, she's just taken her first steps,' Lewis told her proudly.

'We're in for it now.' Jinty sighed. 'Life's never going to be the same again.'

'Andrew got a letter this morning.' Jenny's voice shook slightly. 'He's to go to the hospital at the end of next week to get the results of his tests.'

'That's quick,' Ingrid said.

'That's what I thought. Perhaps too quick. Perhaps it's bad news.'

'It could just as well be good news,' Helen said firmly, looking up from the table, where she was scribbling in an

76

exercise book. She had volunteered to help Lynn Stacy write songs for the school's end of term scarecrow musical, and had brought the book and a biro over to the Gift Horse so she could enjoy a coffee with her friends and also get some help with her task.

'I know, that's what I keep telling Andrew, but then I think . . . he's not been well for ages, really,' Jenny said. 'Tired, and not eating as he used to. I put it down to work, and this business of trying to settle Maggie in; now I wish I had made him go to the doctor long before this.'

'He's a man, not a child. He's the only one who could make that decision,' Ingrid told her. 'It could be all sorts of things, Jenny. Diverticulitis, irritable bowel syndrome, some sort of bug. He can only start to get better from now on.'

'What rhymes with Arbuthnot?'

'A bus stop,' Ingrid suggested.

'It wouldn't fit. Lynn's got this scarecrow called Arbuthnot and it's difficult for rhyming, especially for children.'

'Why would a scarecrow be called Arbuthnot?' Jenny wanted to know.

'He's from the nobility, and he's visiting his ordinary farm field relatives and telling them all about life in the city in this song.'

'Tell her to change it to Pat,' Ingrid said. 'Pat with a top hat.'

'I think I'm going to have to. I wish I hadn't agreed to write the songs, it's not as easy as I thought. But Lynn can be very persuasive, and it's good to be involved in something that's giving my children so much pleasure. Did you know that Kevin Pearce offered to direct the scarecrow musical?'

'Lynn didn't agree, did she?' Jenny said. 'I know he does

well with the drama club, but from what I hear he's dreadfully fussy and quite bossy. Not a good mixture for someone working with kids.'

'That's almost exactly what Lynn said. She sent him packing, nicely but firmly.' Helen noted down a few words before saying, 'Jenny, if you're going to the hospital with Andrew, tell Calum and Maggie to come to us after school.'

'Maggie could come home with Freya,' Ingrid suggested. 'They can listen to music and do each other's hair. That's what girls like doing. I take it that you *are* going to the hospital?'

'Wild horses wouldn't keep me away this time. I want to hear everything that's said to him.' Andrew had insisted on going alone to the Edinburgh hospital for tests, and Jenny had got very little information out of him afterwards.

'Quite right,' Ingrid said approvingly. 'That way your worries will be laid to rest right away.'

'That's what I think too. What about Harry for your scarecrow, Helen? I'm sure there are rhymes for Harry.'

'Ever nicked anything?' Ryan asked casually.

'No!'

'You have, haven't you? Tried it and got caught, didn't you?'

'No I haven't, don't be daft!' Maggie tried to suppress the memory of her attempt, several months earlier, to steal a bar of chocolate from the village store, and her humiliation when Sam Brennan caught her at it and made her hand it back. A few days later Jenny had presented her with a bar of chocolate exactly like the one Sam had caught her with, and she realised he had told on her. If Jenny had been angry and upset, Maggie would have felt she had achieved something, but the loving way she had said, 'It's my pleasure, sweetheart,' when Maggie mumbled her thanks

78

had been so full of forgiveness it had made Maggie want to throw up.

'Why've you gone all red, then?' Ryan was saying.

'I haven't gone red,' Maggie insisted, though she could feel her cheeks beginning to glow. Ryan had been on at her for a while to stay behind when the others took the bus home after school, and her chance had come when Jenny and Andrew decided to spend the day in Edinburgh. When Jenny suggested that Maggie go home with Freya, Maggie had informed her stepmother that a classmate had invited her home for tea, and had watched, with a well-hidden mixture of amusement and contempt, Jenny's face breaking into a wide smile.

'That's lovely, Maggie,' she said. 'What's her name?'

'Fern.'

'You must invite her here, any time you want.'

'Maybe,' Maggie had said, then left to catch the school bus. It was a lot easier to lie to Jenny than to Ryan; perhaps it was because she didn't care what Jenny thought, while she craved Ryan's approval. Perhaps it was because his blue eyes seemed to bore into her head and read her most private thoughts. She hoped he couldn't see anything about the bar of chocolate incident.

'Come here.' He had bought two bags of chips to eat while they strolled aimlessly about Kirkcudbright, and now he crushed his empty bag, seized hers, which she had not finished, and tossed them both into a nearby litter bin before seizing her hand and drawing her into a chemist's shop. The counter was at one end of the shop with most of the floor space taken up by shelved stands.

'Here . . .' Ryan guided her to a stand that hid them from view of the assistants at the counter. 'Lipstick, that's handy.' He picked out a silver tube and opened it. 'Too pink for you. You need something a bit more dramatic.'

'I don't need lipstick.'

'I never said you did.' He selected another tube. 'This is better. Nice strong red. You'd look good wearing that. Want it?'

'No.' She glanced round guiltily. 'Come on, let's go.'

'Hang on, I want to show you something.' He closed the tube and tossed it lightly in his hand. 'You only need to wait until they're busy and . . . Now you see it, now you don't.'

Maggie stared at his empty hand and then at the space where the lipstick had been. 'Ryan, where is it? What did you do with it?'

He spread out both hands, laughing at her. 'Innocent as a baby, me. Search me, if you like. Come on.' He took her hand and drew her up to the counter. 'Let's buy something to make you feel better.'

Maggie wrenched her hand free and fled to the security of the street where she waited, trembling, for him to come out of the shop.

When he eventually swaggered back onto the pavement he said tightly, 'That was a daft exhibition you made of yourself. The woman behind the counter thought you were a shoplifter.'

'Me? Do I look like a thief?'

'Yes, the way you rushed out like a startled rabbit. If I hadn't told her you felt sick she'd have been out after you. I'd to buy you a packet of paper hankies to convince her.' He began to walk along the street and she had to run to catch up with him.

'What did you do with that lipstick?'

'Nothing. It's not my colour.'

'Did you put it back?'

'Stop fussing, Mags. If she'd searched me she'd not have

found a thing. You've got to learn to look folk in the eye and stop blushing. Innocent people don't blush.'

'I can't help it.'

'Learn,' Ryan said, the tight voice returning. He tossed the packet of tissues to her. 'Have them.'

She dropped them into the pocket of her school blazer, then froze. He watched her out of the corner of his eye as she pushed her hand deeper into the pocket before withdrawing the lipstick.

'How . . . When did you . . . ?'

'Told you – it isn't my colour, so you have it,' Ryan said, and ducked round a corner unexpectedly. When she caught up with him he was standing outside a large newsagent's shop.

'This'll do. What do I fancy? Wine gums. Nice and easy to nick. In you go, and remember to look innocent and keep an eye on the staff.'

'Ryan . . .'

'Don't be such a wimp, Mags.' His eyes and voice were suddenly cold and hard. 'You got the lipstick, I want the wine gums in return. Fair trade. Or would you rather just run home to your mummy and daddy? Suits me.' He turned away.

'Wait . . . I'll do it,' she said and he looked back at her. Ryan was the only good thing that had happened to her since she had come to Prior's Ford. The thought of losing him or, worse still, seeing him lording it round school with another girl, choked her. 'I'll do it.'

'Good. Go on then, and don't take all day. And remember to buy something; that stops them from getting suspicious.'

The shop was quiet, but fortunately the man behind the counter, an Asian, was talking on the phone in a swift almost musical language. Maggie gave him a nervous smile and he nodded briefly, his free hand gesticulating as he spoke.

81

Heart thumping and knees shaking, she wandered as casually as she could to the back of the shop, pausing while she was still in the man's sight to pick something up, study it and then put it down again. Then she sauntered round a stand to where she was out of his view.

So far so good, but now she found herself facing shelves of cat and dog food. She looked wildly around and spotted the sweets to one side. Within a minute, a packet of wine gums was in her hand; fumbling with the straps of her school bag she finally managed to push the sweets inside. Mindful of Ryan's order to buy something, she snatched up a pack of chewing gum and hurried to the counter. The man had finished his phone conversation and was waiting for her.

'I'll have this, please.' Her heart was racing and her lungs were filled with cotton wool; she gasped the words out as though she had been racing round the shop at top speed for the past half hour.

'Forty-five pence.'

She groped in her pocket for her small purse and dropped a coin on the counter. Instead of taking it he fixed his dark eyes on hers. 'And eighty pence for the sweets.'

'Wh-what sweets? I didn't take any sweets.'

'I saw you, in the mirror.' He pointed, and she turned to see a large circular mirror positioned in such a way that from where she stood, she could see the shelves of sweets.

Panicking, she rounded on him. 'I didn't!'

He held out a hand. 'Let's look in your bag, dear.'

'No!' She backed away as he started to move round the counter towards her. Just then a woman, middle-aged and harassed-looking, came into the shop, a large bag swinging from one arm.

'Pervert!' Maggie heard herself screeching. 'Dirty old man! I ought to report you!' She turned and ran from the

82

shop, pushing past the woman, tripping over the doorstep and only just avoiding falling on the pavement. She raced down the road, only dimly registering Ryan, who was studying the shop window.

Dodging to left and right, she sped along the street and round the corner, not stopping until she could run no longer. Seeing a narrow alleyway just ahead she veered into it and came to a halt against a brick wall, the schoolbag dropping to the ground as she doubled over, fighting for breath.

When a hand landed heavily on her shoulder she yelped and tried to pull away, but the fingers closed about her arm.

'Relax, it's only me,' Ryan said. 'I didn't know you could run like that. You should put your name down for the school sports day.'

'Did they come after me?'

'Why would they bother for a measly packet of wine gums? Give.' He held his hand out. When she nodded at the bag, he picked it up and riffled through it. 'Thanks.' He took out a sweet, then offered one to her. 'Five out of ten. You almost blew it.'

'There was a mirror.'

'So next time, keep your eyes skinned. Right?'

Once she was on the bus home Maggie began to relax. She had made a mess of things, but at least she hadn't ended up at a police station, and she hadn't made a complete fool of herself in front of Ryan, though she could have done better. She hoped, without much real hope, that he wouldn't expect her to do any more shoplifting.

It wasn't until later she realised the coin she had left on the counter with the chewing gum had been a two-pound piece. No wonder the shopkeeper hadn't bothered to run after her; he had profited in the end.

10

For once, there was none of the effortless chatter that usually flowed when Jenny, Ingrid and Helen were together. Although it was an hour before closing time Ingrid had put up the 'Closed' sign and locked the Gift Horse door. Now the three of them sat in the small back shop, holding glasses of wine they hadn't yet tasted.

'It's not the death sentence it used to be,' Helen finally ventured.

'That's what the nurse said. She's been allocated to us, to answer any questions and so on. Her name's Hope.' Jenny gave her friends a wan smile. 'A good name for a nurse, though to be honest the surgeon didn't really give us much hope.'

'They can't,' Ingrid tried to sound her usual brisk self, but couldn't quite manage it. 'They can't tell you everything's going to be fine until they're sure of it themselves.'

'Whenever I spoke,' Jenny said, 'the doctor looked at Hope and this other nurse they'd brought in to the meeting, but never at me. It was as if he was making sure they memorised everything I said for future reference. Or perhaps he kept expecting me to turn hysterical . . . I don't know.'

'Where's Andrew now?'

'He went back to the office. He said he had work to finish and he wanted time to think.'

'The two of you need to sit down and have a good talk, surely,' Helen ventured.

'I know that.' Jenny stared down at her glass as though surprised to find herself holding it. 'I think we both need time to think about what we're going to say to each other. To accept it's happened. Andrew's got cancer.' She drew in a deep breath, and looked at her friends. 'There, I've said it.'

'Good for you,' Ingrid told her. 'It's only a word; why are people so afraid to say it?'

'People used to just leave a gap in the sentence, or call it, "you know",' Jenny agreed. 'But you're right, Helen, it doesn't have to be a death sentence nowadays, so I'm not going to be afraid to say it. An entire team of experts is looking after Andrew now, and the one thing I did pick up is that they're all as determined as he is to get him well again. As I am, too.' Then, as someone tried the shop door, 'Ingrid . . .'

'Leave it. What action are they planning to take?'

'Well, because of where the tumour is in the bowel, they want him to have a course of radiotherapy and some chemotherapy as well, to shrink it before they operate. They're talking about starting the therapies in July for four weeks, and then they plan to operate in September. At least we'll have it over and done with by Christmas and know where we stand – one way or the other.'

'What about the children?'

'That's one of the things we need to talk about.'

'You know that Helen and I will help you in every way we can.'

'What would I do without you two?'

'Fortunately, you'll never have to find out,' Helen said. Then, 'I have to go; it's almost time for the school to come out.'

'I have to go too. Not a word to anyone until Andrew and I have had time to talk things through,' Jenny said hurriedly, setting the full wine glass aside and gathering up her bag.

'Not a word,' Ingrid agreed, while Helen nodded.

'I feel so helpless!' she said when Jenny had left them. 'I can't even begin to know how she feels. It sounds dreadful, but I almost wished she would cry, so we could at least comfort her.'

'She's in shock. She will cry, but in her own time. And perhaps she'll want to do it on her own. D'you want your wine?'

'No thanks,' Helen said.

When she had gone, Ingrid turned the 'Closed' sign round to read 'Open' and then went into the back shop, where she lifted her own wine glass, looked at its contents, then emptied it and the other two glassfuls into the sink.

'Here you are, hiding in your garden.'

'Working, more like.' Clarissa got to her knees, pulling her gardening gloves off. 'Cup of tea?'

'I wouldn't mind. I wanted to show you something,' Alastair said as he followed her into the kitchen. 'You'll have heard about the Scarecrow Festival the Progress Committee's planning?'

'I have, and it sounds like a great idea.'

'That's what I say. They asked me to rough out a poster

for them, and I came up with two ideas. I wondered if you'd pick out the one you like best.'

'But I'm not on the committee.'

'I know, but I value your opinion, Clarissa. Look . . .' He spread two brightly coloured posters on the kitchen table.

'They're both good. Either would do, really.'

'Be more specific,' he urged her. 'Go on, give me a clue!'

'That one.'

'Not the other?'

'I told you, they're both good.'

'But you prefer that one. Why?'

'I like the way you've drawn in a whole lot of cushiony little fields with a different scarecrow in each one, and a little face in the middle. The other one's all face, and for me it's a bit . . . much?'

'Thank you. To tell the truth, I preferred that one myself. But I just wanted to know what you thought.'

'Show them both to the committee, though,' she said over her shoulder as she fetched mugs and biscuits.

'I've still to tidy them up. I don't have much time because they want the posters all over the village as soon as possible.'

'Leave them rough, as they are. It's about scarecrows,' Clarissa explained as he raised his eyebrows, 'you don't want perfection, you want a certain roughness. And you've got it there.'

'Mmm.' He studied the pictures, then gathered them up. 'What would I do without you?'

'What you did before I came here,' she said as the kettle clicked itself off, gently breathing steam into the air.

I don't want to go back to being without you, Alastair said in his head as he watched her make tea with neat, precise movements. One day, he would have to say it out loud, but not yet. Perhaps not for a long while.

★   ★   ★

87

'We have to tell the children.'

'We're not telling them anything. I mean it, Jen.'

'So you're going through a course of treatment and then have an operation while I'm supposed to pretend that you've just been delayed at the office?'

'I meant, don't tell them until we have to. Calum's all wrapped up in this end of term school concert, and Maggie's got exams on the horizon and I don't want them distracted,' Andrew said; then, gently, 'It'll be all right, Jenny.'

'Promise me!'

'You know I can't do that. Nobody can. But I feel good about the surgeon we talked to, and the oncologist. I've got total confidence in them.'

'Why us?' Jenny burst out. It had been hard, going through dinner and helping Calum and Maggie with their home-work while all the time she was thinking of nothing else but the future, and what it might hold for her family. 'What have we done that's so wicked? Is it because we didn't get married, is that it? How was I to know Neil had died?'

'People get ill, that's all there is to it. Good people, bad people; it makes no difference. They get ill and most of the time they get better.'

'But why us?'

'Why not?' Andrew asked, and for a moment, filled as she was with a rage born of terror, she wanted to rush across the room and hit him. Instead, she curled her hands tightly into impotent fists. 'How can you be so calm about this?'

'Because getting angry isn't going to make the cancer disappear. But the medical people can stop it in its tracks, and I know they're going to do all they can to help me. Losing our tempers isn't going to help.' He came to her and took one of her hands, smoothing the fingers out and then lacing them through his. His hand was warm and strong. 'I have to work with them, Jen, and you have to work with me if we're to come through this. I know we must tell the kids, but not until we have to. We'll need time to decide how we're going to do it. OK?'

She nodded, and when he pulled her into his arms she rested her head on his shoulder.

'Don't leave me, Andrew,' she whispered.

'I don't intend to, not for a very long time.'

'Not at all! Promise!'

'I promise I'll do my best,' he said, and for the time being she had to be content with that.

The official name of the neat row of six small terraced houses fronting directly onto Main Street was Jasmine Cottages, but the local people continued to call them by their former name, the Almshouses.

Built to last in the nineteenth century, they had started life as one building housing the old, poor and infirm who had nowhere else to go and no families to care for them. In the mid-twentieth century the building, no longer required for its former purpose, had been divided into six separate dwellings, each with its own front and back door, living room and kitchen downstairs, two bedrooms and a bathroom upstairs. Plumbing and central heating had been installed. The land at the rear of the row had been left as an open communal space with paths, a grassed area with washing lines and flower and vegetable beds for residents with an interest in gardening.

The renovated houses were still intended for pensioners and, as it happened, the present residents qualified. In the past few decades all but one of the snug little homes had left council control and become private housing. The

89

exception was number one where Mrs Ivy McGowan was a sitting council tenant and, at ninety-three, one of the oldest villagers. Born in the village, Ivy knew everything and everyone.

The open back garden meant that on good days the residents frequently gathered together, each bringing the drink of their choice, and one or two bearing a plate of home-made scones or a sliced sponge cake. On this warm early May day, Ivy had settled herself on the bench outside her back door and they had all joined her, bringing deckchairs and folding garden chairs from the large shared shed. Cissie Kavanagh had provided a platter of pancakes fresh from the griddle and spread with butter.

'Eat them up before the butter melts,' she said, passing napkins round while Robert organised the chairs in a circle, indicating that this gathering was more of a meeting than a social occasion.

'Now then,' he began briskly when they were all settled, 'you'll have seen the posters about the Scarecrow Festival.'

'Couldn't miss 'em,' Ivy grunted, butter running down her chin. 'They're on every lamp post and half the windows. The one in the butcher's window stares me straight in the face every time I open me curtains in the mornin'. What do we want with a scarecrow festival, that's what I want to know. Scarecrows is for scarin' crows. Farmers make 'em and stand 'em in fields.'

'You don't see many scarecrows now, though, do you?' Dolly Cowan said. 'That's a pity.' Dolly had a froth of dyed-blonde curls framing a face that, despite middle age, still possessed little-girl prettiness, possibly due to her large innocent blue eyes. She and her husband, Harold, a quiet man with a long, rather melancholy face, had only been in the village for three years. They adored each other and their

90

two poodles, Minnie and Maxy. When the dogs first arrived the other almshouses inhabitants were concerned, but had quickly learned there was no need. Minnie, Maxy and their owners were very well behaved; both dogs were taken for long walks twice a day and rarely barked, while Harold and Dolly were firm believers in poop scoops and plastic bags.

'That's why the committee thought of the Scarecrow Festival,' Robert explained. Muriel, who had been the one to raise the subject, lifted an eyebrow but said nothing. 'Scarecrows are part of our heritage and Dolly's right, farmers don't use them as often as they once did. All the more reason for country dwellers to keep them alive.'

Hannah Gibbs gave a sudden exclamation and shifted nervously in her chair.

'Are you all right?' Charlie Crandall asked anxiously. Hannah and Charlie, both keen gardeners, were responsible for most of the flowers and vegetables enjoyed by their neighbours, and were also close friends.

'A touch of cramp.' She rubbed one calf vigorously. 'That's better.'

'The idea, as you can see from the posters,' Robert forged on, 'is that every garden and shop window will have a scarecrow, and if anyone feels like making more than one there'll be room for them on the village green and places like that.'

'Are you saying that *we* should all make one?' Harold wanted to know.

'Not necessarily one each, but one at least to represent the Almshouses.'

'Where would we display it? We don't have front gardens, and nobody would see one out here, at the back.'

'We could make small ones and put them in our windows,' Dolly suggested.

'Or one that can sit or stand on the pavement, as long as it didn't get in anyone's way,' Robert added.

After enjoying a cup of the strong tea she loved, and three of Cissie's pancakes, Ivy McGowan had settled her back comfortably against her house wall and slipped into a pleasant doze. Now, surfacing and catching the gist of the conversation, she muttered, 'You can count me out. I've had my fill of scarecrows. Made more of the dratted things than you've had hot dinners, and I'm done with 'em!'

'We wouldn't expect you to actually make one, Ivy,' Robert began. 'Hang on, did you say you'd *made* some?'

'Course I did, every dratted year when my John, rest his soul, was a ploughman. That's why you'll not catch me doin' any more.'

'You still remember how to make them?'

'I could do in the dark with me eyes shut. But I won't.'

'You'd be willing to tell the rest of us how, though, wouldn't you?'

'Don't mind doin' some talkin', just won't be doin' any *doin*',' Ivy said emphatically, and closed her eyes again.

'Well, it's good to have an expert in our midst,' Robert said. 'The first step is to decide on the sort of scarecrow we're going to make. Better start soon, time's marching on.'

'If you don't mind,' Hannah said, 'I'd rather not be involved, not in any way.'

'Oh, why not? It'll be fun!' Dolly couldn't wait to get started.

'Not for me. I don't like – what you're talking about.' Hannah looked at their puzzled faces, then added, 'I've . . . they frighten me.'

'How can they frighten you?' Dolly asked. 'They're only made of wood and straw and cloth and stuff like that. They're not real.'

'I know, I've told myself that over and over again, but – I don't know why – I've always been scared of them. It's some sort of phobia and I just can't help it!'

Her voice rose sharply at the end of the sentence, and Charlie reached out to put a hand over hers. 'It's all right, Hannah, we understand.'

'Would you like me to nip inside and fetch you some more tea?' Dolly offered, while Cissie chimed in with, 'I've got more pancakes in the kitchen, would you like one with some raspberry jam on it?'

'Thanks, but I'm fine,' Hannah said sharply. 'I'm not ill, I just don't like . . .' she hesitated over the word, then took a deep breath before saying firmly, 'scarecrows!'

11

Maggie Cameron was worried. There was an atmosphere in the house these days, a tension that tingled through the air. Jenny and Andrew had started talking earnestly to each other when they thought they weren't being overheard, and breaking off their urgent discussions as soon as she appeared.

Maggie, recalling the time she had been caught trying to take a bar of chocolate from the village shop, was convinced that somehow or other, the shopkeeper in Kirkcudbright had found out her name and address and told on her to Jenny and Andrew.

Perhaps he had gone to the school and given them a description, and they had recognised it. But surely one of the teachers would have spoken to her about it?

'Forget it,' Ryan said when she tried to tell him about her fears. 'Nob'dy knows what you did; only me and I'm not tellin'.'

'There's something going on and I can't think of anything it can be but that stuff I nicked. I wish I hadn't done it!'

'Don't be such a baby! Everyone nicks stuff, it's what

94

teenagers do. If your folks say anythin' to you, look 'em in the eye an' deny it. I've scoffed the evidence, so they've got no proof. Come here,' he said, and drew her into a nearby alleyway, where he shoved her back against the wall and kissed her, pushing himself against her.

'Get off!' She twisted her face away from his and tried to wriggle free but he persisted, his hands pushing inside her anorak and fumbling for the buttons on her blouse.

'Stop it!' Maggie shoved him with all her strength, managing at the same time to hook one foot about his ankle. He stumbled back and almost fell.

'What did you do that for?'

'I'm not in the mood, Ryan. I'm going for my bus,' Maggie said, and managed to escape back into the street before he grabbed her again. She hurried along the pavement, pulling her anorak into place, feeling her face burning, then glanced back to see if she was being followed. But Ryan was walking in the opposite direction, hands in pockets, shoulders hunched and his blonde head tucked down between them. His Big Sulk walk.

For a moment she thought of running after him to apologise but, realising it would only lead to a heavy petting session back in the alleyway, she changed her mind. She didn't want to lose Ryan, but there were times like now when she just couldn't handle his fumbling and grabbing, his breathless demands that she let him go further, his hot wet kisses.

The memory of them made her wipe the back of one hand across her mouth. Sometimes she wanted to go further with Ryan, as much as he said she wanted it, but something always stopped her. It was a step too far, more like leaping across a huge gap than one step, and she knew that once she did it, there would be no going back. She wanted it, and yet it frightened her.

She wished she could talk to someone about it, but there was nobody. Freya MacKenzie, so cool and collected, was the last person she could confide in, and Jenny, the wicked stepmother, was out of the question. She couldn't even write to the local paper's agony aunt column, because the agony aunt was Jenny's friend Helen. After discovering Helen's secret identity a year before, Maggie had written a letter to the agony aunt page under an assumed name, portraying Jenny as the uncaring stepmother. Unfortunately, Helen had realised it was her and shown it to Jenny, who had retaliated with a letter saying how much she loved Maggie. She had slipped it beneath Maggie's bedroom door, and it still lay at the bottom of her underwear drawer. The two of them had never discussed it.

Recalling the letters brought the subject of Jenny and Andrew back to Maggie's mind. She fretted over it all the way home in the bus.

When she got home, Jenny was helping Calum to go over his lines for the school concert. 'Hi, love,' she said with her usual fond smile. 'You're later than usual.'

'Stayed behind with mates.'

'That's nice. Home-made soup and chicken risotto tonight, is that all right?'

'Whatever.' Jenny was a good cook and Maggie loved chicken risotto.

'Would you like something now? A sandwich?'

'No.' Maggie helped herself to an apple from the bowl of fruit kept on the dresser, then stumped out of the kitchen, shoulders sagging in the walk she always put on between the bus stop and the house. Ryan wasn't the only one with a Big Sulk walk. As she went up the stairs she heard Calum and his mother settle down again to their rehearsal.

Calum seemed quite unaware of any added tension in the house. At the moment he was filled with excitement about the concert and the scarecrow that he and his dad were going to make for the front garden.

Maggie waited until she heard Andrew come in from work and Calum coming upstairs to wash his hands before dinner, then she went down the stairs as quietly as she could. They were doing it again, almost whispering to each other, and that strange tenseness was back; she could sense it.

She strained her ears, and thought she heard Andrew say, 'Look love, we've been through a lot worse than this.' Then Jenny's voice rising slightly, wobbling as though she were trying not to cry, 'I don't know if I can do it, Andrew. I don't know if I can go on like this for much longer!'

'You can. *We* can!' he said, and then, as though sensing Maggie's presence, he went on cheerfully, 'Dinner smells great, I'll just put this briefcase away. Hi, Maggie, had a good day?' he added as he came through the hall.

'The usual,' she muttered, watching him go up the stairs.

There was definitely something going on, and it almost certainly concerned her. They knew she was a thief and she wished they would confront her with it, instead of talking about her in whispers!

'Victor's got enough on his plate, I can understand him not being able to help with the cottage,' Alison Greenlees said. 'Tell you what, Ewan, I'll do it. I'll help you.'

'You? But it's going to be a lot of hard work.'

'I'd enjoy it. It'd be fun.'

Her parents were both behind the bar that night, and she and Ewan were enjoying a drink at a corner table. 'It would be great to bring that sweet little cottage back to life,' she went on. 'I can't do any plumbing or electrical work, but I can scrub and paint and sweep and I'm quite good at hammering nails in. As long as I can bring Jamie with me. We could probably find something for him to do as well.'

'Of course you can bring him, if you're sure you really want this.'

'I am. You've done me the world of good, Ewan, making me join the drama club, and get out and about again when I'd become quite scared of other people. And you and your mum have been so good to Jamie. He loves going to the farm. And he loves the worms. We both do. I never thought I would hear myself say that I love worms. But those little red ones in the wormery are really sweet.'

'I couldn't have got it going without you.'

It was true; Alison had taken the time to read all she could about setting up wormeries, and her help had been invaluable. Discovering that Ewan's original idea of keeping the worms in long plastic-lined ditches was over-ambitious for a beginner, she had persuaded him to use sturdy wooden boxes for the time being, pointing out that once the worms started breeding and making compost, they could eventually be moved into the large ditches.

She had put up some of the money to buy the boxes and worked alongside him to prepare the bedding, and she and Jamie had been there to see the first consignment of wrigglers being introduced to their new homes. The young worms were thriving on the pub's unused vegetables, which she blended before taking them to the farm.

'I tell you what,' he said now, 'in return for your helping with the cottage I'll make a Bob the Builder scarecrow for Jamie. What d'you think?'

'He'd love that!' She lifted her glass and touched it lightly against his. 'Here's to our new projects,' she said.

Gracie Fisher, apparently busy at the bar, was keeping an eye on her daughter and Ewan. 'Look at those two, Joe,' she hissed. 'They're celebrating something. Do you think . . . ?'

'No, I don't, Gracie. It's far more likely to be somethin' to do with worms, so don't get yourself excited.'

'I just want to see her settled and happy again.'

'And so do I, but we'll have to give it time, lass. As much time as they need. And from what I've seen of young Ewan,' Joe said, 'he'll take plenty. He's a shy one, but a diamond as well. Yes, Duncan, what can I get you?'

Charlie Crandall banged his gardening gloves together to shake off the loose earth and then laid them neatly together beside Hannah's on a shelf, asking casually, 'Coming in for some coffee?'

'It's my turn, isn't it?'

'Doesn't matter, I've got something to show you.' In his small, neat living room he served coffee before asking, 'Ever heard of Oor Wullie?'

'Your what?' she asked, and he laughed.

'It's well seen that you're a Sassenach. Oor Wullie's a very famous cartoon character. He has a weekly page in the *Sunday Post*, and every other year an Oor Wullie annual comes out in time for Christmas. On alternate years it's a Broons annual – that's Glaswegian for Brown, by the way. They're a family who share the *Post* with Wullie. He was always my favourite and I've got quite a collection of his annuals.'

He handed over a large, brightly coloured book. On the jacket was a picture of a round-faced boy with a mop of spiky yellow hair. He was sitting on an upturned bucket, elbows on knees, chin on hands, scowling into the distance. 'That's Wullie,' Charlie said proudly.

Hannah riffled through the book to find that every page

was filled with one of Wullie's adventures, and each page started and often ended with him sitting on his upturned bucket.

'Why the sudden interest in this character – or is it just that you felt like sharing some childhood memories with me?'

'Have a biscuit. I was thinking,' he said slowly, 'about the festival, and it struck me that since Oor Wullie's such a famous Scottish character, perhaps we should use him as our offering.'

'The penny,' Hannah said, 'has dropped, and I've been tricked. You knew very well that it was my turn to give you coffee.'

'You *have* been tricked, but only in a friendly way.'

'Charlie, you know how I feel about this business. Share your idea with the others; I don't want to be involved in any way.' She laid the annual down.

'Hear me out, Hannah, please. Can you recall why you developed this dislike' – Charlie carefully avoided the word 'fear' – 'of scarecrows?'

She bit her lip, but concentrated on trying to give an honest reply. 'I can't. I just remember seeing one in a field during a walk with my parents, and screaming my head off.'

'Did you have dolls when you were a child?'

'Yes.'

'Were you afraid of them?'

'Of course not.'

'Why not?' he fired the question at her.

'Because they were only . . . They were dolls!'

'Inanimate objects, made of plastic, cloth, wool. Small objects that had to obey your every whim because they weren't real.' Charlie picked up the comic book. 'Oor Wullie's not real, Hannah. And he's not much larger than

100

your dolls. We could find a pair of small overalls and a jersey and stuff them with straw. We could top them with a cushion made from a bit of sheeting, draw Wullie's face on it, give it socks and shoes and hands made the same way as the head, and then sit it on an upturned bucket. Would you be afraid of that? Of something you had made yourself, with me?'

'I . . . I don't know.'

'You wouldn't be, not when you knew exactly what had gone into making it. We could do that one little scarecrow between us – our contribution.'

'Charlie . . .'

'Take the book home and read it. Get to know Wullie. He's a rascal,' Charlie said fondly, 'but he's a nice wee rascal. Scotland loves him and so will you. That's all I ask. That you get to know him. Then we'll decide on the next step when you're ready.'

'Oh my goodness,' Jinty McDonald said as Lewis turned into the road leading to Linn Hall. 'That's never your Molly ahead, is it?'

'It is!' There was no mistaking the jaunty figure striding up the road ahead of them, rucksack on her back and red hair flaming in the morning sun.

'Did you know that she was coming back today?'

'No idea.' He tooted the horn and Molly turned, then waved and stepped back against the verge as the car began to slow.

'She mustn't know that Rowena Chloe's been staying with us at nights, your mother would never live it down! What'll we say?'

Rowena Chloe, strapped into her baby seat at the back, gurgled cheerfully.

'I went down to collect you because you have a bad ankle and brought Rowena with me for the ride.'

'But why would I come to work with a bad ankle? And why would you have her pram in the boot?'

'OK, no bad ankle,' Lewis said swiftly as the car coasted to a stop beside Molly. 'I took Rowena to the village for a walk and collected you while I was at it.'

'Why would you drive to the village to take her for a—'

'Sshh!' Lewis hissed, and jumped out of the car. 'Hi, love, nice to see you. Give me your rucksack and I'll put it in the boot.'

'I can do it.' Before he could stop her, she had opened the boot. 'You've got the pram in here,' she said, surprised. 'Is it all right if I shift this bag?' When room had been found for her rucksack she gave Lewis a long, lingering kiss and then slipped into the rear seat.

'Hi, Jinty. And here she is, my little girl! Hello, Weena! Did you miss Mummy, did you, then?'

Twisting in her seat, Jinty saw uncertainty flicker over the baby's face as Molly leaned towards her. And no wonder, she thought, it's been weeks since the poor wee mite set eyes on her mother! Then as one of Molly's long red plaits swung forward the little girl's face broke into a broad smile. She gave an excited cry and reached out a chubby fist to catch hold of the plait.

'I knew she wouldn't forget me!' Molly crowed, fumbling at the straps that held her daughter securely.

'Wait until the car stops at the house,' Jinty warned her swiftly, but Molly was already lifting the baby into her arms.

'I can't wait a minute longer! We have to have a good cuddle. Oh, I've missed you!'

Not enough to give up your gallivanting, Jinty thought

angrily, while aloud she said, 'Drive carefully, Lewis, and mind the bumps.'

'It's great to see you, Molly,' he said happily as he eased the car up the drive. 'You should have let us know you were coming.'

'I wasn't sure when I'd get here but I got a lift last night on a lorry coming north, and when the driver dropped me off in Kirkcudbright I cadged a ride here in the post van. I phoned the house before we left and spoke to your mother. She didn't say where you were.'

'He took Rowena Chloe for a walk and then collected me to save me the trek to the Hall,' Jinty said hurriedly. 'I'd promised to bring some things that Mrs F needed – the bag in the boot's mine.'

12

Fliss was waiting for them outside the kitchen door, her hands twisting round each other nervously. She pulled the passenger door open as soon as Lewis switched the engine off. 'Lewis, I'm glad you're back. Molly phoned and— Oh, Molly, you're there!'

Jinty bounced from the car. 'We met her on the way, Mrs F. Isn't it lucky that Lewis decided to take Rowena and the pram into the village for a walk, then bring me back with him?' She opened the boot and hauled out the bag that held the paraphernalia required for Rowena's overnight stays with the McDonalds. 'I brought the things you asked for, Mrs F,' she went on briskly. Fliss looked puzzled. 'I'll put the kettle on, shall I?'

'I've got something to show you,' Lewis said once they were all in the kitchen. He took the baby from her mother's lap and put her carefully on her feet, kneeling behind her to make sure that she was steady. 'Now – call her over.'

'Weena. Come to Mummy, Weena. Come on, sweetie,' Molly crooned, then gasped as Rowena took one step towards her, then another and another, arms outspread, managing to stay upright until she reached her goal.

'She's walking! Clever girl!'

'She's been walking for a week now,' Lewis said proudly. 'Back to Daddy, Rowena. There's a clever girl.'

It was a pity, Jinty thought as the little girl started on the return journey, her face wreathed in smiles, that her mother hadn't cared enough to be there to see her first steps.

She had always liked Molly, but over the past few weeks she had come to adore Rowena Chloe. She felt the baby, and Lewis, deserved better than a flibbertigibbet of a girl who seemed to be more interested in her own pleasures than in either of them.

The village was in the grip of scarecrow mania. Primary-school mothers were all busy making costumes for the musical that Lynn Stacy and Helen had written, while Alastair Marshall helped the children make scarecrows to set up in the school playground during festival week.

Farmers were besieged with requests for straw and hay, garden sheds were raided for unwanted timber and chicken wire, and wardrobes for unwanted clothing as the villagers began to prepare for the festival. Ingrid, as enterprising as ever, had set a skilled knitter in the village to turn out cheerful little scarecrow dolls for the Gift Horse.

Busy as he was with the wormery, doing up the old cottage, and his usual farm chores, Ewan McNair was having a lot of fun, making a scarecrow for wee Jamie Greenlees.

'Waste of time,' Victor scoffed, while their father, echoing Ivy McGowan's words, said, 'Why d'you want tae dae that, lad? Scarecrows are useful for one thing only, and no' always that. Ye've more tae dae than make one that won't even scare the birds.'

'I told Jamie I'd do one for him, and I'm doin' it,' Ewan said doggedly. 'He's lookin' forward tae it.'

'It's no' for him at all, it's tae please his mother,' Victor pointed out.

'What if it is?' Ewan was getting tired of pretending that he wasn't interested in Alison Greenlees. 'I'm enjoyin' the work and if Jamie and Alison both like it, that's fine by me!'

Posters had been spread throughout the surrounding area by the Progress Committee, determined that Prior's Ford would be filled with visitors for the special event. Their plans suited Lewis Ralston-Kerr, who decided that the Linn House grounds and the stable shop should be open to the public for the entire week.

'It's the perfect time to launch our new project,' he said at a meeting round the kitchen table. 'The gardens are beginning to look good and people would enjoy just wandering around.'

'And causing damage,' Duncan Campbell put in.

'I doubt that, but we'll be around to keep an eye on things. We could charge a small entrance fee – put up a table at the gate, and you could collect the money, Dad.'

'I don't know about that,' Hector said nervously. 'You're better with people than I am, Fliss.'

'But Mum'll be busy with the teas.'

'The whats?' Fliss asked in alarm.

'I thought we could do teas and home-baking – nothing elaborate, just a scone or a cake with each cup of tea. And soft drinks for the children.'

'But don't you need permission for that sort of thing?' his father asked. 'Now that we're part of this dratted EU you can scarcely blow your own nose without written permission.'

'I've already thought of that. I've had a word with Robert Kavanagh and he says the Progress Committee have it all under control. They'll keep us right. Sam and Marcy can supply us with tea, coffee and sugar at cost price, and we can get soft drinks through them on a sale or return basis. I've found a farmer who'll lend us some trestle tables and benches to put up in the stable yard. The backpackers can act as waiters and waitresses; they'll enjoy that.'

'What if it rains?' Fliss wanted to know.

'Then folk can come in here. It's big enough to take an extra trestle table if it's needed.'

'In here?' Fliss looked round the untidy kitchen. 'But it's not fit for visitors!'

'Believe me, Mum, they'll love it.'

'Lewis is right, Mrs F, people don't often get to see the kitchens of big old houses,' said Jinty, who liked the idea of opening Linn Hall to the public. 'I'll take responsibility for the baking, and I'm sure some of the Women's Institute ladies would be happy to help out, providing we can supply the flour and so on.'

'Ginny, I was wondering if you could man the shop for the week. I'll be there as well, most of the time, but I need to help Duncan keep an eye on the gardens.'

'Of course.'

'What are you goin' tae sell in this shop of yours?' Duncan wanted to know. 'We've no' begun tae sort that out.'

'It'll be on a small scale, of course, but we can manage something – bunches of cut flowers, for instance, and I'm going to package some of those seeds we collected last autumn, since we have more than we need for ourselves. I reckon they'd sell. Ginny, can we have as much produce from the kitchen garden as you can manage?'

'I think we could do quite well.'

'Good. And I'm going to have a word with Ingrid, to find out if she has any surplus stock we could have. We'd sell at her price and she'd get all the money because it's just to keep the shelves from looking too bare. And if anyone can think of other ideas let me know, because we need all the gimmicks we can get.'

'If you ask me, you're riding for a fall,' Duncan predicted.

'A pint in the Cuckoo on the final night says we won't.'

'Two pints,' Ginny put in. 'We each buy you one if the whole thing collapses, Duncan, and you buy us one each if it breaks even.'

'You're on.' Duncan cheered up slightly. 'I can taste that beer slidin' down my throat right now.'

'Dream on, pal. If you like, Dad,' Lewis offered, 'Ginny and I could take turns collecting entry fees at the gates, and you could help Mum and Jinty, and perhaps take a turn in the shop.'

Hector had been listening with mounting uneasiness to his son's plans. He had no objection to the gardens being opened to the public, and he was proud of Lewis and his determination to revive Linn Hall's fortunes, but he was a very shy man and strangers terrified him. On the other hand, he knew that as the head of his small family, he had to pull his weight. 'No, I'll do gate duty,' he said firmly. Surely nobody would want to stop and chat to the person collecting their entry money!

'Do you think this idea of Lewis's will work?' Fliss asked Jinty when they were on their own, Jinty washing and Fliss drying dishes. 'I don't really think we're ready for it.'

'Of course it'll work, we'll all make sure of that. And he's right; the festival's the best time to try it out. I've never seen the gardens looking so good, and if we can cope with

108

backpackers every year, we can manage visitors for a week. They'll be happy enough with a mug of tea or coffee and a piece of home-baking,' Jinty said confidently. 'In any case, I think it'll be good for your Lewis to have something to occupy his mind. That lad's pining for Rowena Chloe and her mother.'

'It's a pity Molly couldn't have stayed on for a few weeks. We all miss the baby. She's a very sweet, contented little thing, isn't she? I'd like to think,' Fliss said wistfully, 'that she's our flesh and blood granddaughter.'

'Have you thought of suggesting a DNA test to Lewis?'

'Good gracious no, we couldn't do that!'

'There's quite a lot at stake,' Jinty said in her straight-forward, practical way as she plucked a gleaming plate from the sink and handed it over to be dried. 'This place isn't as tumbledown as it used to be. You've got some money in the bank, and the way Lewis is going, bless him, there might be something well worth inheriting one day.'

'I know.' Fliss heaved a sigh. 'I've tried to speak to Hector about it, but he's rather hiding his head in the sand. He hates confrontations and having to make decisions, and we both detest the thought of even hinting to Lewis that that lovely little girl isn't his after all. When it comes right down to it, Molly's the only person who knows the truth.' Then hope lifted her voice. 'So if she says that Lewis is Rowena Chloe's father, he most probably is.'

Jinty, who was more streetwise than Fliss, wasn't sure if Molly, a true child of the times, could be certain that Lewis had fathered her baby. But she kept that thought to herself.

13

Hannah Gibbs had to admit that there was a certain mischievous charm about the spiky-haired little lad known to readers of the *Sunday Post* newspaper as Oor Wullie. And Charlie Crandall could be very persuasive when he wanted to be. Before she knew it, she was touring the charity shops in Kirkcudbright for Wullie's trademark white shirt and dark overalls, or, as Charlie called them, dungarees. She had also bought some bright yellow wool to fashion into a cap of spiky yellow hair.

She was enjoying herself, and Charlie wisely refrained from pointing out that she was overcoming her fear of scarecrows. But he did wonder what would happen when July came and she found herself surrounded by them.

When the committee announced that there would be prizes for the best shop-window scarecrow and the best garden scarecrow, friends and neighbours who had until then amicably discussed possible ideas suddenly became tight-lipped, and children were forbidden to tell their friends about the plans their parents came up with. Garden sheds were locked and their windows hung with sacking to deter snoopers.

'I've not seen such a carry-on since that flower show ten years ago, when Jake Paterson accused Fred Langmuir of spying on his greenhouse,' an elderly villager recalled over a pint in the Neurotic Cuckoo. 'Nearly came to blows they did, when Fred won the competition for the best tomatoes. They still weren't speaking to each other when Jake died close to a year later.'

'That's right,' Lachie Wilkins recalled. 'A right carry-on, that was. Fred refused to go to Jake's funeral.'

'You should have mentioned that when the committee decided to award prizes, Lachie,' the first speaker said.

'Truth to tell, Dennis, I forgot about it. And it's too late now to change things. We thought a competition might add a bit of spice to the whole business.' Lachie defended himself and his fellow committee members. 'It isn't our fault if folk take things too seriously, is it?'

'There is that,' Dennis agreed. 'They shouldn't be so childish, should they?'

'Havin' another?'

'Why not.'

'So what ideas have you come up with, then?' Lachie asked when he returned to the table with the drinks.

'Mind your own business!' Dennis snapped, lifting the fresh pint to his lips.

'I haven't had such fun for ages,' Alison Greenlees said happily.

'I wouldn't call it fun.' They were both in the cottage kitchen, Ewan making a draughty window frame wind- and water-tight while Alison, her fair hair covered by a scarf, brushed loose dirt from the kitchen walls.

111

'But it is! Much more fun than serving behind the bar or doing housework. Oops!' She deftly sidestepped as a large spider, dislodged from its web in the upper corner, scuttled down the wall and began to run across the floor. Alison dropped the brush and picked up a plastic tumbler. Trapping the spider beneath it, she slid a piece of card in to act as a floor.

'I don't know why you bother, it'll only try to get back in if the rain comes on. They don't like rain.'

'If it does, I'll put it out again. I can't bear to kill the wee things; they've had this place to themselves for so long they've got squatter's rights. And we can't tell you that you're evicted, can we, pet?' Alison said to the spider as she carried the covered tumbler to an open window. She released it into the long grass beneath then called, 'All right, Jamie?'

Her son squatted on the path beside one of the kitchen chairs, a bowl of soapy water beside him and a nailbrush clutched in one fist. The old flagstones all round ran with soapy water and his clothes were damp. 'I'm buthy,' he said importantly, dipping the brush into the bowl before scrubbing at a chair leg.

'Good for you.' She drew back into the room and returned to her own work. 'He's as happy as a sand boy. Wringing wet, but happy.'

'He's a grand wee lad.'

She nodded. 'I'm going to miss him when he starts nursery school in September. You don't realise how quickly time flies until you watch a child grow up.'

'It'll do him good, mixing with other kids.'

'I know. And it'll give me more time to help you with this place, and with the wormery.'

'You don't have to, you know.'

'But I want to. As I said, it's fun bringing this lovely wee

112

cottage back to the way it was. And I enjoy the wormery, as long as I don't have to touch the worms with my bare hands. Should we try going through my lines while we're working?'

'Best tae wait until we can concentrate,' Ewan said, wishing that he had never offered. Reading through the love scene Alison was to have onstage with another man was a torment, and the bit where they kissed at the end of the play was something he preferred not to think about. He had never in his life envied anyone before, but the thought of seeing, or even imagining, Alison in someone else's arms made him sick with jealousy.

They worked in companionable silence for another ten minutes before Ewan closed the window, tested the repaired frame, then opened and closed the window several times more before announcing, 'Finished. And I think it's draught-free now.'

'Next time I'll wash down the walls in here,' Alison said as they packed up, 'then they'll be ready for a coat of white-wash.' As they left the cottage she turned to look at the sturdy little building sitting in its overgrown garden. 'It's beginning to look less neglected already. Are you going to plant roses round the door?'

'It's being rented out to holidaymakers as an authentic farm cottage, not a chocolate-box picture,' Ewan protested.

'I know, but roses would look so nice there.'

'Then we'll plant roses, once we get to that stage.' If Alison wanted roses, Ewan would make sure she got them.

'It looks so . . . safe, doesn't it? It looks as if nothing horrible could happen to the people who lived there,' Alison said wistfully. Then as Jamie tugged at her hand and announced loudly that he was hungry, the three of them began to walk up the lane towards the farmhouse, where

Jess awaited them with home-made scones and a huge pot of tea.

Jenny and Andrew continued to act strangely and talk in low voices, breaking off as soon as Maggie came within earshot, but still nothing was said about her pathetic attempt to steal from the shop in Kirkcudbright.

She had been practising her hurt look and her protestations – 'I didn't go into his poxy shop and even if I did, he tried to touch me! And I paid for the sweets, he can't deny that. Why do you have to believe him and not me? Nobody ever listens to a word I say . . .' – for so long they had turned into meaningless sounds in her head and guilt began to give way to anger. They had no right to keep her waiting and wondering like this; she had other things on her mind, like exams and Ryan. The exams weren't her main problem, because Maggie had a quick mind that made learning fairly easy. With nothing much else to do but sulk in her room in the evenings, she had put in a lot of studying at the nice desk Jenny had provided.

But Ryan was another matter. He was getting tired of her, she knew it. She had behaved like a baby over the business of the wine gums and she was still refusing to let him go further when they were alone together. He kept reminding her that there were other girls who fancied him and it was true; she could tell by the way they looked at Ryan, and at her when she was with him, that they wanted to be his girlfriend instead of her. What with one thing and another, life was rotten.

She called her grandmother on the mobile phone Jenny and Andrew had given her for her birthday and tears came to her eyes as she heard the pleasure in Ann Cameron's voice. 'Maggie, pet, it's so good to hear your voice! How are you? And the family? And are your exams over?'

'Fine, everyone's fine, and the exams are still to come but I've been studying hard.' That was something she would never have admitted to Jenny.

'You always were clever, even as a wee tot,' her grandmother said proudly. 'You take after your uncle Malcolm there.'

'How's Granda, and Auntie Lizbeth?'

A bleak note slipped into Ann's voice. 'Liz isn't too well just now; but you know how it goes with her, she'll maybe feel much better next week. And your grandfather . . . well, they said it would be a long time before he got his strength back. It frets him badly at times; you know how much he liked to do everything. Mebbe too much, the way things have turned out.'

'I wish I could help the two of you . . . all of you.'

'It does help us all, pet, knowing you're being looked after and that you're happy with Jenny and Andrew, and doing well at the school. Just wait till I tell your granddad and your auntie that you phoned to ask after them. That'll bring a sparkle to their eyes!'

So there was no hope of getting back to Dundee. Maggie felt, when the call ended, as though a lifeline had just been twitched away from her frantically grasping fingers.

It seemed, now, that the only person who had time for her was Ryan. Perhaps, she thought miserably, it was time to forget the people who called themselves family, and concentrate on keeping him happy, at least for the time being.

And so, when he came up with another dare, she agreed to it.

★　　★　　★

115

'Care for another?'

Ginny, enjoying an after-work drink with Duncan and Lewis, had seen the burly young man who was now standing by their table often enough, drinking with other villagers in the Neurotic Cuckoo, and sometimes with young people who did casual summer work at Linn Hall, but he had never spoken to her before. Nor had she ever seen Lewis scowl the way he was scowling now.

'No thanks, we can buy our own.'

'I'd not say no to another pint, Cam.' Duncan drained his glass and held it out.

'Sure. What about you?' The newcomer smiled at Ginny. He had a nice smile.

She glanced at Lewis, who was gripping his almost empty glass as though trying to resist the temptation to throw it at the other man.

'I think we were—'

'Just going,' Lewis finished the sentence for her.

'Come on, Lewis, have a drink with me! It's purely business, if that's any consolation.'

'You and I don't have business to discuss, Cam.'

'We might have.' The young man tossed a large envelope down on the table. 'Take a look at these while I fetch the drinks. Same again all round, OK?'

'I'm going,' Lewis said as soon as the other man had gone to the bar. 'You two stay if you want.'

'Hang on a minute; let's see what's in here.' Duncan opened the envelope and brought out a bundle of postcard-sized photographs. As they spilled across the table the overhead lights caught the glossy paper, turning the coloured pictures into a rainbow. Duncan gave a low whistle as he began to sort through them.

'They're good. Look, Ginny, here's one of the kitchen

116

garden taken from the gate. And this one of the rhododendrons – they're all pictures of the hall gardens, Lewis.'

'What?' Lewis snatched a photograph from Duncan, then picked another up at random. 'Who gave him permission to photograph our property?'

'They're good.' Ginny lingered over the picture of the kitchen garden, its red brick walls glowing in the sunlight.

'Gangway.' Cam had returned; he waited until Duncan had cleared a space before setting down the tray of drinks. Lewis maintained an angry silence until the other man sat down, then he snapped, 'What d'you think you're doing, taking photographs of private property?'

'That's what I wanted to talk to you about. I'm Cam Gordon, by the way, and I already know you're Ginny Whitelaw.' He shook Ginny's hand. 'You've done a great job on that old kitchen garden.' She gave him a puzzled look. 'I work for the firm that's been putting Linn Hall to rights. Look,' he searched through the photographs then handed one to her, 'I took that one from the roof last autumn.'

It was an excellent photograph of the kitchen garden, taken from high above and showing the paths and raised beds she and Jimmy had gradually uncovered from the chaos of weeds and overgrown vegetation that had all but smothered the area.

'It's great!'

'Thanks. Cheers!' Cam took a hefty gulp of his pint then set the glass down and wiped his mouth with the back of one hand. 'As you say, Lewis, I didn't have the right to take those photographs, but it's my hobby – remember? And though I say it myself, I'm good at it. I've heard you're going to start a shop in the stable block, and I thought you might be interested in selling photographs of the grounds

117

and the house.' He spread them out. There was one of the statue in the neglected rose garden, a nymph who had once poured water from an urn into a small pool, and another of the stone summer house overlooking what had once been a lake. In both instances the photographer had concentrated on the subject and managed to exclude the surrounding neglect. Other pictures were in the same vein, showing close-ups of rose bushes in full bloom, small sections of lawn nestling among shrubbery, a distant shot of the house that managed to hide its shabbiness, a stone bench with blue flowers massing behind it, a small-paned stable window with a pot of scarlet geraniums on the sill and the driveway, a cool tree-shaded oasis speckled with sunshine.

'Technically, they're yours, and if you want 'em you can have 'em,' Cam said as the other three looked through the pictures, Ginny and Duncan with enthusiasm, Lewis reluctantly. 'But what I thought was, they might go down well in your new shop. I'm willing to print out as many copies as you need, for fifty per cent of the cost – to be set by you. And I can take more photographs if you want. What d'you say?'

'Go for it, Lewis.' Normally, Duncan Campbell was a pessimist, but not now. 'You've been sayin' you need more stuff in the shop, and what have you got tae lose?'

'I suppose. OK, Cam, let me take these home and show them to my parents. I'll get back to you.'

'Fair enough.' Cam held out a hand and, after a moment's hesitation, Lewis took it.

It wasn't until later the next day that Ginny managed to get Duncan on his own. 'What was all that about last night?' she asked. 'Cam seemed a nice enough man and the photographs are great, so what was wrong with Lewis?'

'It's just one of those daft things,' Duncan grunted. 'The two of them grew up together, never out of each other's company till Cam's dad took him out of school and intae the buildin' firm he works for. Cam was desperate tae stay on at school an' for some daft reason he resented Lewis bein' able tae stay on an' then go tae university, though it wasnae Lewis's fault. Nothin' was ever the same between them after that. Then, when Molly came tae work here an' Lewis fell for her, Cam claimed that he'd already met the lass on a holiday. Hinted that the two of them'd been more than good friends. If you ask me, it was just said tae rile Lewis, and it worked. They went at it in the Cuckoo one evenin' – a right good fight it was, too, till the landlord stepped in an' spoiled it. Maybe this business o' the photographs'll put them right, though. It's crazy fallin' out over a lass.'

14

The problem with being Lucinda Keen of the *Dumfries News* agony aunt page was that Helen Campbell wasn't allowed to tell anyone that she was living a double life. Because the *News* was a local paper, there was a chance she might get letters from people she knew, which hadn't happened as yet. As the editor explained when he offered her the job, nobody would spill out their most intimate problems on paper if they knew the person who was going to read them. He had a point, but it was difficult for Helen to be two people. Only Jenny and Ingrid were in on her secret, because she had sought their advice when offered the page.

Everyone knew she wrote the weekly Prior's Ford news column, and friends and neighbours were good about leaving her in peace on Wednesday afternoons, when she had to meet her deadline. But poor Lucinda, who had a different deadline, was constantly being interrupted.

Today, Helen was pondering over a letter from a woman who suspected that her neighbour's husband was having an affair with the widow across the road. The writer wanted to know whether she should warn the unsuspecting wife or hold her tongue and thus collude with the husband. It was a tricky one, and Helen wanted to get the answer right. She had just come to a decision and was about to key it into her computer when the doorbell rang.

'Oh . . . sugar!' she muttered, wondering if she could possibly ignore it. But after a pause it rang again, and she had to hurry downstairs, completely losing the advice she had been about to give.

'Hello,' Jean Parr said when the door opened. 'It's all right, I'm not here to sell you artificial flowers or clothes pegs.'

'Excuse me?'

'A rather silly joke we travellers have done to death.'

'Oh . . . it's you. Sorry, I was thinking about something else.' Helen collected her scattered wits. 'Come in.'

'I won't, dear, because you're clearly in the middle of something, and I've just popped into the village for some supplies.' Jean indicated the bags she carried. 'We're heading off to pastures new and I wondered if you were still interested in that article you mentioned earlier.'

'Oh, yes, I am!'

'Are you free tomorrow morning? We're planning on leaving in the afternoon.'

Helen's brain raced. If she worked hard for the rest of the afternoon, and if Duncan was willing to help the children with homework in the evening . . .

'Yes, I am.' She would have to be. This chance was too good to miss.

'Ten o'clock?'

'Perfect. Would it be all right if I arranged to bring a photographer from the newspaper?'

'Of course. See you tomorrow,' Jean said, and hurried off.

The travellers moved out of Prior's Ford as swiftly and neatly as they had moved in. Victor, who had taken the afternoon off from the farm in order to help at his future father-in-law's garage, was taken aback when, directing his usual glare at the field as he drove past, he discovered that it was empty.

His car screeched to a halt and a delivery van following behind had to swerve round him and gave an angry blast on the horn. Ignoring the driver, Victor leapt from the car and ran to inspect the property that had just been restored to him. He scoured every inch, only to find that apart from the indents made by wheels, the field was as it had been before the travellers took possession of it. There was not a trace of debris; not so much as a spent match.

He returned to the car and reached the farm just after his father and brother arrived for their dinner.

'The travellers have gone.'

'I know, one of them came to thank us for our hospitality,' his mother said. She nodded at a bunch of flowers in a vase. 'He gave me those, wasn't that nice of him?'

'Stolen from my field!'

'Even so,' Jess said quietly, 'it was a lovely thing to do. I don't often get flowers. Sit down, now, and eat your dinner while it's hot.'

When the meal was over and Victor was about to follow Bert and Ewan out, his mother put a restraining hand on his arm. 'The man who brought the flowers asked me to give you this.'

He took the envelope carefully, as though suspecting it might blow up in his hand. 'What is it?'

'How should I know? It's got your name on the front — it's none of my business.'

Victor stuffed the envelope in his pocket and didn't open it until he was in his own room later. It contained a wad of folded notes, and a letter written in a neat hand.

Dear Mr McNair,

My family and I prefer to earn the right to campsites through work, but since you refused to allow us to help on your farm during our stay, we have no option but to offer you money instead. I trust this amount will be acceptable.

I trust, too, that you find your land in the same condition as we found it. It is important to us that wherever we go, we behave like the guests we are. Travellers, like all other communities, consist of good and bad and nobody should pre-judge.

You mentioned during our only meeting that you are seeking planning permission to turn your field into a permanent caravan site, presumably for acceptable holidaymakers. My advice to you is to consider some other use for it. The area is unsuitable for the purpose you have in mind, and should you obtain the necessary permission, which, to be honest, I doubt, the amount of money you would have to spend on the project would take many years to recoup.

Sincerely
Ruben Parr

Victor crushed the letter and thrust it deep into his pocket before counting the money. It was more than he would have expected travellers to have. He wondered if it had been stolen, then decided to drive into Kirkcudbright first thing in the morning and put it into the joint account he and Jeanette had opened. Should anyone come round asking awkward questions, he would claim the travellers had gone without paying a penny in rent.

When Victor went with his father and brother to the Neurotic Cuckoo on the following Friday evening the place was buzzing. 'Have you read today's *News*?' Gracie Fisher asked as she served them.

'Haven't had time, have I?' Bert grunted. 'Won't get the chance before tomorrow night.'

'Here, have a look.' She pushed the paper over, folded at an inside page. 'She's a good writer, that wife of yours, Duncan. You must be right proud of her.'

'Aye,' Duncan Campbell said morosely. Helen's passion for reading and writing had always puzzled him, but there was no denying that the bit of money she made now she worked for the newspaper helped to augment the small wage he got from his work at Linn Hall.

'Hey, Victor, look at this!' Ewan had picked up the paper and begun to read it. 'Helen's written about those travellers of yours.'

'She has indeed,' Cam Gordon said from the other end of the bar. 'Got them all wrong, didn't you, Victor?'

'We all did,' Gracie said.

'Some more than others, though. Just as well that you never got round to throwin' them off your land, isn't it, Victor?' Cam laughed.

'What are you on about? Here, let me see!' Victor snatched the paper from his brother, picked up the filled glass Gracie had just put down before him, and bore them both off to an empty table, leaving Ewan to pay for the drinks.

The article with Helen Campbell's name in a prominent position took up an entire page, and was written around a photograph of the travelling group that had been the bane of Victor's life over the past month. According to the story, the Parrs spent their winters in comfortable homes in Cumbria, and the rest of the year travelling. Helen had written:

> *Jean Parr told me that she and her husband Ruben had met in a French campsite, and spent their honeymoon there a year later. 'When the children were born,' Jean said, 'we took them camping too, but in a caravan, every summer. As we moved towards four generations we needed more accommodation, hence the buses and other vehicles. As our daughter-in-law is a teacher, we now spend six months of the year on the road. It is of enormous benefit to the children, who have travelled extensively in Europe as well as the United Kingdom. We all love meeting people. Sometimes travelling folk get a bad press, which is so often unfair. Whenever possible, we use our various trades and skills to pay for anything we need so we can feel part of the genuine travelling community.'*

The article finished with: 'Jean and her daughter, mother and daughter-in-law are gathering material for a book about their experiences, and the Parr family have enjoyed their stay in Prior's Ford.'

Victor thrust the paper away as Bert and Ewan joined him.

'Bloody travellers!'

'I told you there was something different about them,' Ewan said.

'Shut up,' snarled Victor.

'Are the children in bed yet?' Jenny asked when Helen answered the phone.

'Just, thank goodness.'

'Care for a drink?'

'I can't. Duncan's gone to the pub.'

'Have bottle, will visit,' Jenny's voice sang down the phone line, then Marcy called from the background, 'We're on our way.'

'Fantastic! I'll get the glasses out.'

'No need, Ingrid's bringing them,' Jenny said, and put the phone down.

No matter how hard Helen had tried to train her children to put all their toys into the large box kept behind the sofa some always got away. She ran to scoop them off the furniture and into the box, then got to the door just in time to see her friends trooping up the garden path. They surged in, Ingrid waving a bottle at her.

'Wow, champagne! What are we celebrating? You and Sam haven't decided to get married, have you, Marcy?'

'The jury's still out on that one,' Marcy said firmly.

'You both really have to stop being so obstinate,' Ingrid told her equally firmly, 'one is as bad as the other.'

'I got my fingers burned once, and I'm not going to let it happen again.' Marcy and Sam ran the village store and lived in Rowan Cottage, next door to Clarissa Ramsay. Neither believed in marriage, and they were both fiercely independent. They had fallen out so badly over the possibility of the village quarry re-opening – Sam for it and Marcy against it – that she had disappeared for the best part of a year. When she finally returned, it was with a set of rules, including separate bedrooms. The rules had been relaxed somewhat, but marriage was still a taboo subject for both of them.

'But Sam's nothing like your former husband,' Helen protested. Before coming to Prior's Ford, Marcy had been married to a man who had gambled every penny she earned. 'He's as steady as a rock.'

'And as wary of commitment as I am. Anyway, we're here this evening to drink to a very successful writer we know, who has just published a very good scoop.' Marcy put an arm about Helen and swept her into her own kitchen, where Jenny lined up four champagne flutes while Ingrid coped with the bottle. The cork popped to a chorus of squeals and Ingrid deftly poured the champagne without spilling a drop.

'To Helen, journalist of the month,' she said when they were all seated in the small living room.

'To Helen!' the other two chorused.

'To me,' Helen said, and took a generous mouthful. 'Mmm, gorgeous!'

'You minx, you didn't say a word to any of us about that article, or about the Parrs moving out,' Marcy accused.

'They didn't want any farewells, and I wanted the article to be a surprise.'

'Which it was. Very well written, too. What did the editor think of it?'

'He was pleased.' Helen tried to sound casual, but couldn't prevent a broad grin from spreading across her face.

'And so, I hope was Duncan?' Ingrid asked.

'Well . . . you know Duncan. I'm sure he was impressed, but he doesn't say much.'

'Typical. A toast to typical men, and the wonderful women who tame them,' Marcy said. She drained her glass, then got to her feet. 'Shall we have another?'

'Why not?' Helen said, and drained her own glass. The champagne had cheered her, but not as much as the know-ledge that she had such good friends.

'You know something?' Jenny said as her glass was being refilled. 'I'm going to miss those people.'

'Our children certainly will,' Ingrid agreed. 'Ella brought the two older children to our house, and even though they're much younger than she is, they knew so much. And they were so well behaved, too.'

'Gregor's been on at us to do up an old bus and go travelling in it,' Helen said. 'I was talking to the children when I gathered material for the article; they know more about our local history than I do, and I've lived here all my life. They showed me the scrapbooks they had done. They never stop learning, but in a fun way. In fact' – she took another gulp of champagne and waved the glass at her friends – 'if I thought my Duncan would agree to it, I'd go out and find myself an old bus and do it up. Think of the material I could collect! Think of the books I could write!' And then, sadly, 'But he won't. I know he won't.'

'That's good, because I would hate to lose you. But once the children are older and Duncan is, perhaps, mellowed, you might manage to get your old bus, Helen,' Ingrid said consolingly.

'I'll drink to that,' Helen said, cheering up.

15

During the first week in June groups using the village hall had to move to the smaller church hall because the drama group was preparing for its summer production. On Monday the sets were put up, on Tuesday a full dress rehearsal was held, and the actual performances would take place on Wednesday, Thursday, Friday and Saturday.

As far as director Kevin Pearce was concerned, the final night could not come quickly enough. For the second year running, Cynthia McBain, the club's leading lady, had been giving him a difficult time over the casting. Cynthia wanted to play the part of the young girl who falls in love with her best friend's widowed father, but Kevin, who normally bowed to her wishes, had given the part to Alison Greenlees. This had led to a delicate situation when Cynthia demanded to know why she was being passed over, as she put it.

'You owe me, Kevin. If you remember, I was denied my proper place in last year's play because of that ghastly woman Meredith Whitelaw!'

'I know, but it's not often we get a proper actress in our

little club – I mean, a professional actress,' Kevin added hurriedly as her grey eyes glittered ominously, 'and Meredith was so keen to play the part you'd been cast in that I could scarcely deny her.'

'But as you recall,' Cynthia's husband Gilbert cut in, 'your friend the professional actress let you down, and if Cynthia hadn't stepped into the breach at the last moment and given the performance of her life you wouldn't have been able to do the show at all.'

'Exactly, Gilbert.' Cynthia tossed her head, somehow managing to convey the impression that her short brown hair was being thrown back like a full mane. 'I feel I'm owed something. And if I take that part it means that Gilbert and I will be playing opposite each other, which would be nice.'

Kevin opened his mouth to protest that since the entire village knew that Cynthia and Gilbert were husband and wife, the audience could well find it difficult to accept them in the play as a young woman involved in a romance with her best friend's father, then wisely decided against it. 'I quite agree, but as I see it, nobody could possibly play the part of the aunt as well as you, Cynthia.'

'And nobody could play the part you've given Alison Greenlees as well as I could.'

'Then I would have to cast Alison as the aunt, and she's too . . .' Cynthia's eyes began to narrow, and a frown set itself between Gilbert's eyes. Kevin struggled to pull himself back from the brink. 'Too inexperienced,' he finished lamely. 'That part must be played by someone who knows exactly how to handle it.'

'It's so difficult, with Cynthia being a school teacher,' he confessed to his wife later. 'Every time she gives me that dragon stare I feel myself falling to pieces.'

'You didn't tell her that Steph McDonald was your first choice for Alison's part, did you?' Eleanor asked. Steph was a remarkably good young actress, but this year, her final school year, she had been too busy with exams to attend rehearsals.

'Do you think I'd be sitting here eating my dinner if I had? I'd be in a shallow grave, stung to death by Gilbert McBain's bees. I'm beginning to wonder if I should give up the drama group.'

'Don't be silly, dear, you love being their director.'

'I used to, but it's all become so . . . complicated. I like Cynthia, really I do, and I think she's a superb actress . . .'

'But she had her forty-second birthday recently and she's getting a little too long in the tooth to play juvenile leads. Everyone knows that.'

'Everyone,' Kevin said miserably, 'except Cynthia. And Gilbert. I know I'm not going to have an easy time of it during rehearsals.' He heaved a sigh.

'I'll stock up on camomile tea,' said Eleanor, who knew that Kevin, like Cynthia, liked to make the most of the small dramas in his life. 'It always helps to calm you down, doesn't it, dear?'

The entire village knew about the delicate situation between Cynthia and Kevin, and they were all eager to see the play. All, that is, except one person. As the time for the drama club's summer show neared, Ewan McNair became distinctly reluctant to be there.

'You go, Mam, and I'll stay home and help my dad. It's no' my sort of play anyway. I like a good thriller.'

'Ye cannae no' go tae the concert, Ewan,' Jess protested. 'We've bought our tickets an' I don't want tae waste them.

And Alison'll be disappointed if ye don't go tae see her on the stage after all the work ye've put in, helpin' with her lines.'

'Aye, on ye go with yer mother,' Bert chimed in. 'Victor'll be here, for once, and it'll do him good tae dae your share of the work as well as his own, God knows you've taken on *his* share often enough.'

Ewan looked at him in despair. His dad rarely praised him, but did he have to do so tonight of all nights?

'Are ye sure, Dad?' he persisted. He wanted to see Alison in the play, of course he did, but at the same time he couldn't bear to think of her playing opposite Gilbert McBain. And, worse still, being held and kissed by Gilbert McBain.

'I said it, didn't I? Stop fussin' me!' Bert snapped, and so Ewan found himself sitting beside his mother in the village hall as the curtain opened on the play, his large hands fisted tightly on his knees.

Every time Alison came onstage he leaned forward slightly, his lips moving as he mouthed her lines and the lines of the people in the scene with her. He had spent so much time working on the play with her that he knew every word of her scenes by heart. And when, near the end, she and Gilbert moved towards each other Ewan closed his eyes, squeezing them shut so tightly that lights flashed against the darkness of his lids and his cheekbones ached with the strain.

As a low murmur came from the audience, indicating that the lovers onstage had finally acknowledged their mutual passion, Ewan groaned softly between clenched teeth.

'She's a grand wee actress,' Jess said as the cast took their bows and the audience erupted into applause, cheers and whistles.

'She is,' agreed Gracie Fisher, who was sitting beside the McNairs. 'It's a pity, Ewan, that you couldn't have been in the play too.'

'Ach, Gilbert made a better fist of it than I ever could.' He was on his feet, impatient to get out of the place.

'Now that's not true at all! You and Alison were very good in last year's play, weren't they, Jess?'

'Aye, they were. And such a bonny couple, too,' Jess affirmed, and both mothers nodded at each other, as though in some sort of conspiracy.

'We'd best be gettin' home, Mam.'

'Are you not goin' to wait for Alison? She'll want to know what you thought of the play, and you could come back to the pub for some supper.'

'I'd best see Mam home, Mrs Fisher.'

'For goodness' sake, Ewan, I'm no' in my dotage yet, and it's still light out. I can manage on my own,' Jess objected, and Ewan had no option but to stay behind with Gracie until Alison appeared in the hall, face flushed with excitement and her lovely brown eyes sparkling.

'Did you enjoy it?'

'It was grand, pet, and you were so real I couldn't believe you were my daughter.'

'Thanks, Mum. What did you think of the play, Ewan?'

'It was very good. And you did well.'

'Thanks to all your help. Are you coming back for some supper?'

'I've already asked him, and he is.'

'Good.' Alison linked her arm in Ewan's. 'I'm starving!'

Two hours later, when he left the Cuckoo, she walked across the village green with him.

'Isn't it a lovely night?'

'Aye. Did ye enjoy the play yerself?'

'I did. The first night's always the difficult one, but now it's over, I'm going to enjoy the next three nights.' They had reached the main street. 'I'd better get back. Good night, Ewan.' She moved easily into his arms, holding her face up for his kiss.

'I'd enjoy it even more if I was playing opposite you instead of Gilbert,' she said when they finally drew apart. 'No harm to him, but with you last year, it felt so . . . so right.'

A shockwave ran through Prior's Ford on the early June morning the graffiti was discovered – a huge, bright blue scrawl defacing the white end wall of the almshouses, the wall nearest to the village green.

'It's a disgrace, so it is!' Ivy McGowan, the oldest resident, had been slumbering peacefully on the other side of the wall when the perpetrator, or perpetrators, had struck in the night. 'It would never have happened in my young day, I can tell you that!'

Her neighbours exchanged glances, but nobody was brave enough or daft enough to point out that in Ivy's young days young hooligans didn't have access to aerosol cans of paint. Instead, Harold Cowan asked if she was sure she hadn't heard anything the night before.

'I never hear anythin',' Ivy snapped. 'I go to my bed early, as you all know, and I sleep the sleep of the just. Always have done, always will do.'

The almshouses residents were squeezed together in Ivy's over furnished living room. Dolly and Harold had brought a large pot of strong tea and some mugs, Hannah Gibbs and Cissie Kavanagh had supplied a pot of coffee each, Muriel Gibson had contributed a large packet of gingernut biscuits, known to be Ivy's favourites, and Charlie Crandall,

134

who found baking therapeutic, had brought a home-made chocolate cake.

Now Ivy took yet another gingernut and plunged it into her tea. 'I could have been murdered in my bed, so I could, and never known a thing. Nor any of you until you saw the milk bottles piling up outside my door.'

'Oh, Ivy, we'd have acted on just the one milk bottle,' Dolly protested, shocked to think that her aged neighbour believed them callous enough to leave her body undiscovered for weeks.

'Should we inform the police?' Hannah wondered, and Ivy snorted.

'What good would they do now? It was a different matter when we had our own policeman livin' here in the village, but now they're miles away and we could all be murdered in our beds before they reach us.'

'Ivy's right. I don't mean about us all being murdered in our beds,' Hannah hastened to add when Dolly gasped and put a hand to her throat. 'I mean about it not being worth calling the police out now. Whoever did it will be well away.'

'You think it might be youngsters from outside the village?' Harold asked.

'Outside, inside, what difference does it make? What's done's done and the police'll never find them now. We'll just have to hope they don't do it again,' Cissie said. 'Not that I think they *will* do it again. In fact, I think that the less fuss we make of it the better. If they think they've upset us, they might come back out of devilment.'

'You've got a point,' her husband said as the others nodded in agreement. 'I've got a tin of white paint in my shed; I'll try to scrub come of that blue stuff off and then I'll paint over it.'

'I'll give you a hand, Robert,' Charlie offered. 'We'll make it as good as new in no time.'

When the two men arrived at the wall, armed with cleaning materials, paint pot and ladders, Alastair Marshall and Clarissa Ramsay were studying the damage.

'Grafitti's one thing,' Alastair was saying, 'but that's just an ugly scrawl. Very unprofessional.'

'We've decided to clean it up and say no more about it,' Robert told them briskly. 'Not worth making a fuss.'

'You're probably right. Want a hand?'

'We're fine thanks, Alastair.'

'At least nobody can blame the travellers for this,' Alastair said as he and Clarissa walked to her cottage. 'Not that any of them would stoop to this sort of mindless vandalism, but there are probably folk in the village who'd be willing to blame strangers rather than suspect their own.'

'You don't get much vandalism in this village, do you? I've never noticed anything before.'

'Hardly ever. The local kids are fairly well behaved, but it could have been youngsters from elsewhere in the area. In any case,' Alastair said as they reached her car, 'it's not all that bad. Here's hoping it's a one-off.'

The two of them had been shopping further afield, where nobody could see what they were buying, and after Clarissa had fetched a large bag from the car they walked round the house to the shed instead of going indoors.

Once inside with the door closed against prying eyes she took a cloth ball, the size and shape of a football, from a shelf and handed it to Alastair. 'What d'you think? I stuffed it with some old sheets I've been meaning to throw out, and stitched on a face last night. It's a bit lumpy, but he's

136

supposed to be an old gardener so I think we'll get away with it.'

He studied the grumpy face with its closed eyes, big nose and down-turned mouth. 'It's good.'

'I've still got some bits of sheeting we can use for hands, and I found the old hat Keith used when he was gardening, so now all we have to do is to make the body.' From the bags she had brought from the car, Clarissa produced a checked shirt, an old tweed jacket, baggy trousers, a pair of shabby shoes and several long lengths of artificial ivy. 'So what's next?'

An hour later the scarecrow leaned against the wall, almost complete. The clothing had been bulked out with straw from Tarbethill Farm before the scarecrow was fitted onto the wooden framework Alastair had put together earlier.

'One last touch.' Clarissa put the old gardening hat on the figure's head. 'There we are, he's all ready to go into the front garden, and I think we both deserve a long cool drink.'

'I can't wait to see the village all set up for the festival,' she said later, setting down a tray on the garden table. 'It's going to look fantastic. And we're all looking forward to the school's end of term show.'

'The youngsters have been working hard on that, and on their own scarecrows. They're going to have quite a few figures in the playground.'

'From what I hear, you've put in a lot of work with them, not to mention the paintings you've done for the Gift Horse.' She handed him his drink. 'I don't know how you found the time to help me as well.'

'Easily. I've enjoyed all of it.'

'I don't know what I'd do without you,' Clarissa said,

and then, suddenly serious, 'Really, I don't. If you hadn't found me that day, sitting on the stile in the rain, goodness knows what might have happened to me.'

'Soaked through, and not making much sense. At first I thought you were out of your mind.'

'I was, in a way. That was the last day of my old life and, thanks to you, the first day of my new life. I never told you what had happened to send me out into the rain that day, did I?'

'You don't need to, it's over and done with,' he said swiftly, but Clarissa was looking back on that last day of her old life.

'I'd been clearing out Keith's papers and I found love letters written to him by my best friend.'

'Oh.'

'They'd started their affair not long after he married me, and it was still going on when he died. Every time he went to visit his son and daughter on his own, he saw her at the same time. He kept it very well hidden; I don't think Steven and Alexandra know about it and, of course, I'll never tell them. They both looked up to their father. Still do.' Then as he said nothing, she returned from the past and smiled at him, reaching out to touch his hand lightly. 'You showed me there are always other avenues to explore. You befriended me, taught me to drive, and gave me the confidence to go off on my travels and get to know my real self again.'

'You don't still have the letters, do you?'

'Lord, no. I burned them and then I phoned the woman I'd believed to be a friend and threw her out of my life. And that felt surprisingly good. To think I'd been on the point of going back to England to be near her because I thought she cared.'

'It must have been hard, finding out you'd been let down by the two people closest to you.'

'It was, but then Naomi said something that completed the healing process. She said we can't lose friends, we only lose people we *thought* were friends.'

'That,' Alastair said, 'is very profound.'

'Isn't it?'

'And very Naomi.'

'And that's when I decided to stay in Prior's Ford, with people like Naomi and you. As I said, I don't know what I would have done without you.'

'You'd have survived,' he said lightly, 'because you're a survivor. Though you might not have been able to make such a good scarecrow without my guidance.'

When Clarissa laughed the years seemed to drop away from her. Alastair loved the way she threw her head back and let the amusement pour free. Today, her skin was flushed by the sun and, unknown to her, there were little bits of straw caught in her brown hair.

She was in her mid fifties and he in his mid thirties, but when he was with her he was never aware of the age difference. It was only when they were apart that he fretted that she was old enough to be his mother, and railed at unkind fate.

16

In Main Street, an hour of hard work was paying off. Robert and Charlie, armed with stiff-bristled scrubbing brushes and plenty of detergent, had managed to remove most of the scrawl, leaving only a faint blue outline. The job had taken longer than they first thought, mainly because of the villagers who came to watch and discuss the vandalism. Now they were applying a coat of white paint.

'It's always easier to clean up graffiti if you can act before it soaks in,' Robert said as they worked. 'And we're lucky in another way . . . it's all along the bottom of the wall. They didn't use a ladder.'

'Maybe it was small kids,' Charlie suggested.

'Could be. There's certainly a half-hearted air about it. When I was buying the detergent I asked Sam and Marcy if any youngsters had bought cans of blue spray paint from them, but apparently not. So it might have been outsiders.'

'Let's just hope they don't come back.'

'Ach, I think it was just a one-off prank,' Robert said easily, sweeping his paint brush along the wall.

'I hope you're right, with the Scarecrow Festival coming soon.'

'Let's not cross bridges before we come to them,' Robert was advising him when Ivy arrived, thumping her walking stick on the ground with each step.

'As good as new, Ivy. Well . . . nearly,' Charlie greeted her cheerfully. The old woman cast a critical eye over the wall and sniffed.

'I can still see a wee bit o' blue beneath the white.'

'We'll have to let it dry, then we'll give it another coat tomorrow,' Robert explained. 'That should do it.'

'Wee middens. They need a good hard clout!' Before either man could stop her Ivy had whacked her stick hard across the newly painted section of wall.

'That paint,' Robert pointed out mildly while Charlie turned away to hide a smile, 'is still wet. Look at your stick, Ivy.'

'Eh?' She lifted the stick and examined the white streak along its length. 'Wee middens!' she shrieked. 'Look what they've done tae my good stick now!'

'Come on, back to your house.' Robert took her by the elbow. 'I'll get you settled and then I'll clean the walking stick for you.'

'Did you hear about the graffiti on the almshouses?' Marcy was asking as she served Jenny.

'I've been away most of the day.'

'Some kids scrawled blue paint over the almshouses wall last night. Robert Kavanagh and Charlie Crandall were in here buying detergent and I think they've managed to clean it off.'

'That's good.' Jenny paid for her purchases and left the shop, her mind buzzing. Maggie had been out late the previous

141

evening, and had hurried upstairs as soon as she came in, to spend ages in the bathroom.

Asked that morning about the sticking plaster on her hand she had snapped back that she had got a paper cut. Now, Jenny began to wonder if the plaster was covering something other than a small cut. Something like a splash of blue paint, difficult to wash off.

Why, she asked herself, should she jump to the conclusion that the local vandal was her Maggie? And to her horror, the answer that popped into her head was . . . why not? Maggie was a closed book, and one that Jenny, already beset by worry over Andrew's health, was terrified to open lest she let out more horrors than she could handle at the moment.

Even so, she couldn't resist asking that evening, 'How's your hand, Maggie?'

'Fine.' Maggie flourished a hand free of sticking plaster. 'No problem. It was only a tiny burn.'

'I thought it was a paper cut.'

Maggie flashed a quick look at her, then said sharply, 'No, a burn. I got it when I was taking something from the oven during the domestic-science class. It's cleared up now.'

'Good,' Jenny said, and Maggie smirked. She had panicked the night before, scrubbing her hand almost raw in the bathroom before finally slapping a sticking plaster over the obstinate stain at the base of her thumb. Ryan had laughed at her when she told him that morning, and sneaked her into the art room during break to remove the tell-tale stain with some turpentine.

'That all?' he had asked, and when she produced the balled-up T-shirt she had pushed to the bottom of her schoolbag and shaken it out to show a blue streak across the front, he had rolled it up again and pushed it into his own bag.

'I'll shove it into a litter bin on my way home. You did OK last night,' he said casually.

She shrugged. She'd got a shock that morning when she saw the ugly blue scrawl over the almshouses wall and realised just what she had done. It had been easy to appear just as shocked as the others then, but now, with Ryan, she felt better about it. Nobody cared about her, so why should she care about anyone else?

Serve them right. Serve them all right!

Jenny was standing at the bottom of the stairs, shouting, 'Maggie! Calum! If you don't come downstairs within the next five minutes you're both going to be late for school,' when the post came through the letter box. She gathered it up, leafing through it as she went to the kitchen. She paused just before she got there, her stomach lurching as she saw the name of the Edinburgh hospital stamped on one envelope.

Andrew was checking the papers in his briefcase as he did every morning without fail. Late-June sunlight flooded through the window, and the microwave hummed cheerfully as it made the porridge.

Jenny liked her yellow and white kitchen, seeing it as a haven of peace and security, but today it suddenly felt wrong. For a brief moment she contemplated putting the post behind the big bowl of fruit on the Welsh dresser and giving him one more normal day, but just then he looked up and said, 'Ah, the post. Anything interesting?'

Silently, she handed it to him, watching his expression change when he saw the hospital letter. He picked up the paperknife from the dresser. Andrew always insisted on slitting envelopes open neatly.

Although they had a small dining room they always break-
fasted at a round table in the kitchen. Jenny moved behind
one of the chairs, both hands clutching its back as she
waited for him to finish reading the single sheet inside.

At last he looked up and said calmly, 'I start treatment
on the tenth of July.'

'Oh, Andrew – so soon?'

'The sooner the better, Jen, and we knew it was going
to happen eventually, love.' He returned to his letter. 'Four
weeks in all, radiotherapy every day, plus chemo during the
first and final weeks.' He smiled at her as he handed the
single sheet over. 'That's good. It means we can enjoy
Calum's school concert and see the start of the Scarecrow
Festival.' He consulted the kitchen calendar before
announcing, 'And we can visit my parents for a few days
after the schools close, to break the news to them.'

'How are we going to tell—' Jenny stopped as she saw
that his gaze had suddenly moved away from her face to
something behind her.

She turned, to see Maggie standing in the doorway.

'There's something wrong with one of you,' the girl said
accusingly. 'It's cancer, isn't it?'

Maggie had been out late again the night before with Ryan.
As had happened on the evening of the spray painting, he
had cycled over from Kirkcudbright, and the two of them
had wandered about the village, which was quiet other than
the buzz of voices from the Neurotic Cuckoo's open door.

Maggie's favourite book was *The Wind in the Willows*,
and her favourite chapter the one where Mole and Rat
were hurrying back to the river on a cold winter's night,
passing lit windows and envying the people snug within.
Ever since reading it she had enjoyed looking in lit windows

on dark nights, not out of nosiness but because she loved the snatched glimpses of people safe and happy in their cosy homes.

Ryan, as always, was bent on mischief, but to her relief he didn't find anything to do this time. When he finally cycled off she let herself into the house quietly and was sitting on the bottom step taking her shoes off before sneaking upstairs when Jenny opened the living-room door and said, her voice heavy with relief, 'You're back, Maggie. Have a nice evening?'

'It was all right.'

'With Ryan?'

'Yeah.'

'You should have brought him in for a cup of tea.'

The lace on the second shoe was knotted, so Maggie wrenched it off and put it down beside its partner, anxious to reach the peace and privacy of her bedroom.

'Night,' she said, and sped upstairs, ignoring Jenny's hopeful, 'Would you like a cup of . . . ?'

This morning, she had come downstairs in her stocking feet and was sitting on the third step, wrestling impatiently with the knot and paying little attention to the murmur of voices in the kitchen until she heard Jenny cry out, 'Oh, Andrew!'

Rising, she limped, one shoe on and the other in her hand, to the door, careful to stay out of sight.

'Four weeks . . . radiotherapy . . . chemo,' she heard Andrew say. 'That's good, it means we can enjoy Calum's school concert . . .'

She knew what he was talking about. The mother of one of her school friends at home in Dundee had had that sort of treatment. Without thinking, she stepped into the doorway to face the two of them.

'It is, isn't it?' she repeated, and when they stared at her silently, went on, 'One of you has cancer. Who is it?'

'It's me, Maggie. But I'll be all right.'

'How long have you known?' she demanded, and saw Jenny turn to look at Andrew, as though seeking guidance. 'You've known for ages, haven't you? Is that what you've been whispering about when you thought I couldn't hear you?'

'We didn't want to worry you until we were sure,' Jenny's voice trembled and her eyes glittered with unshed tears. Relief swept over Maggie at the realisation that they had known nothing about her stealing sweets from the shop in Kirkcudbright, but was then pushed aside by anger at this latest bombshell. As if she didn't have enough to put up with!

'You knew he had cancer and you didn't tell me, or Calum? Your own son? That's . . . terrible!' She felt a sudden lump come into her throat, and a hot feeling at the back of her eyes. Faced with the choice of bursting into tears or flying into a rage, she chose the latter. 'You try to convince me we're a family, and then you keep something like this a secret? Families don't do things like that to each other! Gran and Granda would *never* have done that to me!'

A scuffling from overhead told them that Calum, never good at waking up, was fumbling his way downstairs. Maggie stepped swiftly into the kitchen, closing the door behind her and leaning back against it, one hand gripping the door-knob.

'Maggie, we'll talk about this in the evening,' Andrew said levelly. 'Right now we're all going to have breakfast and then I'm leaving for the office and you and Calum are going to school.'

'We need to talk about it *now*!' Calum had reached the

146

kitchen; the doorknob twisted beneath Maggie's fingers and she gripped it tightly.

'Mum? The door's stuck.' He tried again without success to turn the handle, and then she felt him throwing his weight against the panels.

'Let him in, Maggie.'

'Not until you tell me what's going on!'

'I have bowel cancer and I'm going to have a course of treatment and then an operation. Now you know as much as we do.'

'Mum!' Calum battered on the door. 'Let me in!'

'That's all about *you,* but what about *me*? I suppose you'll want to get rid of me now. I suppose I'll be sent back to live with Gran and Granda.'

Jenny suddenly and unexpectedly lost her temper. 'For goodness' sake, Maggie,' she snapped, 'why does everything have to be about *you*? Andrew's ill and we're all going to have to help him to get better. You're Calum's big sister and you'll have to help us see him through this. And you can start by letting him in and behaving as if nothing's happened. We'll talk about it tonight, the three of us, after he's gone to bed because I will *not* have him upset before his school concert. Now let him in!'

Maggie had never seen Jenny so angry. Sheer shock made her step aside. The door flew open to reveal Calum, flushed and angry.

'What's going on?' He erupted into the kitchen, glaring at the three of them. 'Have you been having one of your arguments again?'

'Just putting a few things right,' Andrew said blandly as the microwave pinged. 'All sorted, old son. Nothing to worry about.'

'That's true, isn't it, Maggie?' Jenny added. And as her

stepdaughter nodded, staring at the floor, 'And now we're all going to sit down and have breakfast because the clock's racing round.'

During breakfast Jenny and Andrew tried to chat about unimportant things while Maggie stared at her food and Calum watched all three of them suspiciously. When Andrew had gone off to work, Jenny sent Calum upstairs to brush his teeth and followed Maggie into the hall, catching at her arm as she moved to the front door.

'You say one word to Calum or anyone else about this,' she hissed, 'and you'll be sorry. Do you understand?'

'Yeah, OK.' Maggie pulled herself free and bolted from the house, gulping down fresh air as she ran towards the bus stop.

17

The school day was like a bad dream. Maggie sleepwalked her way through every class, only dimly aware of what was going on, and during the breaks she kept to herself, spurning anyone who tried to speak to her. Even Ryan was rebuffed, and stormed off muttering, 'Daft bitch!' as he went. She saw him chatting up another girl later, but even that didn't bother Maggie. She felt as though she were locked in a glass cabinet, peering out at the rest of the world.

Jenny, not Andrew, occupied her mind all day. Jenny, almost snarling, 'Why does everything have to be about *you*? . . . You're Calum's big sister, and you'll have to help us to see him through this.' Then later, in the hall, her eyes cold and hard as lumps of ice, 'You say one word to Calum or anyone else about this and you'll be sorry!'

Strangely, although the words and the rage behind them had shocked and alarmed Maggie, they also comforted her. Since their first meeting in Gran's house, Jenny had always spoken in a way that set Maggie's teeth on edge; a blend of anxiety overlaid by sugary kindness, or a maddening 'let's be all girly together'. That morning, for the first time, she had treated Maggie like a real person rather than the little girl she had left behind all those years ago. She had even referred to her as Calum's big sister.

Did that mean that they wanted her to stay in Prior's Ford? And if so, did she want to? Andrew's illness could give her the excuse to insist on escaping back to Dundee, to the family and friends she missed. Back to her old life – except that it wasn't her old life any more. Not with Granda so ill and Gran worrying about him all the time. She felt like the rope in a tug-of-war contest, being pulled this way and that. She could feel the fibres the rope was made of snapping inside her, one by one.

She didn't even know how she felt about having to go back to Prior's Ford after school, but she had no option. Back to what? Talking, more arguments, decisions to be made. Another fibre snapped as the bus carried her closer to the village and she wished that she could shout 'Stop!' and get off and go . . . where?

When they arrived in the village she hung back while the others flowed in a uniformed stream to the pavement, waiting until they had all alighted before making her way along the aisle to the door.

'Never mind, love, worse things happen at sea,' the driver said cheerfully as she stumbled down the steps. 'Tomorrow's another day, an' all that.'

Before tomorrow comes, there's the rest of today to get through, Maggie told him silently.

The others had already set off to their homes by the time she stood on the pavement. Freya had made one or two attempts at conversation during the journey, but after being met with silence every time, she had finally flicked back her long blonde hair and moved to sit with someone more talkative. Freya and Maggie had drifted apart since Maggie had begun to see Ryan, who looked on Freya MacKenzie as a stuck-up snob.

Maggie began to walk towards River Lane, not even hearing her name called, stopping only because a hand on her arm halted her and then swung her round. She saw Naomi Henderson's beaming smile.

'Maggie, I was hoping to see you, and to invite you to the manse for tea.'

'Me?'

'Yes, you. It's all right,' Naomi said as Maggie began to shake her head. 'I've cleared it with Jenny.'

'Oh.' Maggie immediately stiffened. 'So she's asked you to talk to me.'

'It's not so much a question of me talking to you,' Naomi said cheerfully. 'More a question of you talking to me, if you want to. From what Jenny tells me I think you could do with a change of scene and the chance to catch your breath. Ethan's got football practice, so he won't get under our feet. Cold ham and fried potatoes do you? And fried bread because I love fried bread. If you don't, I can easily eat your share.'

At the mention of food Maggie suddenly remembered she hadn't bothered with any lunch. She was about to refuse when her treacherous stomach, presumably hearing what Naomi said, rumbled loudly. Naomi laughed, and handed her one of the two carrier bags she was holding.

'I think that decides it. Come on,' she said, and set off along the pavement, leaving Maggie with little option but to follow.

Maggie had never been inside the manse before; as she went into the narrow hall she was taken aback by the clutter. Ethan's bike leaned against one wall and his schoolbag had been abandoned on the staircase. A coat rack was so well festooned with coats, jackets and hats that it resembled a woolly Christmas tree, and shoes and Wellington boots were lined along the wall opposite the bike. There wasn't much room in which to walk along the middle.

In the kitchen, where every inch of counter was in use, Ethan, in his football kit, leaned against the sink, eating a massive sandwich.

'Hi,' he said indistinctly as Maggie followed Naomi in, and then managed to fit in another mouthful. When Naomi said, 'I hope you haven't bought any fizzy drinks from the village store, young man,' he shook his head and pointed to a tumbler half full of milk.

'Good lad!' The minister cleared a space for both shopping bags and began to unpack them. 'Maggie's come to have tea with me,' she told Ethan, who nodded and then picked his drink up and wandered out of the room, still chewing.

'I try to see that he has a healthy diet,' Naomi said, carrying an armful of shopping to the fridge, 'but it's not easy. At least he's drinking milk instead of something filled with chemicals. He's my cousin's son, and it's like borrowing a favourite book; you feel quite anxious about returning it in good condition.' She opened the fridge door, peered inside, and shook her head.

'Bother, he's taken all the ham. No wonder that sandwich looked so big. I sometimes think that if I put food into a steel box, padlocked it and then buried it at the end of the garden, Ethan would find it and eat it. And he never' – she took out an empty milk bottle and handed it to Maggie, shaking her curly head again – 'thinks to leave the empty milk bottles out where I can see them. Come to think of it, empty milk bottles are the only things he puts away carefully, every time. Lucky I bought some more, just in case. The cat will have its supper, after all. At least he left the boiled potatoes. You can slice them while I get the frying pan going. We'll have eggs instead of the cold meat.'

Something soft brushed along Maggie's ankles, almost causing her to drop the plate of potatoes.

'What . . . ?' She glanced down to see a large marmalade cat at her feet.

'That's Casper, come to see if there's any food going.' Naomi reached into a cupboard and brought out a large frying pan. 'Right, let's cook!'

When they had eaten sitting at the kitchen table, Naomi refilled their mugs with fresh tea and led the way to the living room, where Casper leapt on to Maggie's knee as soon as she sat down.

'Push him off if you want to.' Naomi sat down and put a plate of biscuits on the small table between their chairs. 'He likes to pester visitors but he accepts rejection with equanimity, bless him.'

'No, it's fine.' Maggie stroked the cat's soft warm fur and Casper wriggled into a more comfortable position and began to purr. The sound, together with the casual untidiness of Maggie's surroundings and the meal she had just eaten to the accompaniment of Naomi's memories of her own school and university days, made her feel more relaxed than she had been for a long time.

But she knew that she couldn't allow herself to be lulled into a false sense of security, so she took a gulp of tea, then said, 'I expect I'm here because Jenny asked you to talk some sense into me.'

'Do you need to have sense talked into you?'

Maggie shrugged. 'I'm a teenager, what would I know about sense?'

'Quite a lot, I would imagine. She's worried about you,

153

Maggie. You're unhappy and she doesn't know what to do about it.'

'She could send me back to Dundee.'

'Is that what you really want? From what I've heard, it isn't much of an option, given your grandfather's poor health.'

'What difference does that make?' Maggie suddenly burst out. 'Everywhere I go, people are ill. People die! My mother died when I was born, my dad died when I was eight, and now Granda's ill, and Auntie Lizbeth's ill, and so's Andrew. It's all my fault!'

'Really? You're not telling me that you're a witch, are you?' Naomi asked with interest. 'Or that horrible child from *The Exorcist*?'

'Of course not.'

'Good, I'm glad you realise that, because you're not to blame for what's happened to any of these people, Maggie. You've been very unfortunate, and in my view life's treated you unfairly. I don't blame you for feeling angry and frustrated, but there's no need to feel helpless as well. You can turn things around.'

'Oh yes?' Maggie sneered. 'By waving my magic wand?'

'No. Although a wand would be useful, wouldn't it? I'd love one. I meant by taking control of your own life and dealing with what's happening. For instance,' Naomi went on placidly, 'your family in Dundee wouldn't have to worry about you if they could be sure you're OK here, with the Forsyths. And it would help Jenny and Andrew a lot right now if they knew Calum had a sister to lean on during his father's illness. Which leads me to the reason why I asked you here. The doctors have decided that Andrew's best chance of a full recovery is to shrink the tumour before they operate to remove it. That means he has to have four weeks of radiotherapy combined with two weeks of chemotherapy.'

The thought of it was almost more than Maggie could bear. She bent her head over the cat, stroking him harder and faster. He stopped purring, his tail began to twitch angrily and he dug his claws into her thigh and lifted his head to glare at her. She forced herself to slow down.

'Naturally,' Naomi was saying, 'Jenny doesn't want him to be on his own, and since the hospital's in Edinburgh it would be easier for the two of them to stay there during the week and come home for weekends. It's going to be hard on Calum, Maggie, and she really needs you to be there for him. I've suggested that the two of you spend Mondays to Fridays here during Andrew's treatment. Ingrid MacKenzie would like you to stay with her family. Jenny says you should be the one to make the final decision.'

Casper stretched his magnificently furry legs out, gave a mighty yawn that displayed sharp white teeth and a pink mouth, and then settled down again. Maggie looked round Naomi's well lived in living room, then pictured Mrs MacKenzie's perfect house.

'Here would be OK, if you really mean it,' she said.

Jenny, who had been watching for Maggie's return, opened the door as her stepdaughter was fishing her key from a pocket.

'Hello, love, did you have a nice time with Naomi?'

'It was OK.' Maggie's pretty face was set in its usual scowl. She pushed past Jenny and made for the stairs, pausing with one foot on the lowest tread. 'We'll live at the manse during the week – Calum and me – while you and Andrew are in Edinburgh.'

'You're going to stay in Prior's Ford?'

'For the summer, anyway.'

'Thank you, Maggie,' Jenny said.

Once shut safely in her room, Maggie drew a deep breath and threw her schoolbag into a corner before letting herself flop backwards on the bed. She stared up at the ceiling, replaying the scene, seeing again the relief on Jenny's strained, anxious face and hearing the gratitude in her voice as she said, 'Thank you, Maggie.'

Ever since she had come to Prior's Ford Maggie had felt as though she was expected to be grateful to Jenny and Andrew. To be fair, they themselves hadn't made her feel that way but others had, telling her how *lucky* she was to be part of such a *nice* family. And Jenny's anxious, mumsie attitude hadn't helped.

But now things were different. Now they needed her help. They wanted her to stay in the village so she could look out for Calum while his father was ill. Now it was their turn to be grateful to her. They would owe her if she did as they wanted. But she was going to have to continue to keep them at arm's length because if she changed they would assume everything was going to be all right between them and her, and she wasn't ready for that yet.

She needed time to think about Naomi's intriguing suggestion that she should take control of her own life, and turn things round. It sounded good, but she couldn't quite see how to go about it.

In the meantime, she would have to go on watching her step. It had been so easy at the manse, being her old self, able to speak freely to Naomi, but she couldn't be like that with Jenny and Andrew. Not yet, and perhaps not ever. Why, she wondered moodily, did trying *not* to be friends with people have to be so difficult?

18

Andrew Forsyth hadn't been the only person to receive an important letter that day. At Tarbethill Farm, Jess went through the post as soon as it came in, hoping for a letter from her daughter, giving details of her family's visit to Tarbethill during the school holidays. The letter was there, and she pushed the other mail behind the clock on the mantel-piece for safe keeping, eager to hear Alice's news.

Her face fell as she scanned the two pages. 'Sorry we can't manage a visit over the summer holidays, Mam,' Alice had written. 'Johnny's going to Germany on a school trip for two weeks, and it's going to cost us more than we can really afford. And Becky's decided to work at the stables all through her school holidays to pay for her riding lessons. She's turning into a good wee rider, and we're pleased she's willing to work in order to get what she wants. So it looks as though I'm going to have to stay here all summer. I can't expect Jack to cope with the farm and the kids on his own. This is what happens as they grow up and start going their own way. I'm determined, though, that we'll

157

all come to see you in the autumn, when they get their school holidays.'

The phone rang and by the time Jess ended a long discussion about the next Women's Institute meeting she had very little time in which to get the midday meal ready for her hungry men. The post was forgotten until Victor asked about it that evening.

Jess gave a guilty start. 'Aye, there was somethin' for you, but I was readin' our Alice's letter and the rest of it went out of my head. They'll no' be able tae come this summer after all, Bert, because the bairns have things tae do.'

'Where's my letter, then?' her firstborn asked impatiently.

'They're all behind the clock.'

Victor riffled through the envelopes, tossing a catalogue to Ewan and two envelopes to his father before finding an official-looking letter bearing his own name.

'It's from the planning department. How could ye have forgotten about it all this time?' he asked Jess as he ripped the envelope's flap open.

'It's only been here since late mornin'. It's surely not that urgent,' she began. As he read the letter, she saw the look on his face. 'What's wrong, son?'

'Everythin', that's what! I'm no' gettin' permission for the caravan park. Bastards,' Victor said through gritted teeth as he crushed the letter into his pocket.

'But ye already knew that it would cost too much money tae dae what they wanted,' Jess said.

'Jeanette's father offered tae put up half the money an' go intae partnership with me. I thought his money might get us started, at least. Now it's all come tae nothin'!'

'Nob'dy ever thought it would,' Bert grunted.

'It could've though, Bert. It was a good idea. He'd it all planned out, didn't you, Victor?'

'Aye, but I shouldnae have bothered, should I? I should've realised that field was no use. Dad, could I get the big top field instead?'

'Ye could not! That's one of our best fields as well ye know. Even if it wasnae,' Bert said, 'I wouldnae let ye have it for caravans. It'd mean folk usin' our lane an' comin' past the farmhouse all the time. We wouldnae be able tae call the place our own.'

'There's the field you let me have for the wormery, Dad,' Ewan, engrossed in his catalogue, spoke for the first time. 'I'd thought of puttin' the worms in the furrows I've dug, but me and Alison have decided boxes would probably suit best. The worms need tae be kept warm in the winter, an' I was goin' tae ask ye if I could use the old shed behind the barn. I'll patch it up an' make it watertight.'

'Victor's not gettin' that field either, for the same reason,' Bert said firmly. 'Folk would have tae use the lane tae get to and from it, and God knows the damage they could do. There's only one field suitable, and that's the one ye've got, Victor.' He picked up his newspaper and snapped it open. Old Saul, in his usual spot before the fire, winced at the sudden sound.

'But the council might think that Ewan's field would be better for a caravan park,' Victor argued. 'It's flat – easier tae put pipin' intae.'

'Ye're behavin' like a spoiled wee laddie sortin' through a bag o' sweets tae see which ones he likes best. You wanted that field and I let ye have it. Ye insisted on me signin' a piece of paper tae say it's yours now. We made an agreement and ye cannae go back on it!' Bert said before burying his head in the paper again.

For a moment it seemed to Jess and Ewan that Victor was going to drag his father from his chair. Jess put a hand on his arm, while Ewan tensed, ready to intervene. Then Victor, his handsome face dark with anger, turned on his heel and stormed upstairs.

'Mebbe I should go up an' have a word,' Jess said tentatively.

'Leave it, Mam.'

'Aye, leave it, woman,' Bert said from behind the paper. 'He's got tae learn he cannae have everythin' his own way.'

Half an hour later they heard Victor come back downstairs. Instead of coming into the kitchen he left the house through the rarely used front door and a few minutes later his car engine leapt into life.

It was after midnight before Jess, lying rigidly awake, ears straining, heard the car return. When Victor had come upstairs and let himself into his bedroom, she let out her breath in a long sigh and turned over, nestling against her sleeping husband's broad back. It was a while before she finally fell asleep.

To Lewis's delight and Ginny's secret disappointment, Molly decided to bring Rowena Chloe back to Linn Hall for the Scarecrow Festival.

It was wrong of Ginny to resent the other girl, she knew that, and she despised herself for it. Molly's presence at Linn Hall was none of her business, but it had an upsetting effect on Lewis. He mooned over her like a lovesick teenager, Ginny thought miserably in the dark of the night, and for some reason, Molly disturbed the easy rhythm of life at Linn Hall more than any of the backpackers or workmen did. She seemed to be possessed of a vitality that radiated from her, and caught the attention of everyone in the vicinity.

She certainly caught the attention of the workmen, and was often to be seen perched on the terrace's stone wall, talking and laughing with them when they took their lunch breaks.

To give her her due, Molly Ewing wasn't afraid of hard work. She threw herself wholeheartedly into helping Lewis set up the stable shop, and volunteered for duty in the kitchen garden, where Ginny was potting herbs and cuttings for the shop. As she worked, Molly chattered non-stop about her travels and Lewis and how wonderful Linn Hall was looking now that work was being done on it, until Ginny began to wish the other girl was a budgie she could silence by throwing a cloth over its cage.

'I mean, Weena's an absolute doll,' Molly was saying at that moment, 'a sweet wee thing and I wouldn't want to be without her, but she's limiting, know what I mean? Ever since I left school I've spent the winter and spring working and saving, then come April I'd be off like a shot, going where the mood took me, getting work wherever I could, then back home in the autumn. But you can't do that with a baby, can you? If Mum wasn't working she could look after Weena, but she likes being on the checkout and I can't really ask her to give it up just for us. P'raps I'll be able to take her with me next year, or the year after.'

'Won't you be settled here in Linn Hall by that time?'

Molly wrinkled her nose. 'I don't know about that. I've got to work the wanderlust out before I settle down, haven't I? I don't see Lewis being keen to be away from this place for months, and I suppose I'll be expected to do the lady of the manor stuff. Can you imagine me being the lady of the manor?' she giggled.

'Not really,' Ginny said, and could have bitten her tongue off. But Molly wasn't one to take offence.

'I'm just going to have to learn, aren't I? Eventually.

161

There are still so many places to see first, though. Have you travelled a lot?'

'Not really. France and Belgium, and I spent two months in Australia just after I left school, visiting my father.' It hadn't been a success; her parents had split up when she wasn't much older than Rowena Chloe. Ginny and her father, now completely involved with his Australian wife and teenage children, were strangers to each other.

'I would've thought you'd do lots of travelling, having an actress for a mother.'

'I prefer Britain, to be honest.'

'Do you really? My goodness!' Molly looked at Ginny as though she had just turned into an alien, then whipped round, knocking two flower pots to the ground, as a voice said, 'Hello, Molly.'

'Cam! What are you doing here?'

'Hi again,' Cam acknowledged Ginny, and then gave his full attention to the other girl. 'Hasn't Lewis told you he's going to sell my pictures of the hall and grounds in his shop?'

'No, he hasn't. So the two of you are friends again? Last time we met up in the Cuckoo you were knocking seven bells out of each other.'

'All forgiven and forgotten. Is he around?'

'In the shop,' Ginny told him.

'Good, I brought some more shots.' He held out a large envelope.

'Let me see,' Molly reached for it, but he whisked it out of her reach.

'You can see them along with Lewis. Come here.' He took her by the hand and led her over to an old rain barrel by the garden wall. 'Upsadaisy,' he said, and she squealed as he put his hands on her slender waist and lifted her up to sit on the barrel.

162

'Cam! Lucky for you the lid's on!'

'Luckier for you.' He grinned, unslinging the camera case from his shoulder. 'A nice smile, now.'

When the photograph was taken he lifted her down from the barrel, then the two of them headed for the gate. Ginny, gathering up the pots, spilled compost and delicate plants Molly had knocked over, glanced up to see Cam Gordon put his arm around the girl's shoulders as they strolled along the path.

Seeing them look so comfortable together, and remembering what Duncan had told her about Lewis and Cam coming to blows because Cam had, apparently, hinted he and Molly had once been more than friends, Ginny hoped that trouble and possible heartache weren't lying ahead for Lewis.

Because the primary school's assembly hall wasn't large enough to cope with the expected audience, the end of term concert was held in the village hall.

It had been agreed that rather than send the excited children home after the dress rehearsal they would be fed in the smaller hall, and as Jenny was their main wardrobe mistress she stayed with them while Andrew took Maggie to the Neurotic Cuckoo for a meal before they attended the concert.

It was the first time she had been inside the local pub; secretly, she enjoyed every minute of it, even though Andrew firmly refused to let her have the gin and tonic she asked for.

'I'm sixteen! I'm entitled to have a drink!'

'Only,' Andrew said calmly, 'if I order it for you. And you're still fifteen. We'll both have fresh orange, please, Joe.'

'A wise choice, if I may say so,' the landlord said.

'It's not fair!' Maggie snapped when Joe had gone. She had drunk gin and tonic before, when Ryan had nicked tins of ready-mixed from a supermarket. She hadn't cared for it much; but she'd wanted to find out how far she could push Andrew.

'Who said life has to be fair?' he asked with a lift of an eyebrow. 'It's not exactly treating me kindly at the moment, is it?'

She turned bright red and said no more.

'Actually, that's what I want to talk to you about,' he went on. 'Maggie, I'm really sorry you've had to land in among this cancer business.'

She stared at him, taken aback, and then muttered, 'Can't help it, can you?'

'I'm afraid not. But Jenny was so scared in case you opted to go back to Dundee when we told you, and I want to say we both appreciate your decision to stay here and help us through this business.'

'Got no choice.'

Andrew's face, thinner than usual, split into a wide grin. 'Life can be a bitch, can't it? What I mean is, if you'd decided to walk out on us, we couldn't have stopped you. But with Jenny and I having to spend most of our time in Edinburgh over the summer it's great to know Calum will have you. I know that Naomi will look after him, but it's important for him to feel that his entire family hasn't deserted him.' Then, as their drinks arrived, 'Thanks, Joe.'

'My pleasure. Ready to order your meal now?'

'It's going to be tough, having to break the news to Calum next week,' Andrew said when Joe Fisher had returned to the kitchen. 'That's why we've arranged this caravan holiday with him, while you see your grandparents. It's not that we

164

don't want you there too, it's just that . . . Well, I don't think you'd enjoy it.'

To Maggie's relief, some newcomers stopped at their table to say hello, and by the time they went to their own table the soup had arrived and Andrew introduced the safe subject of favourite books.

Holding her coat for her later, he said, 'Here's a promise . . . I'll bring you here on your sixteenth birthday and buy you a gin and tonic. OK?'

'Are you sure you'll be well enough then?' The words were out before she could stop them, and if she hadn't been slipping her hands into her coat sleeves she would have clapped them to her face in horror at her own insensitivity.

But when she turned to face him, Andrew was smiling. 'I've already promised Jenny I'm going to have a damned good shot at it,' he said, opening the door for her. 'I may have cancer, but cancer certainly doesn't have me. It's going to be tough for all of us, but if we concentrate on winning, it'll happen. Trust me. Now let's go and clap our hands off for Calum and the others.'

The first half of the evening consisted of performances by the school's recorder group and the choir, followed by a fifteen-minute interval to allow the children to change into their costumes for the highlight of the evening – the musical Lynn Stacy and Helen had written between them. On the following day, the final day of the term, the children were to have games in the playground in the morning, followed by the end of term party. For some, like Calum, it would also be a farewell to their primary-school days.

Because the interval would only be long enough for costumes to be donned, make-up for the second half had to be done before the show started. Freya MacKenzie and

Steph McDonald had taken on the job, and now they were working swiftly in the makeshift dressing room, each with a row of children waiting their turn, while a group of mothers checked that the costumes were all in order.

The excitement in the room was so thick it could have been cut with a blunt knife, and the two queues waiting to have their make-up applied were bouncing about.

'Throw a long strip of silk over them both and they would look like those dragons the Chinese use in their parades,' Ingrid pointed out.

'Remember how it used to be?' Helen sighed. 'I loved the end of the summer term: it was the only thing that made going to school worthwhile in my opinion.'

Jenny's eyes were on Calum, jumping about excitedly in one of the waiting lines. 'It's good to see him so happy. I wish we didn't have to spoil it all for him.' Her voice wavered and she gulped before finishing, 'It's going to be the hardest thing we've ever had to do.'

'If it's any help, you'll be surrounded by good vibes from all of us,' Ingrid told her.

'I know, and it does help. I keep wishing that I could jump through time and land in next July. Then I realise that's the last thing I should wish for, because I don't know what I'll find.' She looked at the friends who had gathered into a protective half circle before her, hiding her from the children, especially Calum, then said bleakly, 'I know you're all there for me, but right now I feel as if I'm standing on the edge of a huge dark chasm, knowing it'll only take one slight push to send me over.'

'Take each day as it comes,' Jinty advised.

'That's what Andrew says. I wish I could have his optimism.'

'It's good he has it. It will help the two of you more

than anything,' Ingrid was saying when Calum, climbing into the chair before one of the mirrors, yelled, 'Mum, come and watch this!'

Jenny ran a hand hurriedly over her eyes and went to her son, while the others looked at each other.

'You feel so helpless,' Helen said. 'I wish I could do more for them!'

'Let's start working on that tumour. It's called visual-isation,' Ingrid said. 'We focus our thoughts on it whenever we can, and think of it as an object to be destroyed. Like ten-pin bowling, for instance. The pins are the tumour, and your thoughts are the ball that's going to knock them down, over and over.'

'I was never any good at ten-pin bowling.'

'Then think of something else, Helen. The tumour as a punch ball and you as a boxer, hitting it until it gives up. Anything you like,' Ingrid said impatiently, 'just do it – all of us. Do it for Andrew and Jenny.'

19

As the curtain went up on the first part of the evening's entertainment, revealing the school choir, mothers and teachers who had been working backstage crept into the seats at the back of the hall.

Jenny, spotting an empty aisle seat beside Andrew and Maggie, slid into it as Lynn Stacy walked on the stage, elegant in a black evening gown, bowed to the audience, turned to give her pupils a warm smile, then took her place at the piano.

'Everything all right?' Jenny whispered.

'Yes, fine.' Andrew took her hand in his, holding it tightly. 'Calum OK?'

'He's having a ball,' she said as the music began and the choir, smartly dressed in white shirts and trousers or blouses and navy blue skirts, topped with brightly made-up faces, launched into their first song.

'Did you like it? Was I OK?' Calum wanted to know. The musical had ended to enthusiastic applause, and the curtain was no sooner closed than the children stampeded into the hall to meet their audience, shedding straw everywhere.

'You were great,' Andrew said warmly. 'Wasn't he, Jenny? Maggie?'

'You didn't forget a single line — everyone was terrific,' Jenny assured her excited son, who had whipped off his battered cloth hat and was using it to fan himself vigorously, while Maggie said, 'It was good . . . really.'

Slowly, the hall emptied as children, many still in their scarecrow costumes, were taken home. Jinty, one of the last to leave, turned at the door to look back at the hall.

'I've seen less straw in a barn! I'll need to come in early tomorrow to give it a good clean.'

Steph linked an arm through her mother's. 'I'll help you, Mum,' she said, and then, looking at the rest of the family, 'We'll all help you. We'll set the alarm earlier than usual and come over here first thing.'

'What about our breakfast?' Grant, her twin, wailed. 'I'm no good without some breakfast in me.'

'You'll get fed, but not until after we've helped Mum put this place to rights. Jimmy, while we're doing that you go to the village store first thing and buy lots of rolls and a dozen eggs,' Steph instructed, 'then go back to the house and put the kettle on and start buttering the rolls and frying eggs. Norris and Faith can help you.'

'I'll do that and Jimmy can come over here.'

'I know you, Grant. You'd eat your fill and go back to bed for another half hour. I can trust Jimmy to do as he's told.'

Jimmy smirked, delighted with the compliment, while Grant made a face at his twin.

'You're good kids, all of you,' Jinty said happily. 'Come

on, then, let's go home and get that kettle on. I'm dying for a cuppa!'

'No!' Calum Forsyth said loudly. 'No, no, no!'

'I'd like to agree with you, old son,' his father said, 'but I'm afraid it's yes, and we're all going to have to deal with it as best we can.'

'But it's the summer holidays! We're supposed to have *fun* in the summer holidays!'

'You still can. You like the Reverend Hennessey, don't you? She's full of fun,' Jenny pleaded, 'and Ethan will be there, and Maggie.'

The three Forsyths had been to the nearby town's swimming pool, and now they were back in the large, comfortable caravan they had booked for the week. Calum had been drying his hair when his parents broke the news to him, and now he faced the two of them, his face red, the damp towel slung round his neck and his fists clenched tightly.

'I want to come to Edinburgh with you!'

'Darling, you can't do that. We'll be staying in a tiny flat and spending most of our time at the hospital. You'd be on your own in a place where you don't know anyone.'

'I could come to the hospital with you every day. I wouldn't mind.'

'There won't be room for three of us, and I'll get better faster if I know you're in Prior's Ford, enjoying yourself with your friends.'

'How can I enjoy myself when you two aren't there?'

'We'll be coming home every Saturday morning until Sunday afternoon, so we'll all have the weekends in our own house. You know what the holidays are like,' Jenny coaxed as her son continued to glare, his lower lip stuck

170

out in a way she hadn't seen since his toddler days, 'the time just flies past. Maggie's going to make sure you're all right.'

'You told her before you told me?'

'We couldn't tell you until the concert and your last day at the village school were over. We didn't want to spoil them for you.'

'But Maggie doesn't like me. She hates me!'

'Calum, she's your sister, of course she likes you.'

'Why do you keep calling her my sister? She's not my sister and even if she was, I wouldn't want her to be. And she *doesn't* like me,' he insisted, fighting back tears. 'You don't know what she's like when it's just the two of us. She says I'm just a daft wee boy. I don't want to be left with her,' he shrieked, and before either of his parents could move he was out of the door and running across the field, weaving between the caravans.

'Leave him,' Andrew said as his wife made for the door.

'But where's he going?'

'There.' Andrew pointed out of the big window at the front of the caravan. Calum had reached the low stone wall bordering the field; he scrambled over it, and then perched on top, his back to them and his head drooping.

'Leave him,' Andrew said again. 'I'll go and speak to him in a little while.'

'His hair's still wet. He might catch a cold.'

'I don't think that matters right now, love. If he takes off again I'll follow him, but he just needs to be on his own.'

'Do you think what he said about Maggie's true?'

'I don't know, but when we had dinner together in the Cuckoo the other night I got the impression she was on the verge of becoming a member of the family at last. We can only hope – and put our trust in Naomi.'

They watched Calum for ten minutes, and then Andrew went out to sit on the wall beside him. Jenny stood at the window for a further fifteen minutes while Andrew talked and Calum just sat, head down and shoulders huddled, staring at the ground. Then Andrew returned to the caravan alone.

'We're all going to the Chinese restaurant now, so get your glad rags on.'

'How is he?'

'He'll be all right,' Andrew said. 'He needs time to get used to what he's just heard.' Then, with a sigh, 'One down, two to go. I'm not looking forward to telling my parents our news tomorrow.'

In her grandparents' house in Dundee, Maggie was making herself useful, helping her gran in the kitchen, having long conversations with her grandfather, and visiting her uncle and her aunt, who was going through one of her better phases.

It was lovely to see them all, but she knew now that the Dundee phase of her life was over for good, other than visits. Like it or not, her home was Prior's Ford. She was needed there, and in a way it was good to be needed.

When her grandparents, shocked at her news about Andrew's illness, asked if she would be all right, she smiled and told them that of course she would. 'They need me there to keep an eye on Calum,' she heard herself say. 'I'm his big sister now.'

'He couldn't have better than you, pet,' her gran said, while Granda added, 'You're a right comfort to us all, Maggie lass.'

Alone in her bedroom later, Maggie gave her mirrored reflection an ironic smile. Jenny and Andrew wouldn't believe their ears if they heard such praise being lavished on her. But she had promised to look after Calum, and given the circumstance, it was a promise she had to keep. He wasn't a bad kid, really, so it shouldn't be too hard, especially with Naomi Hennessey's help.

Then the smile faded as the prospect of the summer stretching ahead of her suddenly hit her. She felt as though she were standing on the very edge of a black abyss, about to fall.

She had no idea she and Jenny were sharing the same nightmare.

'So how is Calum now?' Ingrid asked. She and Jenny had closed the Gift Horse for an hour, while Marcy had persuaded Sam to hold the fort at the village store so they could meet Helen for a pub lunch. Between the school holidays and the imminent Scarecrow Festival the four of them had been too busy to meet together.

'He's being very quiet. I wish we didn't have to go off and leave him, but there's no other way to deal with what's happening in our lives at the moment. I'm glad he's going to live at the manse, though, because I think Naomi will be supportive. Not that you wouldn't have been just as supportive,' Jenny added hurriedly.

'We know what you mean. Naomi will watch out for him, and it'll do him good to be with Ethan. Did Andrew's parents offer to take him?' Ingrid asked.

A sudden shadow swept over Jenny's face. 'No they didn't, and if they had we would have refused. The moment the word "cancer" was mentioned they both went into denial so fast that it would have been funny if we'd been in the mood for laughing.' She glanced round the table. 'I was looking at Andrew's father when he told them; his first

173

reaction was one of shock, understandably, but then came open fear. After that, it was almost as if the two of them thought Andrew was contagious. They both started urging him to put his faith in God.'

'Probably the last thing he needs to hear right now,' Marcy said.

'Exactly. When he said that at the moment he was more interested in having faith in his doctors they reacted as though he'd just sworn at them. We couldn't leave fast enough, and clearly they couldn't wait for us to go. So no comfort there.'

'I can understand their rush towards the security of denial,' Marcy told her. 'Parents must find it hard to cope with the thought of losing a child, even a grown child. Not that I'm condoning them, because they should put Andrew and you before their own feelings.'

Jenny lifted her glass with a hand that shook slightly, gulped down a mouthful of wine, then said quietly, but vehemently, 'You could be right, but I feel so angry on Andrew's behalf.'

'What about your own family, Jenny?' Helen wanted to know.

'I'm in much the same boat as Andrew, but at least we're in it together. My parents were always more interested in Glenda, my older sister; I think they only wanted one child so I was surplus to requirements. Once I was married to Neil and off their hands they went to Canada to be near Glenda. She'd moved into a flat with two friends when she was seventeen and I was twelve, then a few years later the three of them emigrated to Canada. She married a Canadian.'

'A Mountie?' Helen asked hopefully. 'Or a lumberjack?'

'There speaks the true romantic,' Ingrid teased her.

'She married a man who worked in his father's grocery

174

store, and now they own it, and another two that they've opened. They're doing quite well. We keep in touch at Christmas and Glenda and my parents send cheques so we can buy Christmas and birthday presents from them for Calum. I wrote to tell them about Andrew, but since they've never met him . . .' Jenny shrugged. 'They've got their lives and I've got mine.'

'But that's wrong!' Ingrid was shocked. 'I would never turn away from Freya or Ella in an hour of need.'

'That's because you love them, Ingrid,' Marcy told her. 'I never got much support from my family, so I know how Jenny feels. Sometimes blood *isn't* any thicker than water.'

'I count myself so fortunate that I've got you three as my sisters.' Jenny added, 'And Andrew. He's the best thing that ever happened to me and I don't know . . .'

Her voice wavered, and Helen put a hand over hers while Marcy said firmly, 'Another glass of wine all round, I think.'

'In the middle of the day? I'll get all squiffy,' Jenny protested.

'Me too, but there are times when being squiffy is acceptable,' Ingrid told her as Marcy went over to the bar.

'Have we made a terrible mistake?' Fliss asked nervously on the day before the opening of the Scarecrow Festival. 'I mean, we don't have anything for visitors to admire; it's not as if we can let them see any part of the house at the moment and I'm sure people expect much more these days for their entrance money than we can give them.'

'They'll enjoy walking round the gardens; Duncan and Lewis and the others have worked wonders with them,' Ginny assured her, 'so there's plenty to see.'

'You've got to remember, Mrs F, that not many people get the chance to walk up the drive of a big house like this,' Jinty added. 'They'll be thrilled just to be here for a little while. And they'll be happy as long as they can have a sit down and a cup of tea once they've done the rounds.'

'And there's the shop, too. It'll all be lovely, just you wait and see,' Molly said vigorously. 'I'm looking forward to it. It's good practice for when me and Lewis own the place, because we'll be ready to open it to the public all summer by then. You can make a lot of money doing that sort of thing.'

'It'll be fine,' Jinty cut in, glaring at Molly. 'I'll join you as soon as I've got the tearoom in the village hall up and running, and Ginny's just across the yard if you need help before I arrive.'

'I'll be in the shop,' said Molly who had opted to take over that responsibility from Ginny, 'and Weena can help you as well, can't you, poppet? Once she comes back from being in the procession.' Molly swooped down on her daughter's playpen. Rowena Chloe ignored her, because she was reaching as far through the bars as she could, shouting, 'Mu-mu-mu . . .' at Muffin, who, not being in the mood to have his fur grabbed by chubby fists, was keeping his distance.

Molly picked her daughter up and gave her a hug. 'She's going to be the prettiest little scarecrow in the village, aren't you?'

Rowena Chloe patted her kindly on the cheek, and then reached out to Muffin again.

'What did Jinty scowl at me like that for?' Molly wanted to know as she and Ginny returned to the shop to organise the shelves. 'Have I got BO or something?'

'I don't think she liked you talking about when you and Lewis owned the hall.'

'Why not? It's going to happen sooner or later, isn't it?' Molly asked, and Ginny had to bite her tongue.

176

20

Prior's Ford was a hive of activity all through Friday and late into the night, and when the sun rose on the following day, it shone on a village that seemed to have doubled its population overnight.

Almost every garden boasted at least one scarecrow, and the stalls and makeshift platform on the village green were set carefully around the Mad Hatter's Tea Party. The school playground held several scarecrow children while the village store had a paper boy in its window and the butcher's had, as was to be expected, a butcher.

From early in the morning the villagers were out putting the final touches to their entries while in the village hall, Jinty and her helpers organised the tearoom.

Signs were put up to show the way to Linn Hall, where Hector and Fliss nervously awaited their very first open day.

By ten o'clock, when the procession was about to begin, Prior's Ford was filled with visitors. Part of the school play-ground and the courtyard behind the village hall had been turned into temporary car parks, but by mid-morning they were filled and cars were parked all along one side of Main Street and in all the side streets. Each time the regular bus arrived it disgorged most of its passengers before moving on.

The procession was to begin from the school, which buzzed with activity as mothers dressed their offspring in their scarecrow costumes, while the brass band hired to lead the procession rehearsed in one of the classrooms.

Lynn Stacy had volunteered to lead the procession, and there were gasps of admiration when she appeared from her office wearing a swirling ankle-length patchwork gown topped by a red silk cape. Her cheeks were heavily rouged and her smile revealed that several front teeth had been blacked out. A battered gold cardboard crown sat askew atop a wig made from bright red wool.

'I,' she announced in ringing tones, 'am the Scarecrow Queen, and here are my attendants.' She clapped her hands and the three other teachers, blushing and giggling, emerged from the office, each wearing a brightly coloured dress, a fun wig and a tiara.

'And you,' Lynn held out her arms to the entire room, 'are my devoted subjects!'

A host of small scarecrows cheered and rushed to surround her, while Helen murmured to Jenny, 'Can you picture Miss Terrell leading a procession through the village dressed like that?'

'Not in a million years. I don't know *how* she managed to persuade the others to make fools of themselves along with her.'

'Exactly. Aren't we lucky to have such a lovely head teacher?' Helen was saying when a surprisingly elegant scarecrow wheeled a buggy containing a small scarecrow into the assembly hall.

178

'Sorry we're late,' Molly Ewing said cheerfully. 'Weena kept trying to pull her wig off so I had to tie it on.' Her daughter scowled, tugging in frustration at her woollen wig and floppy bonnet. 'Well, now we're here, let's get started!'

Fliss had been asked to open the festival, but had managed to get out of it, using the excuse that she had to be on duty in Linn Hall. Naomi, too, managed to avoid the task by offering to run the tearoom in the village hall in order to let Jinty help Fliss. As Hector was known to be too shy to officiate at anything, the Progress Committee had turned in desperation to Lewis, who gave a short but funny speech ending with a reminder that Linn Hall was open and well worth a visit, awarded the Best Scarecrow prize to a blushing five-year-old dressed as a tattered Mary Poppins, and then went off to his duties at Linn Hall, leaving the villagers and visitors to enjoy their day.

'You might have given Weena the prize,' Molly said sulkily as the two of them set off up the hill, Lewis pushing the baby buggy. 'She looked much prettier than that girl, and anyway, what was she doing dressed as Mary Poppins? She wasn't a scarecrow, she was a film star.'

'I couldn't give my own daughter the prize, could I, even though she looked good enough to eat. In any case, by the time I began judging she had pulled the wig over her face, so she wasn't looking her best. And Mary Poppins was a character in a book,' Lewis explained just as Rowena Chloe finally managed to wrench the hated wig and hat off and hurl them over the edge of the buggy with a scream of triumph.

'Imagine folk bein' daft enough to spend time makin' rubbish like this,' Ryan kept saying as he and Maggie wandered round the village.

'I think it's quite a nice idea. It's brightened up the village,' she said, then regretted her defence as he retorted, 'You think so? If you ask me, they all need to get a life. F'r instance, look at that one.'

He drew her to a stop outside a neat semi-detached villa, pointing at a life-sized figure in the middle of the lawn. 'What's that supposed to be? A deep-sea diver? He'd never survive with that over his head instead of a proper helmet.' He sniggered.

'It's a beekeeper and that's what they use when they work with the bees to avoid getting stung. Mr McBain keeps bees.'

'You mean he goes about dressed like that?'

'Only when he's working with the bees.' Ryan's contempt for the festival meant that Maggie felt obliged to keep apologising for the villagers, though secretly, she thought some of the scarecrows on show were very well done. 'Look, he's got a bee scarecrow as well, perched on top of a hive.'

'Daft wally,' Ryan said, the sniggering turning into a belly laugh. To her horror, Maggie suddenly realised both the McBains were standing at their picture window, watching them.

'Come on, there's lots to see,' she said nervously. As Mrs McBain suddenly turned about and disappeared from sight, probably heading for the front door, she grabbed Ryan's arm and began to haul him along the pavement. The star of the local drama club, Mrs McBain was a formidable lady when roused.

'Get off,' Ryan protested. 'What d'you think you're doin', daft mare?'

'Mrs McBain was watching us. I'm talking about the Mrs McBain in the Academy's English department. You don't want to tangle with her.'

'What – Mouthy McBain's married to that nerdy beekeeper? I think I'll go back an' offer my condolences to both of them.'

'Stop it, Ryan; you know what she's like when she gets angry. And she didn't like you laughing at their scarecrow.'

'We're on holiday now, not at the Academy. I'm not afraid of her,' Ryan sneered, but all the same, he allowed her to lead him down the road, though he plucked her hand from his sleeve and tucked it into the crook of his elbow as though showing her who was boss.

As it happened, Maggie had jumped from the frying pan into the fire; running away from the McBains, she had led Ryan towards her own home just as Jenny came through the gate, bearing a large covered tray.

'Hello, Maggie . . . and you must be Ryan. How nice to meet you at last!'

'Is it?'

'Ryan, this is my stepmother, Mrs Forsyth,' Maggie said nervously. To her astonishment, Ryan promptly turned into someone she had never known before.

'Mrs Forsyth, it's my pleasure. Here, let me take that for you.' He whisked the tray from her grasp. 'Where are you going?'

'To the village hall, they've run out of cakes.'

'Lead the way,' Ryan said, and winked at Maggie as the two of them followed Jenny.

When they arrived at the hall, decorated with streamers, balloons and scarecrow pictures drawn by Alastair Marshall and the primary-school children, Jenny insisted on buying tea for the two of them.

'I'll have to go and help in the gift shop, but I've got time for a cup of tea first.' She sat down beside them, to Molly's horror. She was convinced that the sarcastic, sneering

Ryan she knew would break through at any moment, but instead he chatted happily to Jenny, assuring her he was enjoying his visit to the village and was impressed by the hard work that had gone into making all the scarecrows.

'That Florence Nightingale at the house on the green,' he said earnestly, 'is a real masterpiece, don't you think?'

'Yes, Kevin's put a lot of work into it. Kevin Pearce runs the local drama club,' Jenny explained. 'There are going to be prizes awarded for the best garden scarecrow and the best shop scarecrow, and I know Kevin's hoping to win the garden section.'

'I'm sure he will.' When Ryan had first announced he was coming to the opening day of the festival, Maggie had decided that whatever happened, she would make sure he wouldn't meet her family. Now she didn't know how to cope with the situation she found herself in. So she retreated to the sulky silence she maintained when with the Forsyths.

'I wish our area could do somethin' like that, but I live on a council estate,' Ryan was explaining earnestly, 'and the folk there are pretty dull.'

'That's a shame. We might repeat the festival next year, so you'd be welcome to help us to make scarecrows then.'

'Sounds good, doesn't it, Maggie?'

She nodded, not lifting her gaze from the plastic table-cloth, and was relieved when Jenny said, 'I must go. Nice to meet you, Ryan.'

'And you.' He got up smartly and shook her hand. 'P'rhaps we'll meet again?'

'Oh yes, you must come for tea one day. I suppose Maggie's told you my husband's not well at the moment, and he'll be having treatment all summer, but once he gets better we'll look forward to seeing you.'

'I hope he recovers soon, Mrs Forsyth. What's wrong

with him?' Ryan wanted to know when Jenny was out of earshot.

'He's got c–cancer.' It was hard to say the word without stumbling over it.

'Poor sod. She's OK, your stepmum. She's fit,' Ryan said with relish. 'Not like the fairy-story monster you said she was.'

'You don't have to live with her.'

'Oh, I wouldn't mind trying it.' He leered.

'What does that mean?'

'You know what? You're dead easy to wind up, you silly mare. Come on,' Ryan said, picking up the last biscuit from the plate and cramming it into his mouth, spraying crumbs as he went on, 'let's go an' see the rest of the freak show.'

21

To Lewis's satisfaction and his parents' astonishment, their open day on the Saturday had been a success. People arrived in a steady stream from mid-morning until the gates were closed in the evening, wandering round the gardens, taking tea at the tables set out in the courtyard, visiting the stable shop and in some cases, having picnics on the lawn and peering in through the hall's ground-floor windows, which didn't bother the Ralston-Kerrs a bit since the ground-floor rooms were never used.

Many of the men working on the windows were among the visitors, and had brought their families with them.

'I just wanted them to see where I've been workin',' one of them explained to Ginny. 'It's been great, and I wanted to take the chance to have a proper look round myself.'

Several people asked to be shown round the hall, and were disappointed when told that was not possible.

'Perhaps we should think about opening the ground floor next summer,' Lewis said that evening.

'But the rooms are a mess,' Fliss objected.

'We could clean them up. The furniture's still there, and we can point out the house is being worked on. Some of those people today would have been happy to pay a small entrance fee.'

'Lewis is right; most folk never get to see inside a big place like this,' Molly said. 'You'd make a fortune.'

'It'd be hard work.' After a day spent directing cars to what used to be a tennis court, and collecting entry money, Hector was exhausted. He ran his hands through what remained of his hair, making it stand up around his ears.

'We'd need to get people from the village to come in and help. With what we made today,' Lewis said, tapping the shoe box where the takings, counted and recorded, had been stored, 'we could just about afford to pay them, and cover the tea, coffee and baking costs. We'll be up and running next year, you wait and see. I'll try to get Grant McDonald and some of his mates on car-parking duties for the rest of the week,' he added, seeing how tired his father looked. 'Ginny and Molly and I are going to the Cuckoo for a drink in a minute and I'll look in on the McDonalds first. Come down with us, Dad, you could probably do with a drink.'

'I think,' Fliss said, 'that after the day he's had, your father would prefer a nice quiet cup of cocoa. Plus,' she added, when she and Hector were alone apart from Muffin, who was asleep by the fire even though the evening was too warm to have it lit, and Rowena Chloe who slumbered in her pram in a corner, worn out by the day's excitement, 'a tot of whisky. I've been saving some for an occasion like this.'

'Does whisky go with cocoa?' Hector asked doubtfully.

'It goes with pretty well everything,' Fliss assured him, sloshing milk into a pan.

'Hector,' she said later as the two of them sipped their

185

cocoa and whisky, 'things are changing, and I know it's not always easy, but we're going to have to accept the changes. Lewis has the bit between his teeth, and let's face it, the time's coming when he'll take over. Lewis and Molly,' she added, stifling her unease over the prospect of Molly as mistress of the hall. 'Now that the shop's up and running, he has to have visitors to keep it going.'

'It's all too much for me,' her husband confessed. 'I'm not good with people, you know that.'

'But you *are* good with figures. We could arrange for you to keep the accounts while the rest of us deal with the public. As Lewis says, we'll have to bring in temporary staff over the summer from now on, not just backpackers willing to work for bed and board for a couple of months. We'll employ villagers as well, and pay them what we can. You and Lewis could start working out some sort of business plan with the bank manager, couldn't you?'

'I suppose so. But I wish,' he said wistfully, 'we could go back to the way we used to be, with just the three of us and Duncan, and the young people every summer.'

'And the cold winters, and you and me running around upstairs when it rained, putting chamber pots and vases down to catch the drips. At least we're snug and weatherproof now. And Lewis has the baby and Molly to think of . . . he's got no option but to move forward. From now on we have to get used to gradually letting him take control. Nobody can go back, Hector,' Fliss said gently, reaching out to cover his gnarled, liver-spotted hand with her own, red from frequent contact with hot water and detergent. 'The only way is forward, and at least we're doing it together.'

Jenny stared straight ahead as she and Andrew drove out of Prior's Ford, unable to look back at the home they were leaving and the life that had, until recently, been so perfect and might never be the same again.

'Why does it have to be us?' she burst out.

'You're going to have to stop thinking that way and start being positive,' Andrew told her calmly. 'Tomorrow they start shrinking the tumour and as far as I'm concerned I'm in good hands. And things are working out really well, because starting treatment now means we'll be back home to see Calum settled in the Academy before I have the operation. We have to be positive, Jen. Concentrate on the great weekend we've just had.'

It had been a good weekend. The opening day of the festival had been perfect, and that morning they had skipped church for once, and spent the time walking round the village to see the scarecrows. There had been so many, some of them so lifelike that from a distance they could be mistaken for real people.

The end wall at the almshouses sported a basking mermaid, cleverly fastened to the bricks by Charlie Crandall and Robert Kavanagh, with Oor Wullie perched on his upturned bucket outside Hannah Gibbs' door. Further along the small row of houses Darby and Joan, cosy and bespectacled, shared a bench.

An aproned scarecrow swept the village hall steps, a little girl perched on a swing outside the Gift Horse, and a reluctant gardener leaned heavily on his rake in Clarissa Ramsay's front garden, eyes closed and tendrils of ivy growing up his legs. In Ingrid's immaculate front garden a nursemaid pushed a pram with a bonneted straw baby in it, and the smiling Jamaican woman in the manse garden could have been mistaken from a distance for Naomi Hennessey, dressed as she was in Naomi's bright clothes.

Every garden had a scarecrow of some kind: milkmaids,

traditional scarecrows, farm workers, anglers and women sitting on benches knitting or inspecting roses.

Visitors were still pouring into the village, and it was as well that Andrew had had the foresight to book a table at the Neurotic Cuckoo for lunch that day. Demand was so great that Joe Fisher had moved the two scarecrows enjoying a drink from their outside table and seated them in ordinary kitchen chairs, where the Bob the Builder scarecrow that Ewan McNair had made for young Jamie stood nearby, apparently eyeing their beer glasses wistfully.

After lunch, the impressive pirate that Andrew and Calum had made was moved from their garden to the manse, and they had time to see Calum and Maggie settled in before departing for their first week in Edinburgh.

Leaving Calum was the hardest thing she had ever done, Jenny thought before realising that this had happened to her before, years ago when she had fled her bullying husband, leaving Maggie, a toddler, behind. She had had no option then, because Maggie was her stepdaughter, and not hers to take. Now, she'd had to choose between Andrew and Calum. Perhaps this time, torn between husband and son, was the worse of the two.

She slipped a hand into her bag and brought out the set of digital photographs Andrew had taken the day before and printed in the evening. Several were of the procession, with Calum waving cheerfully as he passed the camera. There was one of him triumphantly flourishing a flower vase he had won from the hoopla stall and later given to her, and she and Andrew had taken pictures of each other with Calum and Maggie. As usual, Maggie was scowling, but in every one of the pictures, Calum was happy. At least their final day together for the time being had been a good one for him.

It had been a different matter when they said goodbye

at the manse. He had put on a brave face but Jenny couldn't forget the fear in his eyes and the way his mouth was tightly compressed to hold back tears as he waved goodbye, Naomi's dark hand lying lightly on his shoulder.

'Don't worry, he'll be fine,' the minister had assured them. 'They both will. We'll keep in touch by phone and you'll be back next Saturday.'

Calum was a big boy now, Jenny told herself firmly. At the end of the summer holidays he was going to start attending the Academy, and in December he would celebrate his twelfth birthday.

'Naomi will look after Calum,' Andrew said just then, as though reading her thoughts. 'She'll look after both of them. They'll be OK.'

'I know. It's just that this is the first time we've left Calum.'

'Perhaps it's time he got the chance to be without us for a few days. In just over a year he'll be a teenager.'

'True,' Jenny agreed, and then, as the car sped further and further away from Prior's Ford, she tried to change the subject. 'At least I finally got to meet Maggie's boyfriend, so I feel a lot better about her now.'

'Certainly sounds like a nice lad.'

'He is. Very polite, and good-looking, too. P'rhaps he'll help her to settle down. I so want her to be happy!'

'She will be, given time.'

'I hope so,' Jenny said, then remembered Calum insisting, in the caravan, 'Maggie hates me . . . I don't want to be left with her!'

Maggie surveyed the small room where she was to sleep. It was comfortable enough, with an electric fire and a curtained window, but it wasn't nearly as nice as the room

Jenny had prepared for her when she first came to Prior's Ford. That bedroom had been the best she'd ever had, nicer than the one she had slept in while growing up in her grandparents' house.

She had sneered at it at the time, throwing the furry toys scattered over the bed into the bottom of the wardrobe in order to hurt Jenny's feelings. Sometimes at night, when she felt lonelier than usual, she retrieved a few of them to cuddle in bed, but the next morning they were tossed back in the wardrobe.

Now, she wished she was in that bedroom again, and that she had been nicer to Jenny and Andrew. She had wanted to punish Jenny for leaving her and her father, and she had been so confused it had never occurred to her that it must have been difficult for them to open their home to a teenager they didn't know.

Looking out of the window she saw Calum in the garden below, standing beside the scarecrow he and Andrew had made together, his chin on his chest and his fingers fidgeting with the hem of his T-shirt. He must be lonely too, and she was supposed to look out for him while his parents were away. She could at least make a start on that.

'Cup of tea?' Naomi called from the kitchen as she passed the door. 'I'm making one.'

'Thanks. I'm just going to have a word with Calum.'

'Good idea.'

Calum jumped when Maggie came up behind him and said, 'Hi.' He spun round and his eyes, slightly red around the edges, hardened when he saw her.

'What d'*you* want?'

'Just wondered if everything's all right.'

'Why shouldn't it be?'

She blinked, taken aback by a hostility she had never

190

seen in him before. Calum had always seemed a bit of a wimp, a mummy's boy. It was one of the things that made Maggie enjoy tormenting him.

'He looks good.' She nodded towards the scarecrow. Calum had wanted to make him as like Johnny Depp, the star of the Disney film about pirates, as possible, but Andrew had seized the chance to introduce his son to Robert Louis Stevenson's *Treasure Island*, and the two of them had ended up making a Long John Silver scarecrow, complete with a crutch and a parrot on the scarecrow's shoulder.

'I like his hat, it's fab.' Her hand moved towards the three-cornered hat that Jenny had made, then was drawn back sharply as Calum moved in front of the figure to fend her off. 'Don't touch him,' he snapped. 'If you dare touch him, I'll punch you!'

She stared at him. 'I wasn't going to touch your old scarecrow, you stupid wee boy!'

'Yes you were, and I'm not stupid – I'm not! Don't you ever say that to me again because if you do you'll be sorry!'

'I only meant . . . I'm supposed to be looking after you, can't you understand that? I was trying to be nice, though I don't know why I bother!'

'Don't bother then, because I don't want you to. I wish they'd sent you back to Dundee instead of letting you stay on here. I've got Ethan to look out for me now,' Calum raged, his face scarlet and his fists clenched, 'and if you don't stop teasing me I'm going to make you sorry you ever came here!'

They were staring at each other, Maggie in shock, Calum so angry his fair hair almost stood on end, when Ethan called from the back door, 'Want to play football, Calum? I said I'd meet Ella and some of the other kids at the quarry.'

'Coming,' Calum yelled, and then hissed at Maggie, 'You'd better believe me!' before scampering off.

191

Maggie was looking after him, stunned, when Naomi appeared at the back door, brandishing a mug. 'Ready! It would have been nice to drink our tea in the garden,' she said when Maggie joined her in the kitchen, 'but there are so many strangers out scarecrow-watching that we're better indoors. Every time I go out now I feel the need to keep moving in case I'm mistaken for a scarecrow.'

Her warm laughter filled the kitchen and attracted the attention of the cat, who came in and eyed the mugs hopefully, wondering if biscuits were going to be brought out.

'Calum and Ethan are off to play football at the quarry,' Maggie said.

'Yes, Ethan said. He'll keep an eye on Calum, no need to worry.'

'Calum said he would.' Maggie picked the cat up and buried her face in its warm, silky, comforting fur.

22

'This,' Clarissa Ramsay said, 'is pure heaven. I can't tell you how glad I am you decided to visit.'

'The pleasure's all ours,' Steven told her. 'Chris has been on at me for ages to bring him to see your new home, but with you taking off round the world last year it wasn't to be.'

'Then when I heard about your scarecrows, I decided this I had to see,' said Chris Manson.

'Me and the scarecrows.'

'Strictly in that order,' Chris assured her. 'More wine?'

'I shouldn't really.'

'Yes, you should.' The three of them were lying back in deckchairs in the sun-dappled shelter of the tree in Clarissa's back garden. Now Chris sat up and reached out for the bottle on the round garden table.

'I really should be thinking about dinner,' Clarissa protested as he poured wine into her glass.

'We'll help, and it'll be done in no time,' Steven assured her, holding out his own glass. 'Why not invite your friend Alastair along? He's not met Chris yet.'

'I already did when I heard you two were coming for a few days. He'll be arriving around six.'

'Which gives us loads of time,' Chris said contentedly, settling back into his chair.

'Mmm.' Clarissa sipped at her wine and then closed her eyes, savouring its bouquet and revelling in the warmth of the sun. She felt more relaxed in Steven's company than in his sister's, or even his father's. With both Keith and Alexandra she had always felt slightly inferior, lacking in something, but with Steven she could be herself. She had been delighted when he phoned to ask if he and his partner could drive north to spend a few days with her. Chris, who looked like the rugby player he was, when he could spare the time from his veterinary practice, was a very likeable man, and to her mind, he and Steven were an ideal couple, much more suited to each other than many traditional couples.

Suddenly aware she was under scrutiny, she opened her eyes to see Steven watching her.

'What?'

'You look . . . fantastic. You're glowing.'

'Get away with you!'

'You are,' he insisted. 'You look years younger than that time Alex and I came to sort out Father's papers.'

'I hadn't long been widowed then. Not exactly in the mood to glow.'

'I know, but you've changed so much, Clarissa. You're a different woman. To be honest, when you told us you were going to travel, Alex and I thought you would scurry home within a month, but you didn't. Travel certainly made a big difference to you.'

'That, and living here. I'm glad I decided to stay on in Prior's Ford. I love this house, and the village and the people in it.'

194

'I'm not surprised. Dumfries and Galloway is a beautiful place,' Chris said enviously. 'We're going to have to come here more often, Steven. I can feel my batteries recharging even as I speak.'

'Coming here certainly did Alex good last year. Why did she do it, Clarissa? Did she ever tell you?'

'Just that she suddenly felt the need for a break and couldn't think of anywhere else to go. According to Fliss Ralston-Kerr she did a wonderful job of cataloguing all the items stowed away in the hall while she was here. Dug into rooms and cupboards and drawers that hadn't been looked at for decades, and found all sorts of interesting things. They auctioned off most of them and raised a small fortune.'

'That sounds like my sister,' Steven said lazily. 'Apparently she saw quite a bit of Alastair Marshall, too. She came back speaking very highly of him.'

'Alastair can have that effect on people.' Clarissa remembered how low she had felt the first time she had met him, and how Alastair, without asking questions, had slowly and gently helped her to regain a self-esteem she had thought lost for ever.

'You don't think she fell for him, do you?' Steven asked suddenly. 'I wish she could find someone to share her life with. It might help to rub off the sharp corners and make her happier into the bargain. For as long as I can recall, I've never thought of Alex as happy.'

'I doubt if Alastair's her type. A penniless artist who likes to live in a tumbledown old cottage? I'm sure if your sister ever settles down it will be with a man who can keep her in the style to which she has become accustomed.'

'You could be right, but I hope he can make her happy as well as comfortable,' Steven mused.

* * *

Clarissa woke early on Tuesday morning and lay for a while, listening to the early-morning sounds of the village; birdsong, traffic on Main Street, close by the cottage, people calling to each other across the village green. Thanks to the double-glazed windows the sounds were too faint to be annoying, but loud enough to give her the comforting knowledge that she wasn't alone.

Steven and Chris had set off for home on Monday afternoon, having had a most enjoyable weekend. Clarissa had enjoyed it too, but it was nice, this morning, to know that today she could return to her usual routine. In a minute she would go downstairs and make herself a cup of tea, then take it and the newspaper, which she knew would be waiting on the doorstep, back to bed for a lazy half hour. Later, bathed and dressed, she would have breakfast, probably in the back garden, then walk over to the village store and the butcher's. She might treat herself to a coffee at the Gift Horse, or even lunch at the Cuckoo, then do some letter writing or gardening – perhaps a little of both – in the afternoon.

When she went downstairs, sunshine splashed over the back garden and poured in through the kitchen windows. She filled the kettle and switched it on, then while it came to the boil she went to the front door to fetch her newspaper and milk from the doorstep.

The first thing she saw when she opened the door was her scarecrow, the reluctant gardener Alastair had helped to make (or, rather, that she had helped him to make) sprawled face down on the grass.

'Oh, no!' She left the paper and milk bottle where they were and ran to the still figure, noticing when she got there that the artificial ivy she had wound carefully around his thin legs was now tied about his neck in the form of a noose.

Looking round for the rake he had been propped on, she saw it lying beneath the hedge between her garden and Sam Brennan's.

'What on earth . . . ?' she said aloud, standing up. It was only then she realised the voices she had heard while still snug in bed were louder.

'Morning, Mrs Ramsay.' Robert Kavanagh, on his way from the almshouses, paused to peer over her gate at the prone scarecrow. 'I see they've visited you as well.'

'Who?'

'Vandals, that's who,' he said grimly. 'They were at the almshouses too, some time during the night. And from the look of the folk milling about over on the green, there's other figures been hit too. We're going to have to try to set things right before the visitors start arriving. 'Scuse me.'

He hurried off, and Clarissa, suddenly realising that she was in her dressing gown, retreated to the house, gathering up the newspaper and milk on her way.

Studying her reflection in the hall mirror, she blessed her decision while travelling to have her hair cut short; even tousled and uncombed, it didn't look too bad. And her candlewick dressing gown, though old, covered her from neck to wrists and ankles. Mr Kavanagh hadn't seen her at her best that morning, but at least he hadn't seen her at her worst.

Not that he was likely to care what she looked like, she thought as she made tea and poured cereal into a bowl, the planned half hour in bed forgotten. He was too busy worrying about the scarecrows that morning to notice what a real live woman looked like.

Charlie Crandall's plan to cure Hannah's fear of scarecrows by persuading her to help him to make one had worked well. She had become fond of the Oor Wullie figure they had created, and had even been able to watch the procession on Saturday, and then walk round the village with Charlie to admire the other contributions.

'It's been a good idea after all,' she admitted to him that evening over a meal in her snug little living room. They had fallen into the way of eating together every Saturday evening, one week at her house, the next at his, and occasionally, at the Neurotic Cuckoo. 'It's certainly brought a lot of people in.'

So it came as a shock when Charlie rapped at her door on Tuesday morning when she was eating breakfast, and said tersely, when she opened the door, 'Look!'

Following the direction of his pointing finger, she gasped at sight of the empty upturned bucket by her door. 'Wullie! Where's he gone?'

'That's what I'm off to find out. We've been vandalised, Hannah, and not just us, it looks as though the whole village has been hit. Sam and Marcy discovered it when they went to open up the store this morning, and alerted Robert. I'm off to have a look round.'

'Wait . . . I'm coming with you.'

Charlie looked at the slice of toast in her hand. 'Aren't you in the middle of your breakfast?'

'Never mind that.' She tossed the toast to the lawn for the next passing bird, turned to kick off her slippers and pushed her feet into the pair of shoes she always kept by the door. 'I want to find out what's happened to poor wee Wullie!'

The entire village was in an uproar that morning, with people hurrying about in search of missing scarecrows and returning figures that had been moved. Hannah and Charlie eventually found Oor Wullie sitting in the pram in Ingrid's garden, while the baby taken from the pram was at the Mad Hatter's Tea Party on the village green, perched on the Hatter's lap. The large bee belonging to the McBains had been crammed inside the Hatter's huge teapot, while the beekeeper's hat had disappeared and the balloon Gilbert had used as the head for his scarecrow was relegated to a sad wisp of rubber.

'They could always change it to the Headless Horseman.' Grant McDonald sniggered when he saw it.

'Shut up, stupid!' Steph gave her twin a hefty nudge in the ribs with her elbow. 'Everyone's already wondering if it was any of us villagers who did it; you don't want to make things worse.'

'Us? Our mum'd kill us if we touched a straw of those scarecrows,' protested Grant, who had worked hard with his mother and siblings to create their own entry, a farm labourer.

As it turned out the smiling old lady who was one half of the Darby and Joan couple created by the almshouses residents and on show near Oor Wullie, had been given the beekeeper's headgear, and she herself was now sitting on Darby's lap while her mob cap was crammed over the March Hare's ears.

The figure sweeping the steps of the village hall was found upside down in a wheelie bin, and some of the children's scarecrows in the school playground had been damaged. The little girl sitting on a swing outside the Gift Horse now nestled in the lap of one of the beer drinkers outside the Neurotic Cuckoo, her place on the swing taken by Bo Peep's lamb from the Campbells' garden.

One entire figure was missing. Florence Nightingale had been spirited from Eleanor and Kevin Pearce's garden and was nowhere to be seen. Kevin was one of the first to discover what had happened overnight when he went, as always, to buy the morning newspaper and almost stepped on Florence's lamp, which had been placed on the doorstep. As soon as he realised that the scarecrow itself had gone he rushed back into the house and snatched the phone from its cradle.

'Who are you calling at this hour of the morning?' Eleanor wanted to know.

'The police! Florence Nightingale's gone.'

'Gone where?'

'How could she have gone anywhere under her own steam? She's been stolen! Hello, police?'

The officers who finally arrived studied the note left beneath the lamp. 'I am just going outside and may be some time,' one of them read aloud. 'That's familiar.'

'It's what one of the members of Scott's expedition to the South Pole said before he walked out into the snow to perish,' Kevin told him irritably. 'Clearly the vandal or vandals who did this thought it was funny.'

'Mmm. This lamp looks like quite an old one, sir.'

'It is. I bought it in an antique shop a good while ago. I was going to turn it into a porch light.'

'That surely means that whoever took the figure didn't want to be accused of stealing anything valuable,' said Robert Kavanagh, who was going round the village making notes of the damage done, and had arrived at Kevin's door just before the police car drew up.

'They stole my scarecrow, didn't they? And didn't you say it was the only one that's completely disappeared, Robert?'

'As far as I know.'

'So it must be someone with a special grievance against me. Someone here in the village. Mine was the best, wasn't it, Robert? I was certain to win the prize for best garden scarecrow,' Kevin told the two officers while Robert was still searching for a diplomatic answer. As chairman of the Progress Committee, he had to be neutral.

'But surely, sir, if one person wanted to scupper your chances of winning this prize they wouldn't have troubled to mix up all the other figures?'

'I wouldn't put it past them.'

'So you have an idea as to who it might be, sir?'

'No, I don't. D'you want to take the lamp with you to get it dusted for fingerprints?'

'I don't think there's much point, sir. But while we're here we'll take a look at the other damage.'

'I'll show you round,' Robert said. 'All's not entirely lost. Because we felt that no villager could judge the competition,

201

we got some people in from Kirkcudbright. They came here as visitors on Saturday morning and made their decisions then. We'll hear the results this coming Saturday, so your scarecrow's still got a chance,' he said to Kevin.

'It won't be the same if I don't get her back,' Kevin mourned. 'It took me weeks to get her right, and the clothes were borrowed from the drama club's wardrobe. They've been there ever since we did *Gaslight,* just after I came to the village.'

Villagers raced to and fro all morning, and by the time the first visitors of the day arrived to view the scarecrows things were back to as normal as possible.

'It had to be poor Kevin,' Naomi said at a hastily convened Progress Committee meeting in the Neurotic Cuckoo. 'He's so easily upset.'

'Serves him right for braggin' all over the place about it bein' better than anyone else's effort,' Lachie announced. 'It's only a scarecrow, for goodness' sake. Only a bit of fun!'

'It was certainly a magnificent piece of work,' Hannah put in. 'Eleanor says he started working on it from the first mention of a festival. He takes things to heart so much. Other figures got vandalised, but poor Kevin's scarecrow's disappeared altogether. You don't think there'll be any more vandalism, do you?'

'Surely not,' Muriel Jacobson protested. 'It must be a one-off thing.'

'I wouldn't like to be too sure about that. The thing is,' Robert said, 'who were the perpetrators and where did they come from? Prior's Ford itself or further afield? Kevin's convinced it was someone local, out to prevent him from winning a prize, but I can't agree.'

'It must have happened late at night when everyone was

202

in bed, because nobody seems to have heard anything. Our neighbour's dog barked a few times, but he barks at anything so nobody pays much attention,' Helen put in.

'I don't think it was local children,' Naomi said firmly. Today she wore a loose silky top with green geometric shapes against a scarlet background over a long grey skirt patterned with multi-coloured flowers. It suited Naomi's light brown skin and black hair, and drew admiring looks from people at the other tables. 'I'm not saying they're angels, but most of them were involved one way and another in setting up the festival, and I don't see them trying to spoil it. I made a point of talking to Jinty McDonald and some of the other mums, and they agree with me.'

'Whoever it was, they deserve a good hard thrashing.' Joe Fisher had arrived with a tray of drinks in time to hear what Naomi said. 'But because we live in such a namby pamby country nowadays they'd be more likely to get a pat on the back and a request to try not to do it again. If I'd my way I'd dump all those politically correct freaks on a desert island and leave 'em to bore each other to death.'

'Amen to that.' Pete McDermott picked up his glass.

'OK, Pete, we're here to sort out what's to happen this week, not put the world to rights,' Robert chided him as Joe returned to the bar.

'What did the police say, Robert?'

'There's not much they can do, Helen. No clues, and I think they see it as a daft prank.'

'D'you want me to mention it in my report to the *Dumfries News*?'

'Best not,' Robert said at once. 'If whoever did it reads about it in the paper it might encourage them to come back and have another go.'

Muriel nodded agreement. 'It's not as if any real damage

was done. Only to the scarecrows, and most of them can be put right.'

'Unfortunately,' Naomi said, 'one of the vandalised figures was a Long John Silver that Andrew Forsyth and his son Calum made together. As you all know, Andrew's in Edinburgh right now, undergoing treatment for bowel cancer, and Maggie and Calum are staying with me over the summer. We brought the scarecrow to the manse to cheer Calum up, but it got quite badly vandalised and the poor lad's desperately upset about it. It's more than just a scarecrow to him.'

'As Joe said, whoever did this deserves a good hard thrashing,' Pete McDermott said angrily, 'and I'd be happy to do it, if we ever manage to lay hands on the little blighter!'

'The same goes for me. In the meantime, I suggest we advise anyone who can to take their scarecrows in at night,' Lachie Wilkins said, 'then put 'em out first thing in the morning.'

'Sounds sensible,' Robert agreed. 'And if anyone hears a whisper about who might be behind this nonsense, pass it to the other committee members – quietly. If it *is* someone from this village we don't want any lynching.'

Maggie couldn't rid her mind of the look on Calum's face when he saw the scarecrow sprawled in a flower bed, one sleeve almost ripped from the jacket with silver buttons that Jenny had made specially. The parrot stitched to the pirate's shoulder had disappeared completely as had the crutch. The pirate's three-cornered hat lay on the ground, trodden under-foot and crumpled out of shape.

'We can sort it,' Naomi said, putting an arm about the boy's shoulders.

He twitched away from her. 'I don't want it to be sorted,'

he said in a muffled voice, his chin pushed down towards his chest. 'I want it the way my dad and me made it. Now it's spoiled.' He kicked the scarecrow viciously.

Naomi, Maggie and Ethan looked at each other help-lessly, then Ethan said, 'Come on, mate, let's go and kick a football about.'

Calum nodded without looking up. When the boys had gone Maggie said, 'Perhaps we could try to put it right?'

'I'd leave it for now. It's not really the scarecrow he's upset about, poor wee soul. Calum's got a lot more to cope with at the moment than that,' Naomi said. She put her arm about Maggie's shoulders. 'We're all going to have to treat him very gently this summer.'

She went into the house and Maggie picked up the hat and tried to smooth it out. She desperately wanted to help Calum, but the months of teasing and tormenting she had secretly put him through since coming to live in Prior's Ford meant he didn't trust her.

She took the hat to her bedroom and then went to catch the bus to Kirkcudbright.

Maggie hadn't arranged to see Ryan, but as she was walking along the High Street a voice said, 'Hi, you,' and she looked up to see him standing in front of her, grinning. 'You didn't tell me you were comin' here. You should have given me a ring.'

'I had shopping to do.'

'So how's the Scarecrow Festival goin', then?' he asked, smirking, and with a sinking feeling in the pit of her stomach Maggie knew the suspicions that had flown into her mind as she watched Calum weep over the damaged scarecrow he and his dad had made together were true.

'It was you, wasn't it?'

205

'What was me?'

'You and your mates came into the village last night and messed up the scarecrows.'

'Don't know what you're talkin' about.'

'If that's true, why are you grinning like that?'

'Well, it's funny, isn't it? Someone goin' to all that trouble over a bunch of manky scarecrows. Bet the whole village's got its knickers in a twist this mornin', eh? All rushin' about like ants in their nest, lookin' for bits of scarecrow!'

'How did you know that bits had been scattered about?'

'You said so.'

'I didn't. That was a rotten thing to do, Ryan!'

'Oh, Ryan, that was rotten,' he mimicked her in a falsetto voice. 'Listen to Little Miss Prim!'

'You broke my stepbrother's scarecrow. You made him cry!'

'Poor baby. Time he grew up, isn't it?'

'You don't care, do you? His dad's ill and he's worried sick. He's having a rotten time and you haven't helped.'

'Give it a rest, Mags. Want an ice cream?'

'No, I don't, and even if I did I wouldn't let you buy it for me, or steal it, more likely.'

'Oh, come on, don't give me that shit. You can't stand the little creep, you've told me yourself.'

'Maybe I've changed my mind. Maybe I've decided that a little creep's better than a big one!'

His blue eyes narrowed. 'Stop before you say too much, Mags.'

'It's Maggie. Goodbye, Ryan.'

'Nob'dy walks away from me,' he said as she spun round.

'There's a first time for everything,' she snapped without turning back to him, 'and don't you ever come into Prior's Ford again! You're not welcome there!'

Part of her mind squawked, 'You'll be sorry!' as she strode

off, but the other part told her that she was doing the right thing. She was convinced now that Ryan was behind the vandalism in Prior's Ford; he had probably been checking out the various scarecrows while the two of them wandered round the village on Saturday.

Not that she would tell on him. She might even have ignored what he and his pals had done if they hadn't made Calum cry.

24

'I told you I didn't want anyone to do anything, didn't I?'

'I just wanted to help. He's not badly damaged, and I've steamed the hat and got it back to its proper shape. And I've darned the hole in his jacket, and I bought this . . .' Maggie held out a polythene bag. 'I know it's not as good as the one that's missing, but I found it in a charity shop,' she said nervously as Calum glanced in the bag, then plunged his hand in and drew out a crudely painted plastic cockatoo.

'It's horrible! It's nothing like Long John Silver's parrot!' he screeched. 'How could you even think it looks like his parrot?'

'It was all I could find.'

'But I told you to leave me alone!' He hurled the cock-atoo at her. Hollow inside, it bounced harmlessly against her shoulder and fell to the floor, to be pounced on by the cat. Calum slammed his way out of the door and upstairs; a moment later the door of the room he shared with Ethan slammed shut.

Ethan, alerted by raised voices, came in from the kitchen, a soft drink can in his hand. 'Problems, eh?' he asked sympathetically.

'I don't know what to do with him!'

'Leave him be,' Ethan suggested 'that's what Naomi always did with me at first when I slammed doors like that. Slamming a door's like saying you want to be left on your own to get over whatever's bugging you. Naomi was good at knowing these signs. Good grief, what's this?' He picked up the cockatoo, which Casper had rejected as uninteresting. 'It's ugly!'

'I thought it might replace the parrot on Long John Silver's shoulder.'

'Don't think so. Even a pirate has feelings. Want one?' He held up the can.

'No thanks. I think I'll go out for a walk.'

For the next half hour Maggie walked round the village, shoulders hunched and eyes fixed on the ground. Finally she headed back to the manse, then, deciding she still wasn't ready to face anyone, she went into the church's cool safe dimness.

She was mooching around, studying the stained-glass windows without really seeing them, when she heard a sneeze from behind the vestry door. She went over and tapped on it.

Naomi, finding a manse full of visitors distracting, had filled a flask with coffee and retreated to the peace and quiet of the vestry to start work on her Sunday sermon. At the knock on the door she mouthed a silent, 'Drat,' then put on her most welcoming smile to atone for it as she called out, 'Come on in.'

The door opened very slowly, just enough for a head to peer round it.

209

'Maggie, how nice.'

'I want to confess,' Maggie said in a small voice. 'Where's your confessional place?'

Naomi laid her biro down, realising this was going to be a long session. 'We don't have one. I'm not that sort of minister. This,' she waved a hand round the small vestry, 'is as close as we get to a confessional in the Church of Scotland. But it has its benefits.'

She reached into a desk drawer and withdrew the flask, two paper cups and a small box. 'Coffee and biscuits; come on in and sit yourself down,' she said in invitation and, after a pause long enough to make her think Maggie was going to flee, the girl ventured into the room.

'Hot coffee and chocolate biscuits and good company. There's nothing like that combination for making me feel life's worth living,' Naomi said cheerfully, pouring coffee and putting a steaming paper cup and a wrapped biscuit beside Maggie, who had huddled herself onto the chair on the other side of the desk. She took a mouthful of coffee. 'That's good. Drink yours while it's hot, then tell me what's bothering you – in your own time.'

'You're busy.'

'Not really, just jotting down some notes. I wonder if people realise that a minister's job includes being a writer and an actor, or in my case, an actress. Every week we have to write a sermon and then deliver it with enough passion and enthusiasm to keep even the sleepiest members of the audience alert and on the edge of their seats, eager to hear what's coming next.'

'I never thought of it like that.' Maggie sipped her coffee.

'To tell you the truth, neither had I until now. It might be worth working it into a sermon one day.' Naomi scribbled another note, then picked up her cup.

'I've been horrible to Calum,' Maggie suddenly blurted out.

'I thought you were being really nice to him today.'

'I mean ever since I came to Prior's Ford. He . . . he irritated me. They all did.' Now she had started the words came tumbling out, 'But Calum most of all, I suppose. He kept pestering me to do things with him, share things with him, and I just wasn't in the mood. So I was nasty to him, to make him leave me alone. I kept calling him a baby and laughing at him when Jenny and Andrew weren't there to hear me.'

Her voice shook slightly and she stared down at the fingers clenched round the wrapped biscuit in her lap. Naomi waited, knowing there was more.

'But now,' Maggie leaned forward in her seat, 'you remember when I talked to you before, in the manse, and you said Jenny needed me to stay here so I could help Calum while she and Andrew were away? I didn't want to, but I said I would because I don't have anywhere else to go. That was the only reason. I wasn't going to help Calum at all. I thought you and Ethan could do that.'

'I can understand your thinking. Having a kid brother suddenly foisted on you, hanging round you, must have been annoying.'

Maggie, struggling to find the right words, nodded absent-mindedly, not even realising that Naomi was trying to make her feel better about her behaviour towards Calum. 'But seeing him crying over the scarecrow he and Andrew made together made me feel so sorry for him. He's just a kid, and his world's been turned inside out the way mine was when my grandparents sent me away. And he's never once complained to Jenny or Andrew about the way I was treating him. Not once! That's made me feel worse.'

'I'm glad you've worked things out for yourself. It means you can start afresh with him. Start building bridges, as they say.'

'But he won't even let me help him rebuild the scarecrow, let alone bridges,' Maggie wailed, kneading the still-wrapped biscuit between both hands. 'I've tried to help him. I darned the tear in Long John Silver's jacket and I steamed the hat and got it back into shape, and I looked everywhere for a parrot, but I couldn't find one so I went into a charity shop in Kirkcudbright and bought a cockatoo because it was the only thing they had. But when I gave it to him he just shouted at me. He told me to leave the scarecrow alone, and he threw the cockatoo at me and ran up to his room – to Ethan's room – and slammed the door. Why does he have to be so difficult?'

'Because he's very unhappy and confused right now and he still doesn't feel he can trust you. It's going to take time.'

'How much time?'

'How long is a piece of string?' Naomi asked, and when the girl looked at her blankly, explained, 'What I mean is, nobody knows how much time. Not me, not you, not Calum. You're going to have to be patient.'

'I s'ppose. There's . . . something else. I think I might know who's behind the vandalism in the village.'

'How sure are you?'

'Quite sure . . . I think. Are you certain you don't have a special place where people can confess in private?'

'Sorry. Is it someone in the village?' Naomi asked. Maggie shook her head. 'I'm glad to hear that, at least. You know you can't go to the police without proof, don't you?'

'I don't want to go to the police. I don't want him . . . them,' the girl said swiftly, 'to get into trouble. I just feel bad about knowing, or thinking I know. It makes me feel as if

I've eaten too much and it's lying here in a big heavy lump.' She patted her midriff.

'I know the feeling. I don't have a confessional, but now you've told me you should start to feel better about it. A trouble shared is a trouble halved,' Naomi said. Maggie opened her mouth to protest. 'Let's forget Calum for a minute and concentrate on you. You've had a raw deal from life compared to a lot of other girls your age, but you've done a great job of coping with it.'

'I didn't have much choice, did I?' Maggie muttered, pleased by the praise but aware she didn't deserve it.

'You didn't. It was a case of sink or swim, and God bless you, girl, you swam. But Calum's had a sheltered life compared to yours. Nothing's ever gone wrong before, at least, nothing that couldn't be fixed. Now it's all happening; he's about to move out of the cosy little village school and into the Academy. I imagine he feels like a goldfish about to be taken from its safe little bowl and tossed into a big aquarium filled with strange fish. And on top of it, he's lost his parents for the summer because his father's ill. And he can't do anything to change things. You must know that feeling, Maggie,' said Naomi in her rich warm voice, 'wanting to put things back to the way they were, but not knowing how or who you can turn to for help. That's what Calum's going through for the first time in his life.'

'I suppose.'

'Sometimes the best way to bring people to you is to leave them alone. Let them turn to you in their own time. Give Calum some slack. Offer help with things, and if he refuses, leave it. He needs you, Maggie, but he also needs time to realise you're not teasing him any more. Once that happens, he'll start to trust you. You have to be patient. OK?'

'I suppose. Thanks.'

'You're very welcome, any time. And by the way, I found the parrot on my way over here, lying in the hedge. It's a bit battered-looking but it'll survive, and so will you and Calum. Give me the biscuit.' Naomi took the lumpy, crushed bundle from the girl's hand and replaced it with a fresh one. 'Have this one instead. More coffee?'

'No thanks, I think I'll go now.'

'If you're going to the manse, would you scrape some carrots for me? I'll be over in fifteen minutes.'

Poor little Maggie, Naomi thought when she was alone. It was going to be a long and difficult summer for her; for all the members of that family.

She reached for her notes then picked up a well-thumbed reference book that lived on her desk and began to flick through it. She had helped Maggie, she hoped, and in return, Maggie had helped her with her next sermon.

25

'I've been thinking,' Naomi said thoughtfully over tea, 'that it might be better, Calum, if we put your scarecrow back together tomorrow, so it's ready to move to your garden before your mum and dad come home on Saturday.'

'I want Dad to help me with it. He's the only one who knows how it should be done.'

'But you know as well, don't you? You worked on it with him. And by the time he arrives on Saturday it'll be late morning. It seems a shame to let this week's visitors miss such an impressive scarecrow.'

Calum's lower lip quivered and he bit down hard on it, ducking his head. 'It doesn't look very impressive now.'

'No, poor old thing, but he will once we've finished with him. I know the parrot looks a bit bedraggled, but it can be tidied up. And Maggie's made a really good job of getting the hat back into shape. In fact,' Naomi went on carefully as Calum continued to stare down at the tablecloth, 'I believe that between the four of us, we could get Long John Silver looking as good as new. It would be great if we could keep what happened a secret from your dad. He's probably had a tiring week, getting all that hospital treatment, and if he hears what's happened to the scarecrow the two of you made together, knowing how upset you must have been will make him feel worse.'

'That's true,' Maggie ventured, 'and the festival ends on Saturday, so nobody will be able to see your scarecrow after that.'

'*We* will,' Calum snapped at her. 'Dad says we're going to set him up in the back garden afterwards to keep the birds off the strawberries.'

'Sorry, I'd forgotten.'

'That's a good idea, but it'd be great, wouldn't it, if we could get it back to the way it was so he never knew it had been hurt?' Naomi coaxed.

'I'm up for it,' Ethan said. 'I bet we could make it look as good as new.'

'I'll help,' Maggie ventured. 'We could keep it in the shed tonight, just in case whoever it was comes back, and we'll have lots of time tomorrow to work on it.'

'So what about it, Calum? Want to have a shot at putting things right for your mum and dad?'

There was a long silence, then his head came up slowly.

'I suppose so.'

'Good, that's settled then. I've got a free day tomorrow, and it looks as though the weather's going to stay fine, so we'll start work in the morning. Now then, who's for chocolate pudding?' Naomi asked.

'Hello there, Ewan.'

'It's yersel', Cam. You're out late tonight.'

'I'm lendin' the Progress Committee a hand. Keepin' an

eye out just in case those young bounders who trashed the place on Monday night feel like comin' back.'

'I doubt if they will.'

'Me too, but the committee felt some of us should keep watch for a couple of nights, just in case. No sight or sound of them tonight, though, or last night. I'm about to pack it in.'

'What would you do if you did see them?'

Cam grinned. 'I've got a good strong torch, and the whistle I use for refereeing the kids' football matches. I reckon a few blasts from that would send them packin'.'

'And waken half the village too.'

'Ye cannae make an omelette without breakin' eggs. No need to ask what you're doin' out at this time of night, not when I saw you comin' out of the side door of the Cuckoo, long past closin' time. A wee bit of courtin', eh?'

Ewan felt heat flood into his face, and hoped it was too dark for Cam to notice it. 'Nothin' of the sort, I was just visitin' the fam'ly.'

'I believe you, but most wouldn't. She's bonny lass, Alison, and a nice one as well. A man could do a lot worse,' Cam remarked, then gave a huge yawn. 'I think it's safe for me to go home to my bed now. Goodnight to you.'

'Night, Cam.' Ewan crossed the village green, past the Mad Hatter, the Mad March Hare and the Dormouse sitting silently round their tea table, and set off along the main road, whistling quietly to himself. The Fishers had taken to inviting him for supper about once a week, after the pub closed, and he always accepted eagerly. Joe and Gracie were good company, and it gave him the chance to sit across the table from Alison, sneaking glances at her now and again.

As Cam Gordon had said, she was bonny and he never got tired of looking at her. Recalling how sad she had

217

looked when she and her parents first came to the village, it was grand to see her smile now, a smile that lit up her whole face and made her brown eyes sparkle. He had grown fond of young Jamie too, and when he and Alison worked together in the old farm cottage, which was almost fit for habitation, he had longed to be able to ask her to marry him and bring Jamie to live there with him.

But it would never happen, because although he knew he could never love anyone as much as he loved Alison, he refused to condemn her to the life of hard work and penny-pinching his mother had endured. And he couldn't see a way of making things better.

If Victor had been willing to work with him at bringing Tarbethill back to the thriving farm it had been before they lost their livestock to the foot and mouth epidemic they might just have managed it, but Victor was growing away from his roots. Ewan was convinced that soon his brother would leave Tarbethill altogether, and move to join his fiancée's family in Kirkcudbright. His father had lost heart after the foot and mouth epidemic that had resulted in the wholesale slaughter of animals born and raised on the farm, more like family than livestock to Bert. In the five years since then he had aged alarmingly.

Ewan had just started along the farm lane when the two sheepdogs came scampering out of the darkness to meet him, and his father's voice said, 'Is that you, Ewan?'

'Aye, just on my way back. What brings you out at this time of night?'

'Ach, I couldnae sleep so I came out for a breath of fresh air. It's close in the house tonight.'

'Aye.' He knew, though he would never say it aloud, that more often than not Bert had taken to wandering about the farm until well into the night, unable to sleep.

'I was havin' a wee look at the cottage. Ye're makin' a grand job o' it.'

'It's comin' along,' Ewan acknowledged. 'I thought maybe we could rent it out tae holidaymakers in the summer months.'

'I'm no' sure I'd want tae stay in a wee place like that for my holidays,' Bert said doubtfully.

'Ye would if ye lived in the town or in a city or even if ye came over from another country for a holiday.'

Bert coughed, then turned his head to one side and spat into the darkness. 'Ye're beginnin' tae sound like Victor, with his grand plans for a caravan park. I doubt if that'll work either.'

'We'll just have tae wait and see, eh? Are ye goin' tae walk back tae the farm with me, Dad?' Ewan started to ask, then stopped as the dogs, which had been nosing around the hedgerows, exploring the night-time scents but never straying far from their master, halted at the same instant, heads raised and turned towards the main road.

'What—?' Bert began, but Ewan gripped his arm.

'Shhh. Listen.'

The night was clear and still apart from the occasional call of an owl and the rustle of grass disturbed by small creatures on the hunt for food or, perhaps, escaping from a predator.

'I cannae hear a thing,' Bert whispered after a few seconds. 'But they can.' The dogs were still motionless, their bodies tense.

'I can.' The swish of bicycle wheels on the road. Two, maybe three bikes with their lamps switched off, Ewan guessed, straining his eyes in the direction of the Kirkcudbright road. He caught the faint sound of a voice, then a muffled laugh.

219

'I think it's lads headin' for the village, up to no good,' he whispered into his father's ear.

'We'll see about that! I've got a good torch with me—'

'No!' Ewan grabbed Bert's arm. 'Don't let 'em know we're here. The dogs can scare 'em off.'

'Right.' Bert leaned down towards the animals and murmured a swift command, and they both took off down the lane like greyhounds bounding from a trap at the start of a race. As they went they set up a wild barking. The younger one, not as disciplined as his companion, added an excited howling noise that rang out eerily in the darkness.

Above the noise the animals made Ewan thought he heard a sudden rush of alarmed voices. Then, staring in the direction of the road, he saw a bicycle lamp blink on, followed by another and then two more. The lights danced about frantically, blinking in and out as the machines were turned away from the village.

He touched his father's arm and Bert recalled the dogs with a piercing whistle. Within seconds they were back, tongues lolling and eyes shining in the starlight, eager for praise.

'Good dogs! What in the name of heaven was all that about?'

'I've a feelin' it was lads out to spoil some of the villagers' scarecrows again.'

'Did I no' say that that daft idea would only bring trouble? Scarecrows are for scarin' crows, not for show!'

'Aye, you did, Dad. But you an' the dogs did a good job of scarin' them off, and that's the main thing. Come on,' Ewan said, 'let's get tae our beds.'

Knowing the scarecrow he and his son had crafted would start the week in their own garden, then move to the manse before being brought home again, Andrew Forsyth had made the figure sturdy, yet light enough to move from place to place. Chicken wire formed the basis for the body and limbs, and the clothing was stuffed with old sheets, towels and rags. As a result, it was fairly easy to restore the figure.

Naomi's cheeriness, Maggie's determination to be as nice to Calum as she could, and Ethan's natural exuberance turned the task into a pleasure. By the time Long John Silver had been rebuilt even Calum was enjoying himself.

'Told you we could do it. What a team we make!' Naomi, hands on her ample hips, surveyed the pirate, sprawled in a deckchair with his parrot, carefully washed, his feathers dried and fluffed up by Maggie's hair drier, perched for the moment on his lap. 'Let's have lunch in the garden to celebrate his revival and this beautiful summer day. Ethan and Calum, you two can scrub the garden table and chairs, and set the umbrella up – it's in the shed somewhere – while Maggie and I go to the store to buy something to eat.'

An hour later, after a lunch of sandwiches, fruit juice and individual trifles she gave a contented sigh and tipped her face up towards the sun's heat. 'Food tastes so much better when it's eaten in the garden. Tell you what, let's have a barbecue tomorrow evening, seeing this is festival week.'

'Is there time to plan a barbecue?' Maggie asked doubtfully.

'Yes, if it's a not too fancy. I'll pop to the store later and ask Sam if he can get some extras in for us. He and Marcy can pass the word round their customers, and I don't see why we shouldn't ask everyone to bring a little something with them to help out.' She beamed at the three of them. 'We'll take Long John Silver back to his own garden tomorrow morning so he's there for Jenny and Andrew's arrival home on Saturday morning. And then we can devote the afternoon to getting ready for the barbecue.'

'There's just one thing missing,' Maggie ventured. 'We still haven't found the pirate's crutch.'

'Oh, bother! What are we going to do about that? Is there time to give him a new leg?'

Calum giggled. 'Long John Silver only had one leg. Dad would notice right away.'

'True. He's no fool, your dad, and I expect he's read the book.'

'Lots of times. It's one of his favourites.'

'Mmm. Well, there's only one thing to do,' Naomi declared. 'He'll go into our shed and we'll go into my car, and we'll drive round in search of a forked stick that would fit the bill. Come to think of it, that's probably what the real John used. They didn't have hospital crutches in his day.'

'Calum's dad'll notice the difference,' Ethan pointed out.

'Probably. So I'm going to donate a bag of wine gums to the person who comes up with the best answer to the big mystery.' Naomi looked round the table. 'The Prior's Ford Puzzle – what happened to Long John Silver's crutch? We can all starting thinking of solutions in the car.'

26

'So what's the big secret?' Hannah Gibbs asked as Dolly Cowan poured coffee. A note had been put through her door, inviting her to the Cowans' house for afternoon coffee and asking her, to her surprise, not to mention the invitation to anyone else. It was only when she and Charlie Crandall met on the Cowans' doorstep that they realised they had both been invited.

'You'll find out,' Dolly said mysteriously.

Hannah and Charlie exchanged puzzled glances, then he asked, 'Where's Harold?'

'He's around. You'll see him in a wee while. Ah, here's our other guest,' Dolly said as the doorbell rang. She bustled out, and Hannah raised her eyebrows at Charlie.

'What's going on?'

'Don't ask me.'

'Dolly's positively bouncing with excitement. There's something in the wind—' Hannah stopped abruptly as Dolly reappeared, followed by Cam Gordon.

'Afternoon, all,' the newcomer said cheerfully.

'I've got some nibbles. Help yourself to coffee, Cam, and I'll fetch them.' Dolly bustled into the kitchen, the two dogs, Minnie and Maxy, following close behind her as usual. Once her guests' needs had been seen to she sat down and picked up her coffee cup. 'Now then, to business.'

'What about Robert and Cissie and the others?' Hannah ventured. Dolly shook her curly blonde hair.

'We can't let them in on this, not with Robert and Muriel being on the Progress Committee. They probably wouldn't let us do what we plan to do. And Ivy, bless her, is too old to be of much use. In any case, she might tell someone what we're thinking of and we can't have that.'

'What who's thinking of?' Charlie asked uneasily.

Dolly winked a perfectly made-up eye. 'Wait and see.'

'Why isn't Harold here?'

'He is, Hannah, at least, he will be in a moment. Cam, tell them what you told me and Harold this afternoon in the Cuckoo.'

Cam swallowed half a neat little scone and washed it down with coffee before saying, 'Late last night I was on the village green, keepin' an eye out for anyone who was up to no good when I met Ewan McNair on his way home. By that time I reckoned it was too late at night for vandals, so I went off to my own bed. But this mornin' Ewan told me that when he reached the farm lane his father was there, gettin' a breath of air before he went to bed. The two of them were on their way up the lane when some bicycles came along the road with no lights on, headin' for the village. They reckon it was a group of youngsters.'

Hannah and Charlie both sat forward in their chairs. 'D'you think they're the ones who damaged the scarecrows on Monday night?'

'It certainly looks as if they were bent on mischief, Charlie.

Bert set his dogs to barkin' and whoever it was about-turned smartish an' headed back the way they'd come.'

'I hope the dogs nipped at their heels, cheeky little beggars! What sort of homes do they have, with parents letting them out at that time of night?' Dolly wanted to know.

'I wouldn't be surprised if the parents thought they were in their beds,' Hannah said. 'You know what lads can be like.'

'Oh, I know well enough what lads can be like, and lasses too. It's today's parents I'm wondering about. I reckon I'm lucky with Minnie and Maxy as my children. You don't go dashing off late at night to create trouble, do you, petals?' Dolly crooned, and the dogs, curled up at her feet, looked up at her adoringly.

'So . . . ?' Hannah prompted.

'What? Oh, yes. So we were talking things through in the Cuckoo, like I said, and we agreed that something needs to be done about those little pests.'

'Do the Progress Committee know about this?'

'If you mean Ewan an' Bert hearin' the bikes, Ewan told Robert this mornin' when he was deliverin' the eggs. Robert said we'd all keep an eye out, like we've been doin' every night since the trouble on Tuesday.'

'But we don't think that's enough, do we, Cam?' Dolly chipped in.

'It looks as if those youngsters are comin' in later than any of us expected. If Bert's dogs hadn't been there to scare them away the village green would have been deserted and open to vandalism. But how late should folk stay up on the chance of trouble?' Cam asked. 'Some of us have work to go to in the mornin' and those who've retired are gettin' a bit too old to stay up half the night. In any case, Ewan

225

says that to Robert's way of thinkin' the youngsters got enough of a scare last night, and they probably won't come back.'

'We're not so sure, though,' Dolly said. 'There's only tonight and tomorrow left before the festival ends. Harold and I – and Cam here – reckon they could be up for one last try. And we reckon that whoever they are and wher-ever they come from, they need to learn a lesson and maybe get a bit of a fright. That's why we're keeping the committee out of it, because they probably won't approve of what we're planning.'

Charlie and Hannah exchanged glances then said in chorus, 'And what's that?'

'Before we go into that part of it, there's someone you need to meet. Someone,' Dolly said, 'who has to remain our secret, always. Promise?'

'I'm not sure where this is leading,' Charlie said nervously.

'I'll take that as a promise.'

The almshouses' front doors opened directly into the living rooms; Dolly went to the door leading to the kitchen and staircase, and tapped on it three times. Almost at once she was answered by three taps from the other side.

She whirled round to face the others, grinning broadly as she stepped to one side and struck a dramatic pose, one arm outstretched towards the door.

'Lady and gentle*men*! Presenting the one and only, the world famous – Mr Magnifico!' she said dramatically.

The door was suddenly thrown open and Hannah uttered a muted scream as she, Charlie and Cam stared at the clown standing in the doorway.

Charlie's first thought when Hannah screamed at sight of the multicoloured figure in the doorway was that it wasn't just scarecrows she was afraid of. Although they had been strangers until they both moved into the almshouses, they had since become good friends and he felt very protective towards her.

He reached over to take one of her hands in both of his, holding it tightly. 'It's all right, Hannah, I'm here,' he heard himself say. 'I won't let him hurt you!'

'Of course he won't hurt me,' she said promptly, her eyes still on the new arrival. 'He's a clown, not a monster!' Then wincing, 'Charlie, you're crushing my hand!'

'Sorry.' He released her at once, feeling the tips of his ears go warm as they always did when he blushed. More than once recently he had lulled himself to sleep by imagining scenarios where he rescued Hannah from burning buildings or from men of evil intent. Never once in his fantasies had she ever said, 'Charlie, you're crushing my hand!'

'Sorry, I thought . . . Who the blazes is this?' he demanded to know, desperate to take attention off himself.

'Don't you know?' Dolly was beaming proudly.

'Good grief,' Cam said. 'It's Harold!'

'Give that man a coconut,' said the clown, moving forward into the room with Harold's unmistakable limping gait.

'But why have you never told any of us you were in a circus?' Hannah wanted to know. The coffee cups had been cleared away and now they were all having something stronger to drink.

'And get hauled in to perform at every kid's party or concert in the area? No thanks!' Harold was sprawled in an armchair, Maxy asleep in his lap and a tumbler of whisky in one hand. In his long, loose-fitting jacket with its red, blue and green checks and purple silk pantaloons caught in at the ankle, he looked, Charlie thought, like a pile of brightly coloured washing that had been thrown to the ground when the line broke. His scarlet bowler hat lay on the floor by his feet, which were clad in striped socks and large yellow shoes. 'I'm retired, remember?'

'In any case,' Dolly chimed in, 'my Harold isn't your common or garden party entertainer; he's a professional clown, well known and respected in the business, as well as a talented tight-rope walker.'

'Until the accident that finished my career.'

'I'll never forgive myself,' Dolly said, a catch in her voice, 'for letting you go on without a safety net that night.'

'Give over. I'd been working without the net for months. It wasn't your fault, or mine. Nobody was to blame, girl, it was Sod's Law. Poor old Sod, he gets blamed for everything.'

'Were you in the circus world too, Dolly?' Hannah asked.

'Course I was, that's where me and Harold met. It was love at first sight, wasn't it, Harold?'

'So she claims. I could believe it if I'd been wearing this outfit at the time, but the first time we laid eyes on each other I was just my usual gloomy self. Nobody would ever take me for a clown, would they?' Harold asked his guests. 'That was the fun of it as far as I was concerned. When Dolly first saw me helping to put up the big top she thought I was one of the roustabouts.'

It was true that in his everyday life Harold was quite a lugubrious character, not given to smiling, though he was friendly enough. But now, in full make-up, with a painted red smile covering the lower half of his face he didn't look at all like the man they all knew.

'And what did you do, Dolly?' Charlie asked, and she rose, moved to the centre of the circle of chairs, and pirouetted in a full circle, ending with a deep curtsey.

228

'Dolores and her Dancing Dogs, that was me. We were very glamorous, me and Minnie and Maxy, all in spangles.'

Cam came bolt upright in his chair, choking over a mouthful of beer. For a moment Hannah thought he was overcome by the thought of plump Dolly in spangles and possibly little else, but then he said, 'Your dogs can dance?'

'Oh no, not them, dear. Far too lazy, and far too spoiled, aren't you, sweeties?' Dolly made kissing noises at the dogs, and their ears twitched in response. 'The Minnie and Maxy I had then were their grandparents. Lovely little dancers, weren't they, Harold?'

'Poetry in motion, the three of 'em,' her husband declared. 'I tried to get her to stay on with the circus when my career ended but she wouldn't. She and the dogs gave up everything for me, bless 'em.'

'It wasn't the same without Harold. We'd had such a fantastic life, the four of us.' Dolly's blue eyes were radiant with memories. 'But all good things come to an end, as they say. So we bought a little newsagent's shop and ran it until we retired here.'

'But you kept the outfits.' Hannah had never seen a clown close up before. As she looked at Harold childhood memories of magic visits to the circus came flooding back.

'Just a bit of nostalgia,' Dolly said. 'I can't get into my outfit now, but Harold hasn't put on an extra ounce. I've got photos though; I must let you see them some time.'

'Yes please!' Cam said.

'But you must all promise not to tell anyone else what you've heard and seen tonight,' Harold warned them. 'That's the only reason I let you see me like this – because we've come up with a way to put those dratted vandals off any more thoughts of spoiling our Scarecrow Festival.'

'But,' Dolly added, 'we'll need a bit of help.'

229

'You still think they'll have another go at it?'

'We do, Charlie, and Cam agrees with us. Not tonight, maybe, after being chased off by Bert's dogs, but the festival ends on Saturday and tomorrow night's Friday, so we reckon – Dolly and Cam and me – that they might well have a final go then. And we're going to stop 'em in their tracks. OK?' Harold asked. The others nodded. 'Good. Now then, folks, we're all set for a bit of late-night fun. Let's have another drink, and get down to business.'

An hour later they had thrashed out what seemed to be a workable plan.

'But it needs more than just the five of us,' Hannah pointed out.

'Six of us. We've already agreed that Ewan'll have to come into this,' Cam said. 'And I'm goin' to ask Jinty and Tom McDonald if Grant and Jimmy can stay out late on Friday night. They're both sensible lads for their ages, and if I promise to keep an eye on them and not let them get into anythin' dodgy, I think it should be OK.'

'Do you know something?' Hannah said as Charlie, ever the gentleman, walked with her to her door some time later. 'I'm so glad I decided to retire to Prior's Ford. Between scarecrows and vandals, I've never had so much fun in my life!'

27

On Friday morning Naomi drove the scarecrow to the Forsyths' house while Ethan, Maggie and Calum walked, carrying flowers picked from Naomi's garden as a welcome home for Andrew and Jenny. When the flowers were in vases Maggie went to the kitchen drawer where the shed key was kept. It wasn't there, but after a brief panic they found it in the shed door.

'Andrew mowed the lawn just before they left,' Maggie said over her shoulder as she turned the key and pushed the door open. 'He must have forgotten to take it back to the kitch—' She stopped, then gave a startled shriek and jumped back onto Ethan's foot. 'There's someone hiding in the shed!'

'What? Let me see.' Naomi swept her hopping foster son aside, ignoring his yelps of pain, and threw the door wide.

'Out of there!' she commanded in a booming tone, then found herself face to face with Florence Nightingale, lying back in a deckchair with a trowel in her hand instead of a lamp.

★   ★   ★

The Pearces came to the barbecue bearing gifts to show their gratitude. Kevin made a low bow before presenting his hostess with a bottle of wine and a box of chocolates. 'A thousand thanks, gracious lady!'

'She's in good shape, then?'

'Perfect, and happy now she's been reunited with her lamp.'

'It was actually Maggie who found her, so she shall have the chocolates. Share them with Ethan,' Naomi said as she handed the box over, 'to make up for bruising his foot. And don't believe him when he claims he will never play football again. As for the wine . . . I accept it with thanks, kind sir.'

'These are from me.' Eleanor handed over a batch of freshly baked gingerbread and a large rhubarb tart, adding, after looking round to make sure her husband had moved out of earshot, 'You will never know how grateful I am. I've had Kevin going on all week about that dratted scarecrow!'

'Well done, you,' Naomi said quietly to Maggie when they were clearing up after their visitors had gone.

'What for?'

'Helping make Calum feel better.'

'Oh, that!' Maggie shrugged, hiding her pleasure. She had had a lovely day, just being herself and not having to put on a sulky face.

'He really enjoyed today, and it's set him up for seeing his parents tomorrow.'

'I was thinking about tomorrow,' Maggie began tentatively. 'Perhaps it would be best to let Calum and his mum and dad have the weekend to themselves. I don't mind staying here – if it's all right with you.'

'Maggie, it would be absolutely fine with me, but I'm not going to let you do it.'

'Why not?' Maggie suddenly reverted to a sulky face and whiney voice.

'Because you're not really thinking about what's best for the Forsyths, are you? You're thinking about what's best for you.'

'I wasn't!'

Naomi's rich laugh rolled up from deep inside her, as it always did. 'I wish I had a mirror out here, so you could see your pouting lip! Is this what poor Jenny's had to put up with?'

'No!' Maggie snapped, and then, as the minister continued to laugh, she felt her own lips curve. 'Well, maybe,' she conceded.

'Poor Jenny, it seems I'm seeing a better side of her step-daughter than she has so far. Sit down for a minute.' Naomi took the girl's hands in her own and seated herself on one of the garden chairs, leaving Maggie with only two options – to sit on the neighbouring chair or topple over on to Naomi's ample lap. She sat down on the chair.

'You're nervous about seeing them tomorrow, aren't you?'

'A bit. I don't know what Andrew'll be like. He might not feel up to coping with me as well as Calum. And . . . it's been so good here,' Maggie confessed, suddenly close to tears. 'I'm tired of problems! I just want to be me!'

'Of course you do, but hiding here, where you feel safe and where you're able to be yourself, isn't the answer. You're not a child any more, Maggie love. You have to face up to life. You've worked wonders with Calum today, and now you have to make your peace with Jenny and Andrew. He'll be fine, by the way. Jenny says he's coped really well with the therapies – tired, but that's to be expected. He'll be looking forward to a quiet, peaceful weekend.'

'That's why I should stay here!'

'I thought we'd dealt with that argument,' a slight edge came into Naomi's voice. 'You're going home tomorrow to be with your family, and you're going to be fine. Jenny and Andrew will want you there, believe me. As for me,' the beaming smile split the minister's face again, 'I'm already looking forward to getting you and Calum back on Sunday evening. You may not realise it yet, Maggie Cameron, but you can light up a room when you're in the right mood.'

With people coming and going all the time during the barbecue, nobody noticed some of the almshouses residents leaving earlier than expected. That night, they had more important things than a barbecue on their minds.

'I wish we could have rubbed our faces with boot blacking like commandos,' Dolly Cowan said wistfully a few hours later, when the village had settled for the night. 'I've always wanted to smear boot blacking all over my face.'

'Me too,' Ewan McNair agreed.

'What's the point of that?' Hannah wanted to know. 'It's Harold they're going to see properly, not us.'

'They might see us somewhere at a later date and recognise us,' Dolly pointed out.

'Hardly, since we're all wearing stocking masks. I can scarcely make you out and I'm sure I know you better than any vandals,' Charlie said consolingly. Then, glancing round the dimly lit interior of Cam Gordon's big 4x4, he chuckled. 'We look like a right set of idiots. I would like to put it on record that this is the first and the last time I will be decked out in women's stockings and floaty scarves.'

'I'd like to put it on record that I haven't had so much fun for years,' Hannah said. 'It'll be such a pity if nobody tries to get into the village. Anyone want a sandwich?'

'Not worth the fuss of getting the stockings off and then on again,' Dolly said, and there was general murmur of agreement.

It was almost midnight, and the 4x4 was parked in dark shadow cast by a clump of trees almost opposite the Tarbethill Farm lane. Cam and Ewan were in the front with Harold, in full clown costume, between them. Hannah, Dolly and Charlie were in the back, all of them wearing stocking masks and with as many light scarves as the women could collect between them pinned to their dark clothes to convey, they hoped, strange outlines should they be called to move about outside.

'Are you absolutely certain, Charlie,' Harold wanted to know, 'that you have never dressed as a woman?'

'Absol— well, there was one Hallowe'en—'.

Cam's mobile phone rang and they all fell silent as he spoke to Grant McDonald who, with his brother Jimmy, was on lookout in a field half a mile up the road.

'Bikes, they think about half a dozen of 'em, on the way here. We're in business, people. Let's get going – and don't forget anything!'

They poured from the vehicle, taking care to close the doors quietly. Cam and Ewan raced to the tractors that had been driven into the fields on either side of the road earlier, while the others lined up on the roadway itself, Harold in front and Dolly, Hannah and Charlie several feet behind him.

They waited in total silence until they were rewarded by the hiss of bicycle tyres on tarmacadam and the low murmur of voices, with the occasional giggle.

As the bikes swept round the bend a hundred yards from the lane entrance Ewan and Cam, communicating by mobile phones, switched on the tractors' headlights at exactly the same moment. The vehicles had been carefully placed that afternoon so the beams met, uniting to highlight the motionless figure of a clown in the middle of the road.

Rubber squeaked on the roadway as the bikes came to a sudden stop, two of them colliding and clattering to the ground. A babble of voices came from the unseen riders.

'It's one of their scarecrows, isn't it?' someone said. 'They've put it there to give us a fright.'

'It scared the shit out of me,' another young voice said tremulously. 'Come on, let's go home!'

'Who's afraid of an old scarecrow? We'll run it over. Come on, get a—' The speaker gurgled to a stop as the clown began to dance, twirling and whirling in the middle of the road, moving slowly towards the bikers. Other shadowy figures moved in behind the clown, just close enough to his spotlight for the intruders to see what appeared to be rags fluttering about their shapeless bodies. They, too, capered about in a weird, uncontrolled dance, chanting and filling the night with the sound of sticks beating on drums and metal lids.

It was all too much for the boys. Their nerves in shreds, they turned their bicycles about as one and pedalled away from the village as fast as they could go.

As arranged, Harold and his followers continued to caper, sing and bang pot and bin lids in the spotlight in case any of the intruders felt brave enough to look back. The tractor lights didn't go off until Cam and Ewan got word from the McDonald boys that the riders had passed them at speed and were out of sight.

'Let's go!' Harold made for the 4x4, and by the time Grant and Jimmy appeared out of the darkness his jacket, hat and wig had been stowed in a bin bag and most of the greasepaint had been wiped from his face.

Cam rolled his window down as the boys' cycles came to a smooth stop by the 4x4. 'Well done, lads!'

'That was great!' Jimmy beamed. 'We really put the wind up them. Me and Grant jumped out from behind the hedge and shone our torches under our chins as they came past. They were pedalling fast enough to win the Tour de France.

I bet their pants'll be well soaked when they get home!'

'Serve 'em right,' his brother said. 'Pillocks!'

'D'you lads have to get home right away?' Charlie asked.

'Should do, but we don't have to,' Grant assured him. 'Mum knows we're with Cam. Is there somethin' else you want us to do?'

'I want everyone to come to my place for a well-deserved celebration before bed.'

'You're on,' Jimmy crowed, and the two of them went off into the night as Cam started the engine.

'Not me,' Ewan said, opening his door. 'I've got early milkin' in the mornin'.'

'I feel as if we've struck a blow for pensioners, as well as for Prior's Ford,' Dolly said as Cam did a three-point turn. 'For once the oldies have got one over on the teenagers.'

'We should have T-shirts,' Hannah giggled, 'with "Pensioner Power!" on them. It's a pity we can't let everyone know about this.'

'We have to be like the other superheroes and keep our identities secret,' Harold cautioned. 'Speaking of secrets, can you let me off at the end wall, Cam? I'll slip in the back door and get rid of the rest of this outfit and the last of the greasepaint.'

'What's going on there?' Jenny asked as she and Andrew drove past the field where, the year before, the villagers had held an Easter party.

Andrew flicked a swift glance at the group of men in conversation. 'That's a theodolite – remember when someone was checking out the old quarry and Calum thought he was taking photographs with a theodolite? Someone's surveying the field.'

'I think Victor McNair was one of the men. It must mean he's received planning permission for that caravan park he wants. It's a shame – the field was good for village events like the Easter egg festival.'

'Things change, whether we like it or not.'

'I suppose so, but it's a pity,' Jenny said. She slowed down to make way for a group of strangers crossing Main Street from the village green. 'Look at the place! I've never seen so many people here at one time!'

The village green was swarming with visitors, some photographing the scarecrows, some sitting at the tables outside the Cuckoo and the Gift Horse, while others picnicked on the green or wandered about, admiring the neat houses with their bright summer gardens.

'Looks as though the festival worked. It's great to be back,' Andrew said as she eased the car along slowly, giving people time to cross the road.

'I wish we didn't have to go away again so soon.'

'So do I, love, but it's only for three more weeks.'

She shot a sidelong glance at him. 'I wish I could be as strong as you are about all this.'

'You are. We both have to be, for the kids as well as for each other. And you have to admit,' Andrew went on with a sudden change of subject, 'that this is a great place to come back to.'

As the car turned into the standing area before the garage the front door opened and Calum came dashing out. As soon as Jenny got out he threw himself at her, hugging her so tightly she could scarcely breathe.

'We've missed you!' She finally managed to ease herself free so she could hold him back and look at him. 'Are you all right?'

He nodded, blinking hard, and then said gruffly, 'I'm fine. Are *you* all right?'

'Of course we are.' Andrew came round the car, holding

out his arms. After a moment's hesitation Calum hugged him gingerly.

'It's OK, I won't break,' Andrew assured him. 'But let's see if you do,' and he gave his son a bear hug that had Calum squealing for mercy, while Jenny went to Maggie, who hesitated on the steps, a tentative smile hovering around her lips.

'We've missed you both so much.' She put her arms round her stepdaughter without thinking, and felt the girl stiffen. 'How are things?'

'We're all right, both of us. Naomi's been very kind.'

'I knew we'd left you in safe hands.'

Andrew joined them, one arm draped about Calum's shoulders. 'Hello, Maggie,' he said easily, putting the other arm around her waist and dropping a kiss on her cheek. 'Great to be back.' He glanced across at the scarecrow. 'What happened to Long John's crutch?'

'It got stolen and he was knocked down.'

'Calum, we agreed not to say!'

'It just came out.'

'What's been going on here?' Jenny wanted to know.

'Whatever it was, he looks fine. Was it just him?'

'No, it happened all over the village. We had night raiders,' Calum announced importantly. Maggie shook her head at him. 'But we managed to put him back together and most of the other scarecrows were mended as well. We found Florence Nightingale in our garden shed yesterday.'

'Good heavens, Andrew, it looks as though they had a lot more fun during the week than we did.'

'We can find out about it over lunch.'

'Maggie and Naomi made a casserole. It's in the oven.'

'I can smell it, and I'm starving,' Andrew said, ushering the others indoors.

239

28

'We've missed both of you so much,' Jenny said when she and her husband had heard the week's news, 'but it was good to know you were being well looked after. How was it at the manse?'

'It was OK. I quite liked sharing a room with Ethan.'

'Did you have a good time, Maggie?'

She lifted her shoulders in a slight shrug. 'It was all right,' she said, and was unable to stop herself from adding, 'I suppose.' Old habits died hard.

'There were loads of people around the village when we arrived this morning. It looks as though the Scarecrow Festival's been a success in spite of the vandalism.'

'We've had people here all week. It was quite funny sometimes,' Calum said, grinning. 'Like when you saw someone coming along and you kept still and they weren't sure if you were real or a scarecrow until you moved. And the playground at the quarry was filled with kids we didn't know. There are a lot of pictures in the *News* for you to see.'

'We're going to take a walk round the village this afternoon, aren't we, Jenny? I want to see the scarecrows before they all disappear.'

'Linn Hall's been open to the public all week,' Maggie said.

'Let's go there, Andrew. I've never seen the place close up.'

'Leave the washing-up until later,' Andrew suggested. 'We'll take a stroll round the village, then fetch the car and drive to Linn Hall to save time. I believe there's to be a big party in the village hall tonight.'

'Won't you feel too tired for that?' Maggie asked. She had been expecting him to be greatly changed, but he was much the same as usual, other than looking tired.

He smiled at her. 'No, I'm fine, really.'

'Dad,' Calum blurted out, 'did it hurt?'

'The treatment I'm getting? Not a bit,' Andrew told his son calmly, 'I've brought the leaflets they gave me; you can both have a look at them later if you like.'

Calum nodded. 'It helps to know what's going on,' he said solemnly.

'Of course it does. We only feel afraid of things when we don't understand them. The chemo made me feel very tired didn't it, Jen? When I got back to the place where we're staying I slept like a log for two hours every time, but after that I was fine. I'm only getting chemo during the first and last week.'

'Someone told me to give him ginger tea after chemo,' Jenny chimed in, 'because sometimes people feel a bit sick after the therapy. So I bought some ginger root and grated a teaspoonful into a mug, then added hot water and let it steep for a while before giving it to him.' She wrinkled her nose. 'I don't like ginger, but luckily Andrew does. After drinking it down and then having his sleep he was quite hungry, so it definitely worked.'

'What's radiotherapy like?' Calum asked. 'Greg Campbell

241

said that it's got something to do with listening to radios but that can't be right, can it?'

Andrew, about to take a drink, only just managed to grab a napkin before spluttering tea over the table. Jenny gave a shout of laughter, and Calum eyed them both with suspicion. 'He was wrong, wasn't he? Wait till I tell him he was wrong!'

'He *was* wrong,' Andrew said when he got his breath back, 'but I suppose it was a good guess. It's to do with invisible radio waves that go right inside and make the tumour shrink . . . we hope.'

'But it doesn't hurt,' Calum persisted.

'Not a bit and it doesn't last very long either. It's a bit like getting an X-ray. We'll go over the leaflets together after we get back.' Andrew looked round the table. 'Ready to go?'

The Scarecrow Festival ended with a big party in the village hall. The place was packed, and every household supplied something for the buffet. During the early part of the evening everyone was there, from the oldest to the youngest for the prize-giving.

Kevin Pearce, to his delight, won best garden scarecrow with Florence Nightingale, while Marcy and Sam took the best shop-window award for their cheeky-faced paper-boy scarecrow. Runners up included the Gift Shop's little girl on her garden swing and the McBains' beekeeper. Calum almost burst with excitement when Long John Silver won a commendation. The Mad Hatter's Tea Party took first prize for the best group, with the almshouses' Darby and Joan in second place.

Halfway through the evening Fliss, Hector and the older villagers began to drift homewards. Jenny and Andrew followed soon after; Andrew had been surrounded by well-wishers all evening but, as he explained to everyone, he had been looking forward all week to a good sleep in his own bed.

'Why don't you stay on, Maggie?' Jenny suggested, and when the girl hesitated, Ingrid added, 'We'll walk you back home later. It seems a shame to have to leave now.'

'OK, thanks.' The young backpackers from Linn Hall had appeared in force, and Maggie had been up for every dance, quicksteps and foxtrots as well as the stamping, cheering group efforts like the Dashing White Sergeant, Strip the Willow and the more sedate barn dances. She was having a wonderful time, and when Freya told her quietly in the ladies that she had seen Ryan Kearney in Kirkcudbright the day before, hand in hand with a girl from Maggie's class, Maggie shrugged and said, 'Doesn't bother me. I've finished with him.'

'Really? I'm glad. I know he's one of the best-looking boys in the school and he's got oodles of charm, but I've always thought you could do better than him.'

'Have you?' Maggie was genuinely surprised.

'Of course. You're smarter than he is, and you're so pretty and—'

'Me?'

'Come here.' Freya caught Maggie's arm and turned her towards the mirror. 'I look pale and insipid beside your lovely dark hair and those big brown eyes. Smile – go on,' she urged when Maggie hesitated. When Maggie smiled self-consciously at her reflection she said, 'See how your whole face lights up? You never smiled when you were going with Ryan, and that's because he liked to look sarcastic and you were trying to be like him. You'd be surprised at the number of people in our class who want to be friends with you, but they were put off because of Ryan.'

'You're not serious!'

'I am.'

243

'I always thought you were prettier than me.'

'We're both pretty in our own ways. I'm fair, you're dark. We're like a matching set, in a way.'

'I wish I had gorgeous red hair like that girl Molly who's going to marry Lewis Ralston-Kerr.'

'You're prettier than her,' Freya scoffed. 'Don't you think she's a bit . . .' she glanced round to make sure nobody had come in before saying in a low voice 'tarty in that tight black top and that bright green skirt? I can't see her as the lady of the manor.'

'He's quite good-looking, though. And I like the way he looks at her. All . . . adoring.'

'He's not the only one; half the boys can hardly take their eyes off her, Grant McDonald especially. Come on,' Freya slipped her arm through Maggie's, 'let's go out there and take their minds off her!'

Giggling, they headed for the door.

'You know that every male in this room between seventeen and eighty is jealous of me, don't you?' Lewis said as he and Molly circled the dance floor. She lifted her head from his shoulder and smiled up at him, looking, he thought, like a cat that had just finished an entire bowl of cream.

'No harm in that. You're the one who's got me, aren't you?'

'Mmm.' The only one who worried him was Cam Gordon. Cam had taken some excellent shots of the estate, and he and Lewis were becoming friendly again in a reserved way, but he was still suspicious of Cam where Molly was concerned. He knew the pair of them had met before Lewis knew Molly, and although he didn't know how close they had been then, he fretted over what might have occurred between them.

'Enjoying yourself?'

'It's been OK, but I'm taking Weena back home tomorrow.'

'Tomorrow?' He stopped abruptly and another couple bumped into them. 'When did you decide that?' Lewis wanted to know when they had disentangled themselves and were moving to the music again.

'This afternoon. I phoned Dad to ask him to fetch us now that the festival's over.'

'Phone him first thing tomorrow and tell him I'll take you home – if you're determined to go.'

'Sure you can spare the time?' There was a slight edge to her voice.

'Of course.'

'Can you stay over?'

Lewis thought of all the work he had planned for the next few days. 'Yes, if you like. Why are you in such a hurry to leave?'

'Because I'm *bored*.' Her kissable red mouth pursed into a pout. 'The festival was fun, but now it's over it'll just be work, work, work again. And I'm aching to go somewhere different. A group I met up with two years ago are heading for the South of France the week after next and I've decided to go with them.'

'What about Rowena Chloe?'

'She'll be fine. Mum's best friend's offered to babysit when Mum's at work. She's dotty about Weena. I wish you could come with me, Lewis. You'd love it.'

'I can't, there's too much to do here.'

'See what I mean? Work, work, work.'

'You want me to get the place up and running before we get married, don't you?'

'That won't be for ages yet. You know I want to live a little before I settle down.'

The music had stopped and they stood alone in the middle of the floor. Looking over Molly's red head, Lewis saw Cam Gordon watching them. As the music started again the other man took a step towards them.

'Let's dance,' Lewis said hurriedly, swinging Molly into his arms and away from Cam.

'You should be dancing with some of the other women,' Alison said as Ewan claimed her for the next dance.

'I don't want to dance with anyone el— Sorry!'

'It's all right,' she assured him, though her toes were stinging. He had taken a step forward when he should have taken a step back, and their feet had had a head-on collision.

'I've not had much dancing experience. Cows don't seem to be interested in quicksteps.'

'I don't suppose they are. I can teach you, if you like.'

'Did you do a lot of dancing in Glasgow?'

'Mmm. It used to be famous for its dance halls, but there aren't as many of them nowadays.'

A sudden thought struck Ewan. 'Would you like to dance with some of the other men?' The possibility hadn't occurred to him before. Every time the music struck up and he saw a man start towards Alison, instinct made him rush to claim her first.

'No, I wouldn't.' It was the truth; even though Ewan was clumsy, she cherished every moment spent with him. Not so long ago she had been certain she could never care about another man after losing her husband, but Ewan had broken down the walls she had built round herself.

Without realising it she began to lead and, with Ewan obediently following, they moved together easily and comfortably.

★ ★ ★

When the music finally ended and the remaining revellers went out into the cool dark night the MacKenzies walked Maggie home. A dim light burned in the hall, the rest of the house was in darkness.

'Got your key?' Ingrid asked.

'Yes, thanks.' She went up the garden path and opened the door before waving to the group at the gate. They moved off as she let herself into the house. In the kitchen, she poured herself a glass of milk and made a sandwich, humming and moving about the kitchen as though she were still dancing.

Grant MacDonald had danced with her twice, and said she was a good dancer. Grant wasn't nearly as good-looking as Ryan, but he was nice, and he was going to be a famous footballer one day. Soon after moving from primary school to Kirkcudbright Academy he'd become the football team's star player, and his games teacher had persuaded a scout from Dumfries Thistle Football Club to watch him play. Grant had been invited to training sessions for youngsters at the Thistle ground and had done well enough to be signed up as a possible future player.

Grant might have been ogling Molly Ewing, Maggie thought happily as she finished her snack, but it was Maggie he had danced with.

She put glass, plate and knife on the draining board, hesitated at the door and went back to wash them, then went upstairs to bed.

Jenny, lying awake, had heard the front door. After a while, Maggie's bedroom door opened and closed quietly. She gave a sigh of relief and turned over to cuddle against Andrew's back.

'Mmm? Everything all right?' His voice was heavy with sleep.

'Maggie's home. I couldn't sleep until I knew she was back.'

'The cost of having a teenage daughter,' he mumbled.

'I know,' Jenny said, and fell asleep.

'Ginny, the night's young yet, and we've got a date,' Lewis said as the hall began to empty.

'We have?' Confused, she looked at Molly, who was hanging on to Lewis's arm possessively.

'Absolutely!' He put his free arm through hers and the three of them left the village hall and started along the road.

'Where are we going?'

'You've forgotten, haven't you?' He steered both girls across the village green towards the Neurotic Cuckoo's brightly lit windows.

It seemed to Ginny that most of the villagers had called in at the pub to continue partying. Lewis whisked round the place, gathering up spare chairs and squeezing them in at the table where Duncan Campbell sat with some of his cronies.

'Evening, all. Now then, Duncan,' he went on when they were all settled, 'I believe the first round's on you, old lad.'

'On me? That'll be the day!'

'No, *this* is the day. Cast your mind back to early May when Ginny and I were planning to open the hall's gardens and the stable shop to the public and you claimed it wouldn't work. What was the arrangement we came to?'

'Oh yes!' Ginny suddenly recalled, 'we agreed we would each buy you a pint if you were proved right.'

'And you would buy each of us a pint if we proved you wrong,' Lewis agreed. 'So here we are. Three pints, please, and as you said at the time, I can feel that beer sliding down my throat.'

'Aw, f . . . lippin' heck,' Duncan groaned.

29

'Before the sermon,' Naomi said to her congregation the following morning, 'I would like to ask Maggie Cameron to read the passage my sermon is based on.'

A ripple of interest ran through the filled church, and then heads began to turn as Maggie remained rooted to her seat.

'Go on, darling,' Jenny whispered, squeezing her step-daughter's hand.

'I can't!'

'Yes, you can,' Andrew leaned across Calum to assure her. 'You can do anything you put your mind to.'

'I should explain,' Naomi said from the pulpit, 'that Maggie's in shock because I didn't prepare her for this. Maggie, you're among friends and we're all looking forward to hear you read the passage.'

There was another murmur, this time of agreement. Maggie stumbled to her feet and managed to make her way up the aisle without falling over. She climbed the steps to the pulpit, where Naomi put an arm about her.

'Only a few words, and I know you'll do it beautifully,' she whispered, a dark finger marking the spot. 'The name of the book, the chapter, the verse, then the words.'

Maggie swallowed hard, gave an experimental cough, then drew a deep breath. 'Hosea, chapter eleven, verse four,' she said as clearly as her fast-beating heart allowed. 'I led them with cords of kindness, with bands of love.'

'Thank you, Maggie,' Naomi said and, as she made her way back to her place, Maggie suddenly realised that on either side of the aisle people were nodding, smiling and mouthing, 'Well done,' at her. By the time she reached her seat her face was poppy red.

As she spoke of the abiding power and strength of love and sincerity Naomi's voice flowed over her attentive congregation like a soothing balm, filling the small church to the rafters. It seemed to everyone there that she took time to single each one of them out for a special glance as she spoke. She ended by asking those present to concentrate their thoughts at least once a day on Andrew Forsyth and his family at a time when they most needed compassion and love.

As the congregation left after the service the Forsyths were surrounded by well-wishers.

'Ye look well, Andrew,' Jess McNair said warmly.

'I feel fine, and I'm being very well-looked after into the bargain.'

'The hospital staff are so kind to him – to both of us,' Jenny added as Andrew was claimed by another well-wisher, 'but it's good to be back home, even briefly. I see Victor got his planning permission.'

Jess and Ewan, by her side, gave each other puzzled looks, then Jess shook her head. 'No, it was refused because he couldnae afford tae dae all the work they insisted on. They said the field wasnae suitable.'

'Oh . . . we saw him in the field with a group of men when we arrived back yesterday morning. One of them was using one of those things surveyors use – I never remember the name. Perhaps he's found a better use for the field.'

'What other use can there be for that field?' Jess wondered as she and Ewan walked back to the farm.

'I can't think of one. I'll talk tae Victor when I get the chance, an' try tae find out what he's up tae. Best not tae say anythin' tae Dad till then.'

But Ewan had a good idea as to what his brother was planning, and the very thought of it sickened him. He would have to speak to Victor as soon as possible.

'That sermon on Sunday was aimed at me, wasn't it?'

'Actually, Maggie, it was aimed at a lot of the people in the congregation, and I hope that, like you, most of them took it personally. One thing I will admit,' Naomi said serenely, 'was that the talk with you in the vestry last week gave me the theme and, for that, I am very grateful.'

It was Monday, and Maggie and Calum were at the manse again, while Andrew was about to start his second week of therapy.

'Actually, it was a good sermon.'

'Thank you. I have to do some parish visiting this afternoon, so could you make a start on the dinner for me if I'm not back by four?'

'OK, just tell me what needs doing.'

'Do you know something?' Naomi said. 'It's great, having someone who can help out like this. Ethan tends to listen, nod and then forget about it. If you ever feel like taking up housekeeping as a career I want first refusal.'

When Naomi had gone out Maggie went to her room

251

and read for a while before wandering downstairs to see if any television programmes were worth a look. To her surprise she found Calum in the living room, so deeply absorbed in a book that he jumped when she said, 'I thought you were with Ethan.'

'He's meeting friends in Kirkcudbright.'

'What are you reading?'

His face went red and he slammed the book shut then clutched it to his chest, his arms folded tightly across it. 'Nothing. None of your business!'

'French?' He hadn't realised that the book was held with the title in full view. 'You're learning French?'

'Shut up! It's nothing to do with you,' he snapped, trying to push past her towards the door.

'Hang on a minute.' She detained him with a hand on his arm. 'If you want to learn French, I can help you.'

'I can manage by myself.' He struggled, then when she clung on he stamped on her instep.

'Ow!' She bit her lip in pain, but kept her hold on him. 'Why do you have to be so difficult when I just want to help you?'

'Because I don't trust you.'

'But—' she began, then stopped and tried again. 'OK, I can understand that. I'll admit I've been nasty to you in the past, but I've been trying to show you I'm sorry and want to make it up to you.'

'Why?'

'Because being nasty all the time's very tiring, and because with your parents in Edinburgh, we've only got each other. And if you're thinking of stamping on my foot again you should know that next time I'm going to hit back.'

He hesitated, then pulled free and thumped on to the sofa.

'That's better.' Maggie sat down beside him, rubbing her foot. 'Let's start again. Are you trying to teach yourself French?' He nodded slowly, eyes fixed on his knees. 'Why? You'll be learning it once you start at the Academy in August.'

'It's a – a promise.'

'To who? Whom?' she corrected herself.

Calum dug his chin hard against his chest and mumbled something.

'What did you say?' All she could see was the back of his head; a wisp of fair hair, so like Jenny's, was curled into the nape of his neck in a way that reminded her he was still young and vulnerable. Then his chin suddenly came up, his face tight with a mixture of anger and embarrassment, blue eyes glaring at her.

'God, that's who,' he yelled. 'We've got a deal, him and me. OK?'

Now she understood. 'It's for your dad, isn't it? If you promise to learn French, God'll make him better.'

'So?'

'Why French?'

'Cos I thought God might like it better if I did something really hard like learning French instead of trying to be better at football. My dad likes French. I saw him reading a whole book in French once. And I knew Ethan had a French book in his room.' His glare dared her to laugh.

'Actually, that book's not for beginners. I've still got my first French book at home.'

'It won't do me much good at your gran's, will it?' He was still on the defensive.

'No, not at Gran's; at home in Mill Walk. I'll fetch it later. My aunt Lizbeth started me off with a French song.

I had to learn how to sing the song properly and what the words meant. It was a great idea. I could teach you.'

'I'd rather wait for the book. You'd probably teach me to sing daft things so everyone'd laugh at me.'

'You can be so annoying, Calum! Wait until I tell you about what happened to me when we started French at school. D'you know what RSVP means? You get it on the bottom of invitations,' she went on when he shook his head, 'and someone told me it meant "Reply Soon, Very Pleased".'

'Pleased about what?'

'That's what I wanted to know, and they said, pleased to be invited. It sounded all right to me, so when we started French lessons and the teacher asked if anyone knew what RSVP meant, my hand went up at once and I said it meant "Reply Soon, Very Pleased". But it's really "*Répondez, s'il vous plaît*" – "Please Reply". She had the whole class laughing at me. It was terrible. I cried in the playground afterwards and got laughed at again. I'd never do that to anyone. Now, listen to this . . .'

She cleared the piano seat of its usual pile of newspapers then sat down and, after a few false starts, began to play a melody.

Calum went over to stand beside her. 'I didn't know you could play the piano.'

'I used to get lessons when I lived with my gran and granda.'

'Why don't you get lessons now?'

'Duh! There isn't a piano at Mill Walk and I need to practise if I'm getting lessons.' She finally managed to play the melody all the way through, and nodded her satisfaction.

'Listen, and I'll sing it in French, then in English. *Frère*

Jacques, Frère Jacques, Dormez-vous? Dormez-vous? Sonnez les matines! Sonnez les matines! Ding, dang, dong. Ding, dang, dong! Now I'll sing it in English, "Are you sleeping? Are you sleeping? Brother John? Brother John? Morning bells are ringing! Morning bells are ringing! Ding, dang, dong. Ding, dang, dong!"'

'Sounds daft.'

'Not when you sing it properly. It's called a roundelay, or something like that. Hang on . . .' Maggie darted into Naomi's study, returning with a writing pad and a pen.

'I'll write the words in French, then English. Then I'll teach you what the French words mean and how to say them, and after that, we'll try singing them.'

Two hours passed in a blur of pronunciation, song and giggles before Maggie thought to glance at the clock.

'Good grief, it's after four and I said I'd get the dinner started. Come on, in payment for your first lesson, you can scrub the potatoes. We'll do more French some other time if you want.'

She reached the door, then glanced back to see Calum, clutching the book and the sheet with 'Frère Jacques' written on it, hesitating, brows pulled together and teeth nibbling his lower lip.

'What's wrong?'

'How can I be absolutely sure you're not going to teach me something rude?'

'For goodness' sake! I've got a French–English dictionary at home too. You can keep it for the time being and check every single word in it if you want. Come on, Naomi'll be home soon and I promised her!'

'Doing deals with God,' he said as he trailed to the kitchen after her, 'can be quite complicated.'

255

'You don't need to tell me that.' Maggie delved into the vegetable basket.

'Are you doing a deal too?' he asked in surprise. She nodded. 'What is it?'

'To be a better sister to you.' She dumped a bag of potatoes on the draining board and turned the tap on. 'And it's as difficult as French. Make sure you scrub them well.'

It was only later, getting ready for bed that she realised she had referred to Mill Walk as 'home' without noticing.

30

Two days passed before Ewan got the chance to have a talk with his brother. A dry-stone wall in one of the fields needed repairing, and Bert sent his sons to see to it.

'I can dae it mysel','Victor protested. 'I'm better at stone-wallin' than Ewan is.'

'I know that, he's goin' along so ye can show him how. Go on, now, an' don't come back until the job's well done. I'll go up there mysel' later tae make sure ye've both been workin' hard.'

As the two of them left the farmhouse Bert put a hand on Ewan's arm, holding him back to let Victor move out of earshot before saying, 'I'm sendin' you with him tae make sure he works hard. I don't know what's got intae him these days – it's as if he's laid his brain down and cannae mind where.'

'He gets worse every day,' Victor grumbled as the two of them trudged to the wall. 'I'm sick o' bein' treated like a child wi' no sense.'

'He's worried about how we'll manage tae keep the farm goin'.'

'That's no reason tae take it out on us. Folk in prison have a better life than we do.'

They worked hard for the next two hours, gathering up the tumbled stones and packing them tightly together, then filling the gaps with smaller stones and gravel. Ewan was surprised to see the difference in Victor as he worked on something he enjoyed doing. Every stone had to be carefully chosen, every space between the larger stones had to be firmed up and smoothed off before the next part of the wall was tackled.

When the gap was securely filled, the two of them hunted for flat stones to finish it off. Only then did Victor take his cap off, run a forearm over his face, and announce they were free to enjoy the Thermos of tea and the packet of sandwiches they had brought with them.

They dropped on to the grass and leaned their backs against the wall as they ate and drank. The fields sloped away in front of them, and from their high position they could see the river, the farm buildings and the main road. Prior's Ford's roofs were clustered to the left, looking from that distance like a toy village. Ewan could see the village green and the Neurotic Cuckoo. He wondered what Alison was doing at that moment, and whether she was thinking of him.

Victor threw the last of his sandwich to a bird that had been hopping around nearby, emptied the dregs of his tea on the ground and began to screw on the Thermos top. Ewan remembered the talk they must have. There could be no better time for it.

'Wait,' he said as Victor began to scramble to his feet.

'What is it?'

'Mam and me were speakin' tae Jenny Forsyth after church on Sunday, an' she says that she an' Andrew saw you an' some other folk on Saturday in that field Dad gave ye.'

'Did she?' Victor was standing now, feet planted apart, the sun behind him so that his face was in shadow. 'What about it?'

'She said there was someone surveyin' the field. What's goin' on, Victor?'

'What's it tae you or Jenny Forsyth what I dae with my field?'

'Surely Dad's got a right tae know?' Ewan persisted. In answer, Victor turned and began to stride towards the farmhouse, the old rucksack containing the Thermos and the tools they had used to repair the wall bouncing on his back with every step.

'Victor!' When his brother paid no heed, Ewan scrambled to his feet and hurried after him. Catching up, he grabbed Victor's arm and swung him round.

'Get yer hands off me!'

'Not until you tell me what's goin' on. You're plannin' tae sell the land for buildin', aren't ye?' Ewan said, and when Victor continued glaring at him, lips compressed, he repeated the question, his voice rising. 'Aren't ye?'

'It's my land!'

'It's Tarbethill land!'

'Dad gave it tae me.'

'For a caravan park.'

'You know I couldnae afford the plannin' permission, but it's still my land tae use as I like!'

'Ye're goin' tae sell it for development, aren't ye?'

'What if I am?'

'You promised Dad you'd never dae that!'

'For God's sake! It's a worthless piece o' ground. We cannae plant it, we cannae graze animals on it—'

'It's still part o' Tarbethill!'

'Stop goin' on about Tarbethill!' Victor said, losing his

259

patience. 'The only thing that field's fit for's buildin'. The man that's buyin' it reckons he can get a dozen houses on it, mebbe more. An' he's got plannin' permission because he can afford tae dae whatever the council wants.'

'Ye've got a buyer already?' Ewan asked in disbelief.

'The deal's goin' through at the end o' the week. When I lost the chance of a caravan park Jeanette's dad came up wi' the idea. He's in the Rotary Club an' he knew a man who was lookin' for land tae develop. Me an' him – Jeanette's dad – are goin' intae partnership.'

'What sort of partnership?'

'He's helpin' me tae sell the land for a good price and in return I'm buyin' a partnership in his business. That means that me an' Jeanette can get married sooner. An' our names are down for one o' the houses that's goin' tae be built.'

'What's Dad goin' tae say?'

'I'll deal wi' that when the time comes.'

'D'ye think I can keep quiet about it now I know what ye're goin' tae do tae him an' Mum?'

'I'm past carin'.' Victor shook Ewan's hand from his arm and headed downhill again, sheep scattering before him.

Ewan charged after him again but this time, as he grabbed his brother's arm, Victor swung round and drove his bunched fist, with all his weight behind it, into Ewan's face.

The brothers had often fought before, but never as ferociously as they did that day, neither showing the other any mercy. The struggle raged on for a good ten minutes before Ewan gained the initiative, throwing Victor on his back then holding him down with one knee, blood dripping from his nose to mingle with the blood on his brother's face.

For a few minutes they were both too busy sucking air

into their lungs to speak, then Ewan managed to gasp out, 'Ye'll tell Dad the truth when we get back home.'

'Mind yer own business!' Victor snarled. Ewan grabbed two handfuls of hair and began to thump his brother's head against the ground. 'All right, all right! Get off me!'

Ewan got to his feet, swaying slightly, and offered Victor a hand up. It was ignored as his brother rolled away from him and got onto his hands and knees.

'Are ye all right?'

'Get away from me!' Victor snarled.

Ewan pushed his hair back from his face, picked up the rucksack and headed towards the farmhouse below. The sheep, who had regrouped to watch the fight in mild surprise, drew back to form a gap which he staggered through.

It was mid-afternoon when he reached the farmyard, and there was no sign of either of his parents. He went into the byre and knelt to sluice his head under the cold-water tap. The water ran pink into the drain and he kept splashing handful after handful over his face and head until it ran clear. After using his jacket to dry himself as best he could he combed his bruised hands through his hair in an attempt to smooth it back. When he had made himself as respectable as possible he went into the kitchen, where his mother and father were drinking tea.

Jess, cradling her mug in both hands, said as he came in, 'There you are, Ewan, pour yersel' a mug. Is Vic—' She glanced up. 'Dear God, what's happened tae ye?'

'Nothin'.' The effort of shaping the word opened up his split lip and he felt warm blood trickle down his chin.

'They've been fightin' again,' Bert growled. 'For pity's sake, ye're grown men. Is it no' time the two o' ye began tae behave like it?'

261

'Here . . .' Jess hurried to the dresser to fetch a clean teatowel. 'Put that against yer mouth while I get the first aid box. Where's Victor? Is he all right?'

'As fit as I am.'

She looked deep into his eyes and knew from what she saw there that this was no ordinary squabble. 'What happened?'

'It's up tae Victor tae tell ye,' Ewan said through the towel pressed against his mouth.

'Whatever it was, it's bad. Look at your hands,' she was saying when Victor came in. He hadn't made any attempt at tidying himself and his mother let out a scream at the sight of his face, masked with crusted blood, one eye puffing up and the cheekbone below it split and still oozing.

'What the hell took the two o' ye tae this state?' his father bellowed as Victor stamped over to the sink and snatched up a teatowel draped over the rim to dry.

'Wait till I get a clean one, that might have germs,' Jess told him hurriedly, but he ignored her, dousing the towel liberally in cold water before wiping it over his face.

'Sit down an' let me see tae the two of ye,' she ordered, but Bert banged his fist on the table.

'No' till I get tae the bottom o' this, woman. I sent you two out tae mend a wall and ye come back lookin' as if ye've spent the time throwin' it at each other instead!'

'Yer wall's mended an' Victor's got somethin' tae tell ye.'

'Later,' Jess said.

'Now!' Bert thundered.

Victor fended off his mother's attempts to treat his injuries. 'Aye, now. Let's get it over wi'. Dad, I'm sellin' my field tae a builder.'

'Ye're what?' Bert asked in disbelief, while Jess became motionless, one hand still reaching towards Victor, her face suddenly blank with shock.

262

'I'm sellin' the field—'

'Ye're not!'

'I am, Dad. It's all settled an' the contract's bein' signed at the end of the week. There's goin' tae be a dozen houses on it, mebbe more, and one o' them's for me and Jeanette. Her dad's been helpin' me with the business end o' things and some of my share o' the money's goin' tae buy me a partnership with him. I'm done wi' farmin'.'

31

'What did ye say?' Bert asked his firstborn.

'It's over, Dad. I'm done wi' farmin'. This place is dead on its feet an' the sooner you admit it the bet—'

As he launched himself at his elder son, Bert let out a roar that made the dishes on the dresser ring. Jess and Ewan moved as one, Jess throwing herself before Victor while Ewan grabbed his father.

'Let go o' me!' Bert bellowed. 'I'm goin' tae finish the job you started!'

'Dad, it's done!' Although his father was elderly and worn down by worry, sheer rage had given him added strength. Ewan held on as best he could while he was thrown around like a rat in a terrier's jaws. The two of them crashed into the table, and a chair went spinning. 'Dad, don't make things worse!'

'Worse? How could killin' him make things worse than they already are?'

Victor set his mother aside and steadied himself, facing his father. 'Let him go, Ewan. If it helps him tae fight me

264

I'm ready for him. But I'll defend mysel' – mind that, old man.'

Ewan sensed the fight going out of his father. 'Ach, what use would a fight be?' Bert shook himself free of his younger son and turned away, groping, as though blind, for a chair. He found one and lowered himself into it. 'Ye've betrayed me, Victor, an' ye've betrayed yer mother and yer brother as well as Tarbethill an' the generations that've built up this farm.'

'For God's sake, man, why don't ye wipe the stars from yer eyes an' go outside an' take a good look at the place,' Victor told him ruthlessly. 'It's dyin', can ye no' see that? In fact, it's as good as dead. There's nothin' here for me an' Ewan once you've killed yersel' wi' overwork. This is the twenty-first century, an' farmin' in this country's been destroyed by disease an' stupid, stranglin' laws. I deserve better than this, an' I'm goin' tae get it. I'm sellin' the one bit o' land that's legally mine an' I'm goin' tae use the money tae make a decent life for me an' Jeanette. An' ye cannae stop me. I'll share some o' the money I get wi' ye if it helps, but I'll go no further than that.'

Bert lifted his head and Ewan's breath caught in his throat as he saw how old his father had suddenly become. But Bert's eyes were still alive, blazing at Victor. 'Take yer thirty pieces o' silver,' he snarled, 'an' get out o' here now. Ye're no son o' mine an' I never want tae set eyes on ye again.'

Victor turned his head and spat blood into the sink, then looked back at his father. 'That suits me,' he said, and headed through the door leading to the inner part of the house.

'Bert,' Jess said tremulously, 'ye cannae mean it. He's yer own flesh an' blood. We can sort it out.'

'It's said, an' it's meant and it's over,' her husband told

her, going to the outer door. 'He's no part o' this farm, or this fam'ly.'

'Mum,' Ewan said as the yard door slammed behind Bert, and Jess turned towards the inner door, 'let it be. Dad's right, things have gone too far tae be mended.'

'I'll no' see my fam'ly torn apart like this!'

'Ye've got no choice, and neither have I.' He picked up the bloody towel he had dropped on the floor and held it under the cold tap, then squeezed it out and began to dab gingerly at his face. 'Mebbe somethin' can be worked out later, but no' just now. Victor's goin' tae Jeanette and her fam'ly. They'll take him in, and that's what he wants. We'll have tae find some way o' pickin' up the pieces without him.'

She looked longingly at the door Victor had gone through, then turned to the first aid box on the table. 'Sit down and let me see tae ye.'

Right then all Ewan wanted was to be on his own, but he knew the only way to help his mother at that moment was to let her feel useful. So he shrugged out of his jacket and began to unbutton his shirt. 'Thanks, Mum.'

'For God's sake, son,' she said as the shirt came off, revealing a muscular torso stained with the beginnings of massive bruising interspersed with scarlet weals, 'what's he done tae ye?'

'No more than I did tae him. Most o' it's from rollin' about over stones, an' I think we were in a bed o' nettles at one time.'

'Sit down,' she ordered, opening the box. 'Dear heaven, it's like bein' mother tae Cain an' Abel!'

'No' quite.' Ewan sank into a chair, suddenly aware of how exhausted he felt. 'At least we're both alive.'

Then he drew his breath in sharply as she began to dab iodine on to a deep scratch on his back.

★   ★   ★

When Ewan's wounds had been tended, he returned to work while, with trembling hands, his mother tidied the kitchen and soaked the bloodied clothes and towels in cold water and salt, rubbing hard until the stains were almost gone. She had done this so often after scraps between her sons, but never before with the sense that it would be the final time.

She had just finished when Victor came downstairs and into the kitchen, carrying a full holdall.

'Listen tae me, son—' She tried to stop him, but was pushed aside, albeit gently.

'Don't try tae change my mind, Ma. I've been wantin' out o' this place for most of my life, an' now I've got my chance I'm takin' it.'

'But not like this! Not wi' bitterness splittin' up the fam'ly!'

'It's the only way, with him bein' so pig-headed.'

'Can ye blame him? His whole life's been spent tryin' tae keep Tarbethill goin'. He loves this place.'

'More fool him.' His eyes were on the door and she could feel his yearning to walk through it.

'Ye'll break his heart, Victor!'

'Better his heart broken than my spirit, an' that's what it'd have come tae,' Victor told her coldly. He reached a long arm behind her as she made a second futile attempt to block his exit, and pulled the door open with such force that it hit her hip and sent her off balance. She came up against the wall, then spun round and ran outside as he was throwing his bag into the rear seat of his car.

'Victor, listen tae me!'

He pulled open the driver's door and got into the car, jamming the key into the ignition and revving the engine. Hens ran out of the way, squawking and fluttering their wings as the car took off, almost brushing past his mother. She caught a glimpse of her boy's face, set as hard as stone, the skin bone-white in the patches between bruises and smeared blood, and then he was gone.

Jess ran after the car, but by the time she reached the top of the lane it was halfway to the road, bouncing and juddering through holes and spraying gravel in its wake. At one point the rear wheels skidded and the car began to slew round before Victor, wrenching at the wheel, managed to get it under control. Then it reached the end of the lane and turned on to the road without stopping. Brakes screeched and Jess's hand flew to her mouth, but Victor kept going, out of her sight and on his way to Kirkcudbright.

Immediately afterwards, Sam Brennan's van passed the end of the lane, heading into Prior's Ford.

Jess returned slowly to the kitchen, where she slumped on a chair, staring at the wall. Old Saul, who had hidden behind one of the armchairs during the confrontation between Bert and Victor, emerged cautiously and crept up to her, pushing his grey muzzle against her thigh and whimpering softly.

She stroked his head. 'It's all right, pet,' she reassured him. 'It's all right now.'

But it wasn't, and she didn't see how it could ever be right again.

Sam Brennan glanced round the village store as he brought the first box of supplies in from the van. Seeing there were no customers to overhear, he said, 'I think something's wrong at Tarbethill.'

'What d'you mean, wrong?' Marcy was restacking the shelves.

'I nearly had a collision with Victor McNair on my

way here. You know how he nurses that precious car of his up and down the lane to avoid the potholes? This time he came down from the farmhouse like a rally driver. It was lucky for me I saw the car's roof bouncing up and down above the hedge and slowed the van, because he came out onto the road without stoppin' to look, cut right across in front of me and took off towards Kirkcudbright like a bat out of hell.'

'Maybe he was late going to see his fiancée.'

Sam shook his head. 'He wouldn't drive like that just because he was late. And his face when he passed me – I thought at first he was wearing some sort of mask, but when I think of it, it was more like bruises. I glanced up the lane when I passed and I think I saw Jess there, as if she'd been runnin' after him.'

'You don't think he was rushing to get help? Should we phone the farm to find out if things are all right?'

Sam shook his head. 'Best not. They'd know to ask for help if they needed it and, anyway, if you ask me, it's a domestic situation. Victor's never been keen on the farm, and it's got worse since he got engaged to that lassie with the wealthy father. We should keep quiet about this and not spread gossip,' he advised her as he went back out to the van.

'Can I join you? I'm Lynn Stacy, the local headmistress,' Lynn added as Ginny looked up from the seed catalogue she was studying. She had had a busy day in the kitchen garden, and had walked down to the pub for a drink, still in her working clothes, though she had washed her face and hands.

'Of course.' She closed the catalogue as Lynn sat next to her, putting her own drink down.

'I've got a favour to ask you. I visited Linn Hall during festival week, and I was particularly impressed by the work you've done in the kitchen garden. When I was a little girl I used to play with a child whose parents had a place very like Linn Hall, and my visit brought back so many memories. They had loads of gardeners, and I'll never forget their daughter's nursery – nurseries, I should say, because she had a night nursery where she and her nanny slept, and a fantastic day nursery packed with toys, a huge rocking horse and the most beautiful doll's house I have ever seen.'

'My goodness!' As a child Ginny had lacked for nothing, other than close contact with her parents, but her many comforts had never stretched to two nurseries and such gorgeous toys.

'Anyway, to get back to the point, they also had a kitchen garden very like the one you're working in, though, of course, it was well looked after by the gardeners. I loved that too, with all the fruit trees against the walls, and the smell of the herb garden and the colours of all the fruit bushes.'

'I'm hoping, if I can keep on working there and the Ralston-Kerrs find the necessary money, that this one can be restored to its former glory.'

'Oh, I hope so too! But what I wondered was . . . could I possibly bring the school children to see the garden in September? And if so, could you find the time to tell them about everything and explain what you've done so far, and what you hope to do in the future? They had a wonderful time visiting the wormery Ewan McNair's started at the farm, and now we're making one of our own. I think it's so important for my children to get interested in what other people do, especially work that's going on in their own village.'

'I'd love to, but I'd have to ask the Ralston-Kerrs' permission.'

'Of course. And if they agree, find out how much they'll charge.'

'Oh, I don't think they would—'

'Then tell them they must,' Lynn said firmly. 'We have a small budget to cover special outings and if the Ralston-Kerrs are going to allow you to give up a couple of hours to teach my children about growing fruit and vegetables they must be paid. As I understand it, they've had to struggle really hard to keep that place going, and if they're planning to open the grounds to the public eventually they must start to think commercially. One pound per child at least.'

'If you're sure . . .'

'I'm sure,' said Lynn.

32

'Why,' Alison Greenlees wanted to know drowsily, 'would anyone want to holiday abroad when we live in such a wonderful country?'

'Because we've got weather that changes more often than a fashion model does?' Ewan suggested. Then, slapping at a bare forearm, he added wryly, 'And midges.'

'I offered you some of my midge repellent.'

'I'm a farmer. Farmers don't use midge repellent. We're used to the wee bug— beasties. Nor do we sit about on the ground in the dark, usually.'

'But it's so beautiful at this time of night, isn't it? Look at those stars, Ewan; it's like being underneath a huge dark sequinned veil. It's perfect!'

'Sometimes I wonder if you ever grew up, Alison Greenlees!'

'And sometimes I wonder if you were ever a child, free to just enjoy life instead of having to work all the time.'

'We didn't work *all* the time, just most of it. That's part of being a farm child. Me and Victor had a good childhood – what I mind of it.'

The two of them had been whitewashing the cottage's interior walls, and when it got too dark to see, Alison had opened the old hamper brought from the pub and produced sandwiches and a flask of coffee, insisting they sit outside on the grass, which Ewan had recently mown, to enjoy their nocturnal picnic.

'I suppose we'd better get moving,' she said reluctantly.

'Another five minutes.' Ewan let himself flop back on to the grass while Alison linked her arms about her knees and looked up at the stars again. An owl hooted somewhere and a car passed along the road at the end of the lane, but otherwise everything was silent.

When she had first come to Prior's Ford as a grieving widow Alison had been convinced that although the blood continued to course through her veins her life had ended with her husband's. But the village and the people who lived there, especially Ewan, had somehow managed to put her together again. She would never forget Robbie, her first love and Jamie's father, but now it was as though the happiness she had shared with him had been carefully and lovingly tucked into a box like the precious thing it was in order to make room for Ewan, who had taught her that true love can come more than once.

'Ewan,' she said, suddenly filled with the need to tell him how she felt. Her only answer was a light snore, and when she turned to look down at him she saw in the starlight that he was asleep, one arm thrown above his head.

She moved carefully to a position where she could bend over him. He was exhausted. Now Victor had left the farm, Ewan and his parents had to work non-stop to keep things going. And winter, when the cows had to be brought in from the fields and be cared for in the barn, and spring when the ewes started to lamb, would make their lives even more difficult.

She risked dropping a light kiss on his forehead. He stirred and murmured something, then fell back into sleep.

'Ewan?' She laid a finger gently on his lips and as always happened with Jamie, his eyelids flickered, then opened. He smiled drowsily up at her. Suddenly realising where they were, he sat up quickly.

'What . . . ?'

'You fell asleep.'

'No, I didn't. What time is it?'

'Time we were going,' Alison said, wishing the two of them could stay there, alone and free of all responsibilities, for ever.

'It's in the *Radio Times* for next week!' Jinty erupted into Linn Hall's kitchen, breathless from running up the hill and along the drive. 'Next week! Ginny, why didn't you tell us?'

'Tell you what?' Ginny had brought in some vegetables for lunch and stayed to clean them at one of the two large stone sinks.

'Your mother's play, of course.' Jinty dropped her two shopping bags and sank into a kitchen chair, fanning her hot face with the magazine.

'Surely not. She never said a word to me.'

'I should remember I'm getting too old to run like that. Look.' She laid the magazine on the table and thumbed through the pages, stabbing a finger on the one she was looking for. 'It's right here, see?'

Fliss, who had been mixing pastry, wiped her hands on her apron and went to look over Jinty's shoulder. 'It's here right enough, Ginny. "*Roses in December*, a period drama." And your mother's name's in the cast list. "The Duchess of Ravenhill, Meredith Whitelaw." We must see that!'

274

'My neighbour got her *Radio Times* last night and came round specially to tell us. I got ours this morning when I was in the village store. Everyone's talking about it — we'll all be watching,' Jinty assured Ginny, who had dried her hands and come to look at the page.

'You're right. It's strange she didn't mention it the last time she phoned.'

'What's she doing now, Ginny?' Jinty wanted to know.

'She's been auditioning for several parts, and she's doing some part-time teaching at a drama college. Perhaps she thought she had already told me about next week.'

'It'll be so exciting to see someone who's actually lived here on the television screen. Gracie Fisher says they'll show it on the pub's television set. It'll be a nice change from football.' Jinty sniffed.

'It makes sense. Everyone who goes in to watch the play will buy at least one drink,' Fliss pointed out. 'We'll be there. We really ought to get a television set soon. They don't cost as much as they used to, do they?'

'I'm not sure Andrew will like this,' Maggie said doubt-fully, looking out of the window at the garden where Ethan and Calum, assisted by several other youngsters, were tying balloons to the gate and all along the fence.

'Oh, come on, we've got to welcome them home in style.' Naomi, who had been polishing furniture for all she was worth, came to put an arm about Maggie, while Helen added, 'We just want to show how pleased we are that they're back for good.'

'Until he has to have the operation.'

'Jenny said he coped really well with the therapy, which means the operation has a good chance of success. He'll be asleep all the time, and very well looked after when it's over. He's going to be OK, I feel it in my water,' Helen said, then frowned. 'What does that mean?'

'I don't know, but it's probably better not to ask,' Naomi advised her. 'Maggie, love, why don't you go and lend Ingrid a hand?'

All the Forsyths' friends had turned out to make their homecoming special. Ingrid was in the kitchen, arranging the flowers donated from most gardens in vases donated by neighbours, since the Forsyth vases couldn't cope with the huge pile of blossoms. Marcy and Sam had given enough food to keep the family going for a week and Jinty was in the kitchen preparing a homecoming lunch. Their evening meal, a steak pie, a huge bowl of soup and a trifle, was already in the refrigerator.

Jimmy MacDonald was putting the finishing touches to the garden while Maggie, Helen and Naomi turned the house into a showplace.

'She's a worrier, isn't she?' Helen asked quietly when she was certain Maggie couldn't overhear. 'I hope she's not going to be so pessimistic when Andrew and Jenny are back. They need all the positive vibes they can get.'

'She's scared to look on the bright side. Think about it – she's an orphan, she's here because her aunt and her grandfather are ill, and now Andrew's got cancer.'

'You're not telling me that she thinks she's a sort of Typhoid Mary, are you?'

'Wouldn't you, in her shoes? I've had time this summer to get to know her; she's a decent girl at heart, but a very scared one, too.'

'Now I feel awful! We've all been sympathising with Jenny because Maggie was so difficult. In never occurred to any of us to wonder why. Could you tell Jenny what you've told me?'

276

'I intend to – when she's ready to hear it. She's had a bad time, too. But Maggie's loosening up. When they first came to stay with me, Calum was so suspicious of her but she's tried hard to win him over and now he's more relaxed in her company. I'm sure the two of them are planning something together, but I don't know what it is. We'd better get a move on, Helen, they could be here soon.'

She looked round the spotless living room and sighed. 'Why can't I manage to make the manse look like this? But on the other hand, if I did, Ethan and I would only turn it back into a mess within the hour.'

'How are you feeling?'

'The same as I felt when you asked me five minutes ago. Absolutely fine.'

'I just wondered when I saw that your eyes were closed. I still think we should have waited until tomorrow to give you the chance of more rest. Chemo and radiotherapy can be exhausting.'

'Tell me about it,' Andrew said wryly. 'Been there, done that, got the T-shirt.'

'Oh, very cool, dude!'

'I used to think those flip remarks were irritating, but actually, they roll off the tongue quite pleasantly. Perhaps the therapy's turning me back into a teenager.'

'Please don't let it do that to you; one teenager in the house is enough. Look at that,' Jenny said as they passed a road sign, 'only five miles to Prior's Ford. We're nearly home!'

'And you're as keen as I am to get there. I'd rather sleep well in my own bed tonight than rest all day in Edinburgh.'

'Our own bed – wonderful! I could never live out of a suitcase. I like to have my bedtime routine with everything I need close to hand.'

'Me too,' Andrew said. 'Oh drat, there's a giveaway. I'm not turning into a teenager after all. Still the same old safe-living fuddy-duddy I was before.'

'But you're *my* old fuddy-duddy.'

He laughed, and as she drove on Jenny realised how easily they had fallen into the habit of teasing each other over the past four weeks. Perhaps it had become some sort of protection against what was happening to Andrew, and what might happen in the future.

As they neared the entrance to Tarbethill Farm Andrew sat up, looking about him.

'Look at all those stakes in the field. Victor must have got his planning permission. I'm surprised; I don't think that field's right for caravans. It'll cost him a fortune in draining and access and so on.'

'I hate to see the countryside being changed.'

'Now who's an old fuddy-duddy?'

'Guilty, and proud of it. I want it known officially that I am against change, other than clothes. Remember the Easter egg hunt? We had a lovely day in that field.'

'Yes, we did,' Andrew agreed. As they arrived in the village he said, 'And at last, we're home.'

'Until the end of September. I wish we didn't have to go back to Edinburgh.'

'One final trip, to finish off.' Andrew put a hand lightly on her arm. 'Jen, let's just take the days one at a time and enjoy being back with the kids. We'll both be here to see Calum settled in the Academy. I'd have hated to miss out on that.'

Jenny, turning the car into River Lane, nodded, privately wondering why he had made that reference to them both being there to see Calum make the move from primary school to secondary education. Did it – could it mean that he anticipated a time quite soon when such happenings would only be supervised by her, rather than both of them? A nasty, all-too-familiar hand clutched at her stomach, the fingers digging in, tightening until she began to feel she was suffocating. Forcing her lungs to drag in a deep breath, she felt the hand ease its grip slightly. Although Andrew was being incredibly positive about his prognosis she tended to seize on every remark he made, analysing it in search of a hidden meaning. 'Stop it,' she told herself sharply as she negotiated the corner that took them into Mill Walk estate.

'Oh my God!' Andrew yelped, sliding down in his seat while Jenny stared in disbelief at the great mass of coloured balloons festooning their gate and fence. A group of excited children stood on the pavement with Calum in their midst, flourishing a paper Union flag. Neighbours were gathered in small groups along the pavement while Naomi, her mouth stretched from ear to ear in a grin the size of a slice of watermelon, stood in the garden with Maggie, Marcy, Helen, Ingrid and Jinty and Jimmy McDonald.

'Drive on,' Andrew begged. 'Drive past them and back to River Lane to give me a chance to get over the shock.'

'Don't be daft, we can't just sweep past them. Sit up and smile.'

'Just don't ask me to do a Queen Mother wave. What is Calum doing with that flag?' Andrew moaned through a set smile.

'Be glad he didn't get hold of a skull and crossbones.' Jenny, rescued from her slide into worry over Andrew's earlier choice of words, banged the horn as she drove slowly past the beaming neighbours. Then they were at the gate and she was out of the car and Calum was hugging her as though he would never let go, and she was home and safe.

'This,' Andrew said sternly to Naomi when he had been

hugged fiercely by his son, more sedately by his foster-daughter, shaken hands with all his well-wishers, and finally landed in the minister's warm embrace, 'is your doing, isn't it? And you did it because you knew that all I wanted to do was to creep home without a fuss. You're a troublemaker.'

'How dare you!' She pushed him back so she could beam up into his face. 'I am a woman of the cloth and I would never arrange such a nauseating exhibition of open affection! I only came along to enjoy it. You look as fit as a fiddle.'

'I feel as fit as a fiddle.'

'Oh doodle,' Naomi said, linking her arm in his and leading him indoors, 'if I'd known how good you were going to look I wouldn't have gone to all the trouble of masterminding this welcome home shindig.'

33

When the greetings were over and the Forsyths were left on their own Calum asked his parents to sit down.

'I have something to say to you,' he announced, taking his place in the middle of the living room.

'You've not decided to forget about the Academy and get a job instead?' Andrew asked hopefully and Maggie, who had been quiet since their arrival, was startled into a giggle.

'Dad, I'm not old enough to work!'

'Sorry, I forgot. Go ahead.'

Calum cleared his throat, paused for a minute, hands clenched tightly by his side, then said slowly and clearly, *Je suis content de te voir à la maison et tu as l'air bien. Tu nous as beaucoup manqué, maman aussi. Pour compenser ton absence, nous passerons un joyeux Noël ensemble. J'espère recevoir un cochon d'Inde comme cadeau de Noël.*

There was a moment's stunned silence before Andrew began to clap, with Jenny and Maggie joining in. Calum, poppy-red, collapsed into a chair, a great whoosh of relief escaping from pursed lips.

'That was *magnifique*! When did you start speaking fluent French?'

'While you were away.' Calum tried to sound nonchalant, but his eyes were shining.

'My French is nonexistent,' Jenny admitted. 'What did you say?'

'I know exactly what he said, but why don't you tell us, Calum? In English this time.'

Calum wriggled about until he was able to drape his legs over one arm of his chair. 'I said – "Hello, Dad, it's good to see you back home again, and looking so well. We have missed you and Mum very much. We will all have a good Christmas together to make up for it. I hope to get a guinea pig for Christmas."'

'That,' Jenny said, 'is quite incredible. How did you manage to learn so much in just a few weeks?'

'Maggie helped,' Calum said, and it was Maggie's turn to go red.

'I didn't do anything.'

'She taught me how to sing "Frère Jacques",' Calum explained, 'and she played it on the manse piano and we sang it together. That's how I started learning.'

'I didn't know you played the piano, Maggie.'

'She's good at it, Mum,' Calum said proudly, oblivious of the irritated glance Maggie shot at him. 'She got lessons before, but she can't play here because we don't have a piano. She showed me how to find all the words in a dictionary she lent me, with French and English in it, and wrote down little sentences and made me find the meaning of the words in the dictionary and taught me how to say them properly.' He ran out of breath and paused to suck more in before finishing. 'It was fun.'

'Well, I think the two of you are amazing.' Jenny got up

and kissed the top of her son's head, then turned to Maggie, who gave a casual one-shouldered shrug and muttered, 'Whatever.'

'What about the guinea pig?'

'We'll see,' Andrew said. 'Christmas presents are supposed to be surprises.'

'But it's better to be surprised by something you want than by something you didn't want so much, if you know what I mean.'

'We'll see,' Andrew said again. 'But since we're on to the subject, is there anything you'd like for Christmas, Maggie?'

She hesitated, then said almost reluctantly, 'A kitten would be nice. I like Naomi's cat.'

'Duly recorded,' Andrew told her.

'Calum and Maggie seem to have grown closer while we were away,' Jenny said as she and Andrew settled into bed.

'Seems like it. I wouldn't be all surprised if Naomi isn't behind it. She's a wise woman.'

'Maggie's still quite stiff with us, though.'

'Give it time, love. It'll come.'

'I asked her how Ryan was when we were stacking the dishwasher this evening; you know, the boy she was going out with, and she gave that shrug of hers and said she'd outgrown him. Pity.' Jenny climbed into bed. 'When I met him during the Scarecrow Festival I thought he was really nice. And polite. And good-looking.'

'Hey, let the girl choose her own boyfriends. You've already chosen me, remember?'

'You don't think I'm turning into a mumsie mum, do you?'

'Heading in that direction.' Andrew got into bed and kissed her cheek before collapsing with a contented sigh on to his pillow. 'Beware, that way be dragons.'

'Are we really going to give Calum a guinea pig? And Maggie a kitten?'

'Why not? Kids should have pets.'

'It's surprising we didn't know about Maggie having piano lessons. I'm going to phone Anne tomorrow to ask her how keen Maggie was on her music. If she enjoyed it, why can't she go on having lessons here? And in order to keep up with practising—'

'She would need a piano.'

'Or we could give her one of those keyboards. They seem to be just as good from what I hear.'

'D'you really think she'd prefer that to the kitten she asked for?'

'We could get the kitten too, as a family pet. Maggie could be put in charge of looking after it.'

'Whatever,' Andrew mumbled, and fell asleep.

The Neurotic Cuckoo was filled on the evening when the period drama featuring Meredith Whitelaw was due to be shown on television and the same channel was being shown on every television set in every house in the village.

Joe and Gracie Fisher had rented a large screen for the occasion, one that Joe had taken quite a shine to when it was delivered that morning.

'It's big enough for a cinema. Don't think it's going to stay,' Gracie warned him.

'But look at this . . .' Joe switched channels. 'It's so real! You could swear those horses were going to race right out of the screen.'

'That's what I mean. Folk want to sit of an evening and have a drink and talk to each other. I don't mind having a television set in the bar, Joe, but not one that makes our customers feel as though a horse race is going to trample them under hoof at any minute.'

'It's not all horse racing.' Joe changed channels again, saying wistfully, 'It would be grand for football games.'

Gracie, trying to work how many sandwiches, nuts and bags of crisps might be needed, shot him a cold look. 'What would be grand for football,' she snapped, 'would be putting it back to Saturday afternoons with sensible players who don't earn thousands of pounds whether they win or not. It's a game, for goodness' sake, not something to make a song and dance about.'

Joe, who had heard her views hundreds of times before, sighed quietly to himself and switched channels yet again. 'There you are — a bunch of women doin' what they do best — talkin'.'

'Joe, will you give over switching channels and get that crate I asked for from the cellar?' Then glancing at the screen, Gracie said in disbelief, 'Is that a pimple she has on her cheek? And her skin looks coarse; it never did before.'

'That's cos our old set doesnae show ye anythin' in detail. We could mebbe put it into our livin' room, just for us?'

'That big thing in our wee living room? We'd have to move all the chairs against the opposite wall, and it'd frighten the life out of wee Jamie. Switch it off and get on with what's to be done if ye want to be ready for the rush tonight. That,' Gracie finished as her husband reluctantly did as he was told, 'goes back to the shop tomorrow.'

The Ralston-Kerrs asked Ginny to go to the pub with them, but she shook her head. 'I've got a wee portable set in the caravanette; I'll just watch it in there.'

'It'll be more fun with a crowd,' Lewis coaxed her, but she was adamant. She was uneasy about the play; normally Meredith Whitelaw expected her daughter to take an interest

in her career and lavish praise on her after each performance, but not this time. There must, Ginny thought as she
settled down in her snug mobile home with a cup of cocoa
and a packet of chocolate digestives, be some reason why
she had been silent this time.

When the play started she turned the sound up and sat
forward, the cocoa cooling as she waited for her mother's
appearance. The costumes were magnificent, the actors good,
the sets perfect. Only one thing was missing – Meredith
Whitelaw, former star of the popular soap opera *Bridlington
Close*. Although her name was in the opening credits, she
had still not appeared.

Ginny took a gulp of cocoa then glanced up at the screen
in time to see a raddled old crone limp on the set, mumbling
to herself and lashing out at the other actors with her cane.
It was only when the old woman tossed her head in a
familiar gesture, almost dislodging the ridiculous wig that
looked even older and more in need of restoration than its
wearer, that she recognised her mother.

'Oh my Lord!' Ginny breathed. Meredith had always had
a fixation about her appearance and would never accept a
role that made her look unattractive. Even as Imogen
Goldberg, grandmother and matriarch of a large family in
Bridlington Close she had been an elegant, smartly dressed
matriarch, giving fresh hope to hordes of tired, child-minding
grandmothers throughout the country.

What made things worse for Ginny was the fact that
beneath the deliberately overdone and garishly applied
make-up and the ghastly wig, she was seeing the old woman
her mother might well become.

In the Neurotic Cuckoo, there had been occasional calls for
the past hour of 'Is that her?' 'No, I don't think so.' 'I thought

she was one of the principal characters. Where is she?'

When the old mad woman appeared, the arguments became even more frenzied until Gracie hurried into the living room to fetch her *Radio Times*.

'The Duchess of Ravenhill is played by Meredith Whitelaw,' she announced, returning to the bar, magazine in hand. 'It's her all right.'

'I'll be blowed,' a voice said. 'She's nothin' like the woman we knew. P'raps our Meredith Whitelaw was an impostor.'

'She's an actress,' Fliss protested. 'Actors and actresses need to know how to change themselves completely. I think she's doing a magnificent job.'

There were nods of agreement, and everyone settled down and turned their attention back to the screen only to find that Meredith had gone.

'She kicked the dog and a butler led her out of the room,' a woman who had continued to watch the play told them. 'She'll probably be back in a minute.'

But to their disappointment the play ended five minutes later with no further sight of Meredith.

'Three minutes of looking at someone we didn't recognise at first wasn't worth the cost of hiring that big screen, or the bother of putting it up,' Gracie said tartly to her husband when they were closing the bar later.

'You've got to admit it brought in a lot of punters, though. We made enough tonight to more than cover the cost of the screen,' he pointed out. She continued to stand there, arms folded across her bosom, giving him a look he knew very well, until he shrugged and capitulated. 'I suppose I ought to get them to collect it tomorrow?'

'I suppose you ought,' Gracie agreed, and went off to make some supper.

34

Meredith's television appearance was the talk of the village store the next morning.

'I thought she was good,' Marcy said. 'I didn't even realise it was her at first and that shows she's a proper actress, doesn't it?'

'That's what my Steph said,' Jinty agreed. 'But I was disappointed we only saw her once, and that wasn't for long.'

'Only a bit part, really.' Cynthia McBain smirked, then scowled when someone said thoughtlessly, 'It was a pity we never saw her on our own village-hall stage, wasn't it?'

The small group of women crowding round the counter shifted uncomfortably, as Cynthia snapped, 'If you ask me, judging by last night's performance it was a blessing she let poor Kevin down the way she did last year.'

'I thought she made her mark, even though she wasn't on screen for long,' Eleanor Pearce put in.

'Really? And what did poor Kevin think?' Cynthia wanted to know.

'The same as I do,' Eleanor told her sweetly. In actual

fact, Kevin had been behaving like a child on Christmas Eve all through the previous day. As the time for the play approached he had forbidden Eleanor to work on her sewing as she usually did when listening to the radio or watching television,

'It might distract you.'

'It never has before.'

'Then it might distract me. I want us both to concentrate!'

So she had put her work aside and watched Kevin inch forward on his chair as the play progressed until he was sitting right on the edge, leaning forward, fists clenched on his knees.

'Where is she?' he kept wanting to know, and when the deranged old woman finally appeared, squawking and screeching and laying about her with her cane, he refused at first to believe it was the same glamorous Meredith Whitelaw he had known. By the time Eleanor had convinced him, Meredith was being escorted from the scene by the butler, never to return.

'Never mind,' Eleanor consoled him when the play was over, 'at least we recorded it, so you can watch it any time you want.'

'Yes,' he said unhappily, and went to bed, leaving Eleanor to drink her bedtime cocoa alone.

'I suppose,' Cynthia was saying now, 'she's reached the age where she has to take what parts she can. I'm told television cameras can be quite cruel to ageing actresses. If you ask me—'

She stopped suddenly as Ginny came into the store.

'We're just saying,' Jinty called to her, 'how good your mum was on the telly last night.'

'Wasn't she?' Ginny smiled. 'Pity it was such a short scene, though.' She had tried ringing her mother after the play, only to be told by the housekeeper that Meredith had gone abroad for a short holiday just before the play was aired. No, she hadn't said where, and although she had phoned a few times to enquire about phone calls and post, she hadn't said a birdie about when she was coming back, not a birdie.

'When you're next speaking to her tell her how much we all enjoyed her performance, will you?' Eleanor said sweetly.

'Thank you, I will.' Ginny picked up a basket and disappeared behind a shelf, while Marcy got on with the task of dealing with the queue at the checkout.

The start of a new school year meant that several of the children in Prior's Ford donned new uniforms, joined the queue at the bus stop and then drove past the primary school, some looking at the playground longingly while others scarcely gave it a glance as they headed for the 'big school'.

Calum was one of the youngsters looking forward to the new adventure. He had already begun to master French thanks to Maggie, and his dad was home and looking like his old self.

'It's harder on us than it is on them,' Helen said sadly as she, Ingrid and Jenny watched their children being borne towards a new future. The three of them had been lingering near the bus stop on the pretext of going shopping. 'Gregor was quiet this morning, and a bit pale.'

'Calum was better than I'd expected. It happens so quickly, doesn't it? One minute you're taking them to their first day at primary school and the next you're buying an Academy uniform for them.'

'Ella couldn't wait; she's hoping to get into their football team. Our mothers survived it and so will we,' Ingrid said briskly. 'Come on, let's get the shopping over.'

'Hang on a minute.' Helen, who had noticed Jenny trying to hide a sudden rush of tears, put an arm about her. 'Calum's going to be all right, Jen. You saw how excited he looked when the bus left.'

'It's not Calum.' There was a break in Jenny's voice. 'Not only him, I mean.' She sniffed back more tears and wiped a hand over her eyes. 'It's just . . . we were so happy not all that long ago, then suddenly the world just fell in on us. We had all that worry with Maggie, and I know she's getting easier but now there's Andrew, and I'm so frightened and . . .'

'It's going to be all right, we're sure of it, aren't we, Ingrid? The two of you have been fantastically brave, and Andrew looks so well.'

'But it's not *knowing!*' Jenny told the two of them passionately. 'It's living all the time on the edge of this deep dark crevasse, knowing that if I lose him I'll probably fall in and then what'll happen to the children? Why us? What have we done to deserve it?'

'Blow the shopping.' Ingrid took Jenny's arm and turned her towards River Lane. 'Let's go to my house and have coffee with whisky in it.'

Grant and Steph McDonald's schooldays had ended in July. For Grant the future looked good; four years earlier he had been signed up with Dumfries Thistle Football Club, training at their ground in the evenings. The club had offered him a full-time contract when he reached his sixteenth birthday, but after speaking to his teachers at a parents' night, Jinty had put her foot down.

'You're a clever lad and you're goin' to stay on at school. I want you to get all the education you can before you think about football full time.'

'Och, Mam, it's what I've always wanted to do! What

d'you think, Dad?' Grant appealed to his father, who put his newspaper down, blinking in surprise. Jinty made all the decisions in the McDonald family and that was the way Tom liked it.

'Tell him he's stayin' on at the Academy, Tom,' she ordered.

'He'd make good money if he left school and went to the Thistle.'

'That's not what I want you to say! Too many of those lads who get paid a fortune have no idea what to do with it other than drinkin' and womanisin', and that's not what I want for our Grant!'

'Sounds good enough to me,' Grant put in, then yelped as his mother slapped his head. 'I was only jokin'!'

'It wasn't funny. When you get to the stage of earnin' the daft money they pay footballers now – *if* you get to that stage – I want you to be able to treat it with respect.'

'The way I see it, Mam, if I was earnin' good money doin' what I love – playin' football – you wouldn't have to work so hard. It's time you had a better life.'

Jinty's eyes softened as she looked up at her handsome son. 'You're a good boy, Grant, but I've never minded workin' to give you all a decent start in life. What would I do with myself if I didn't have work to go to? Football's not like other careers. Sometimes it doesn't last long and that's why I want you to have other strings to your bow – and if you try to tell me you're a footballer and not an archer,' she added as her son opened his mouth, 'you'll get a clout on the other side of your head to match the first one. You're stayin' on at school, Grant, and that's final. Isn't it, Tom?'

'Aye, if you say so,' her husband muttered. Speaking for himself, which he didn't dare to do, he was all for Grant bringing in as much money as he could. For one thing, it would make Tom's life easier, and for another he relished the prospect of having free season tickets to all the Thistle's matches. But he knew better than to say so, and it was decided.

Grant did well at school and when he finally left he got his full-time contract.

Steph, knowing her parents couldn't afford the money needed for drama college and a career that might or might not result in her being able to earn her own living, decided to train as a nursery nurse at a college in Dumfries, while working as a checkout girl in a Kirkcudbright supermarket at the weekends.

'You sure you're not takin' on too much?' Jinty fretted.

'It's fine, Mum. I can study at nights and I'll enjoy the weekend work. I'll be meeting folk all the time. And like you said to Grant when he wanted to sign up with the Thistle when he was sixteen, it's important to have a good education and another career choice to fall back on. Anyway, I love kids. You know that. Acting can wait – I've got plenty of time and I'll get there in the end.'

'What about Miss Whitelaw? She offered to help you when she was livin' here last year. She even thought you were worth teachin'. P'raps you should write to her.'

'Och, she'll have forgotten all about me by now. And anyway, I'm not going to cadge off other folk. I'll do it on my own, in my own time.'

'You're a lassie to be proud of, Steph,' Jinty said with a slight tremor in her voice.

'I take after my mother,' Steph replied.

A week after term started an excited crocodile of children shepherded by Lynn Stacy and her staff left the primary school. They marched along the main road and into the

Crescent, turning at the Neurotic Cuckoo to walk uphill towards Linn Hall. Along the drive they went, eyes widening and fingers pointing as the house came into view. When they reached the back of the hall they found Ginny and Lewis waiting to introduce them to the kitchen garden.

Two hours flew past, during which the children toured every part of the walled area, carefully recording the names of plants in their notebooks. They played with Muffin, who was overcome with excitement at finding so many new friends, and filed into the big kitchen, wide-eyed, to eat the biscuits and juice supplied by their head teacher. They were fussed over by Fliss and Jinty and met the backpackers who had not yet moved on. Jinty managed to coax Hector from the pantry, where he was pretending to be doing the books, and he appeared long enough to smile shyly at the youngsters and say, 'Enjoying yourselves, are you? Good, good, that's the ticket!' before scuttling back to his bolt-hole. Duncan kept well out of the way, pointing out to anyone who cared to listen when the visit was announced that if he wanted to see a crowd of noisy kids all he had to do was stay at home.

As the children filed down the drive, each one carried a seedling he or she had potted under Ginny's careful guidance.

Two days later Lynn Stacy delivered a packet of letters to the hall, together with the hope that the visit might be repeated on an annual basis.

'The children loved every minute of it. Some of them have drawn pictures for you to put on the kitchen walls,' she said before hurrying back to her duties.

At the tea break, everyone crowded round the kitchen table to read the letters and admire the pictures, many of them of Muffin.

'Just as well he's so hand-knitted-looking,' Lewis said, staring at one picture made up of a scrawled brown ball with a tail. 'Most of 'em have you down to a T, old lad.'

'Who's that?' Fliss peered at a drawing of a long-legged woman with a pot in one hand and a steaming kettle in the other.

'I think it's you, Mother.'

'Really? How sweet.' After another look at the picture, Fliss added, 'I absolutely must do something about my hair.'

'Bless their little cotton socks!' Jinty cooed as she read the letters, all brimming with appreciation. 'My Faith and Norrie are still talkin' about the visit, and they're so proud of those wee plants you gave them, Ginny. They think you're magic.'

'According to these letters we're going to have all the gardeners we need in about fifteen years. You were brilliant, Ginny,' Lewis marvelled, and she flushed with pleasure.

'It was fun. Perhaps next year when the grounds are open to the public we can let children who visit take a seedling home. We could charge fifty pence a time and still make a small profit. And I'd like to have a good look at that dammed-up water at the top of the hill to see if we can do something about it.'

'So you're coming back?'

'If you want me to.'

'Absolutely,' Fliss told her warmly.

'Ginny, we couldn't do without you now. I tell you what,' Lewis said, 'I'm going to build you into the business plan for next year and see you're paid a proper wage. Would you be up for it?'

'I certainly would!'

'How long have we got you for this year?'

'Until the end of October,' Ginny said happily. 'I think

should spend some time with my mother over the winter, but I'll be back in the spring.'

Since the village had been rocked by Meredith Whitelaw's appearance on the TV, Ginny had been phoning her mother's flat once a week, always getting the same reply from the housekeeper – Meredith was enjoying her holiday abroad and had not yet decided when she was returning home. For the first time in her life Ginny was worried about her mother. It wasn't like Meredith to disappear like this; Ginny was concerned that the shame of being seen by her fans not only as an old mad woman, but an old mad woman who had been on screen for less than five minutes, had upset her badly.

It was a shock, therefore, to hear Meredith herself give her phone number in a brisk voice when she next rang.

'Mother?'

'Genevieve, darling, how lovely to hear from you. I was just about to phone you. How are things up in the wilds of Scotland? Still grubbing around in that garden?'

'Yes, and I'm returning next year. Mother, where have you been?'

'Having such a lovely time in Spain. That's what I was going to tell you.'

'I've been worried about you.'

'About me? Why on earth should you be?'

'Because you disappeared without a word after that play was shown on television and nobody seemed to know where you were. I thought you might be upset about – well, about the part you played in it.'

'Oh, that,' Meredith said dismissively. 'Not at all, it was a really interesting little cameo part, such fun to do. And I got some nice reviews. Didn't you see them?'

'I've been too busy to read reviews.'

'I'll have them photocopied and sent to you. But never mind all that, I've got the most exciting news! I've got a new television series lined up and it's going to be filmed in Spain, starting in April. I wouldn't even have known about it if I hadn't been over there,' Meredith prattled on. 'There I was, sitting by the hotel pool having a drink, when who should spot me but Oliver Donovan!'

'Who?'

'The man who used to be producer on *Bridlington Close* in the early days. If Oliver had still been there my character would never have been killed off. He told me so himself; said that Imogen had been the very core of that soap and it hasn't been the same since. Not that I would know since I don't watch it. Incidentally, he congratulated me on my part in the costume drama. But the thing is, he was over there on business, looking for settings for a new series he's planning about expats living in Spain. One thing led to another and I'm going to be in it. Isn't it thrilling?'

'What sort of part?' Ginny asked cautiously.

'A lead, of course. I've seen the first scripts, and I'd say that I'm *the* lead. Imogen Goldberg stepping out of the shower, as Oliver put it. Alex Weir and I are playing husband and wife. I've always wanted to play opposite Alex Weir,' Meredith said happily. 'Just think of it, Genevieve, months and months of lovely sun and I'm being paid lots of money too. How lucky is that? Oh – by the way, do pass on my news to all my darling fans in that sleepy little village you've become so fond of.'

35

Andrew Forsyth went into hospital during the last week of September for his operation. As before, Jenny went with him and Calum and Maggie moved back to the manse.

The two of them were subdued and anxious, but on the third day of their stay Naomi met them at the door when they arrived back from school, her round face wreathed in smiles.

'Jenny phoned half an hour ago to say Andrew had a scan earlier, and the treatment he had last time has worked. The tumour's shrunk even more than they'd hoped.'

'What does that mean?' Calum asked nervously.

'It means the therapy's done exactly what they wanted it to and that will make the operation much easier.'

'So he'll be all right?' The boy's face lit up, then dimmed as Maggie said, 'That's not definite, is it?'

'Not entirely, but at least there's a better chance of it. Your mum sounded really happy when she phoned,' Naomi told Calum, 'and she says your dad can't wait to get the operation over with and get home soon.'

She glanced at Ethan, who took his cue. 'Coming to play football, Calum?'

'I think I'll work on some French first,' the boy said, heading upstairs.

'OK if I play the piano for a bit?' Maggie asked.

'Of course. Macaroni cheese and chips for dinner,' Naomi said to their backs as they both hurried off.

Wilfred McIntyre stumped up the farm lane and went towards the barn and the sound of hammering to find Bert McNair working on a piece of metal.

'Aye, Bert.'

'Aye, Wilfred.' Bert nodded towards his former employee, hefting the hammer in his hand. 'Damned gate in the top field got a bump from the tractor the other day and now it's hangin' wrong. I reckon the hinge just needs puttin' back into place.'

Wilfred studied the hinge. 'Looks as if you've got it about right. Need a hand with the gate?'

'If ye've got nothin' better tae do.'

'I've never got anythin' better tae do these days,' Wilfred said as they left the barn, the two dogs trotting at their master's heels. 'Ye've not got beasts in the top field, then?'

'Not right now, but the sheep'll be goin' in there soon.'

'I was thinkin',' Wilfred said as they climbed up towards the top field, 'maybe you could do wi' a hand round the farm, Bert.'

'Oh aye? Got anyone in mind, then?'

'I might be seventy-three next birthday, but I'm still as fit as a youngster.'

Bert gave the other man a sidelong look. Wilfred wasn't tall, but he was broad, with a muscular torso and limbs and spade-like hands that could, when necessary, deal with a ficult cow or hold a newborn lamb safe. Even what ould be seen of his bushy white hair, springing out from beneath his cap, gave the impression of vigour. Wilfred was never seen without his cap, and it was rumoured that he even wore it while sleeping. If asked about this, his wife, Maisie, also full of energy at the age of seventy, always replied, 'D'ye think I'd let the man keep a dirty cap on day an' night? He's got four, all the same.' Which didn't answer the question.

'I don't doubt ye, Wilfred,' Bert said now. 'Is this you askin' for your job back?'

'Part-time just. Three or four days a week. I've got intae the way o' doin' gardens for some o' the neighbours and I'd not want tae let them down.'

'An' what would Maisie have tae say if I got ye back here' wi' me?'

'It's like this, Bert. Me an' Maisie never believed in divorce, but that was when I was workin' an' out of the house all day. Now things are different I think we're both beginnin' tae change our minds. An' you could probably dae wi' an extra pair o' hands now Victor's turned intae a townie.'

'That's a terrible business, Wilfred – terrible. It's upset Jess no end.'

'I'm no' surprised. But even as a wee laddie Victor was never bothered about the place. Not like Ewan at all. I mind *him* helpin' me when he was no higher than one of thae dogs. Mind the time we found him eatin' the scrapin's from the hen houses?' Wilfred gave a deep chuckle. 'Neither up nor down after it, too. I knew then that he was a born farmer, and I've been proved right.'

'He didnae put ye up tae this, did he?'

'O' course no'!' Wilfred lied indignantly. 'Everyone knows Victor's deserted ye, and that you an' Ewan an' yer missus

cannae run the place on yer own, no' wi' winter co⸱
in, an' the animals needin' tae be brought from the fiel⸱

Bert nodded, then said, 'Wilfred, I cannae afford tae pa⸱
ye, man.'

'Ach, me an' Maisie manage fine on our pensions, and
she was always good at makin' a pound go a long way. I'd
settle for Jess's midday dinners; she's a grand cook, though
I'd never dare tae say so in front o' my Maisie. So what
d'ye say?'

Bert hesitated, then spat on the palm of his hand and
held it out. 'Done.'

'Good,' Bert responded, and they gave each other a hand-
shake that would have crushed the fingers of most men.
'Now then, let's get that gate hung!'

Maggie's stomach churned non-stop throughout the day
Andrew went through his operation. Naomi had insisted
that she and Calum attend school as usual rather than wait
and wonder at home, but Maggie sat through each class
without seeing or hearing anything. She couldn't eat her
lunch and kept to herself during the breaks.

Once again she was faced with a 'what if' situation.
What if Andrew died? Would she be expected to stay on
with Jenny and Calum, or would they want to be left on
their own? If they didn't want her, could she go back to
her grandparents? Did she want to do that, if it were
possible?

She had become used to Prior's Ford without realising
it. Freya was now her best friend, and she liked the Academy.
She was almost old enough to be independent but she
wasn't ready for that – not yet. She needed to be with
people she knew. She needed to feel safe.

Perhaps Naomi might let her stay at the manse. She chewed

er fingernails and found herself making promises she ght not be able to keep: if Andrew got better she would y much harder to be the sort of daughter Jenny wanted; ney would go girly shopping together; she would take the furry toys out of her cupboard and let them live on her bed. No, that was too much! Not the furry toys!

There was still no news when she and Calum arrived back at the manse.

'That's only to be expected,' Naomi said swiftly as she saw the colour ebb from Maggie's face. 'He was down for an early-afternoon operation and these things take quite a long time. Jenny'll phone as soon as she has news.'

Maggie, Calum and Ethan were watching television in the early evening when the phone rang. The three of them jumped and looked at each other uncertainly as the ringing stopped.

'Naomi's answered it in the study,' Ethan said, and the room became so silent that when Calum swallowed, the sound seemed to ring out.

No more than three minutes passed before Naomi came to them, but it seemed, to Maggie, like an eternity.

'It's all right, Calum; your dad's through his operation and doing well. Your mum wants to speak to you on the phone in the study.'

'Is he really all right?' Maggie asked when Calum had bolted from the room.

'As all right as he can be right after major surgery. Jenny says the surgeon was pleased, and that means a lot. She wants to speak to you when Calum's had his turn.'

'To me?' Maggie was taken aback. 'Why?'

'Why not?' Naomi asked.

Calum reappeared, beaming. 'Mum wants to talk to you, Maggie.'

Maggie didn't realise her hands were sweating unt. telephone receiver almost slipped out of them and lan on the floor. She tightened her grip just in time.

'Hello?'

Jenny's voice almost sang down the phone. 'Maggie? He's awake and talking already and the surgeon's really pleased with him. They said the tumour had shrunk so much they could scarcely see it and they think it all went very well indeed. Calum's too young to hear those details, but I wanted to tell you.'

'Oh, right. That's good.'

'Is everything OK there?'

'Yes, fine.'

'He'll be in hospital for another two weeks at least, and Naomi says she'll bring the two of you over to stay the weekend after next so you can visit him, then she'll fetch you on the Sunday. Not this weekend, because Andrew's got tubes all over the place and we don't want Calum to see him like that.'

'Right. Jenny?'

'What is it, love?'

'I don't like furry toys. D'you mind that?'

'Of course not. They'll go to a charity shop as soon as we get home.'

Jenny had wanted to tell her the important things she couldn't tell Calum, Maggie thought as she put the receiver back on its cradle. She had treated Maggie like an adult, and like a daughter. And she had understood at once about the fluffy toys.

When Maggie didn't return from the study Naomi waited for twenty minutes before going to the kitchen to make cocoa. She gave the boys theirs and then took two mugs

s on a tray and tapped on Maggie's door. 'Cocoa
marshmallows.'

Maggie opened the door, then climbed back on to the
ed with her cocoa.

'Are you all right?'

'I don't know. I feel . . .' the girl hesitated. 'I feel strange.'

'Ill strange?'

'No, more like different strange. It started right after I
finished talking to Jenny. She said she wanted to tell me
things she couldn't tell Calum because he's too young.'

'What she said didn't upset you, did it?'

'No of course not. It just made me feel . . . strange.'

Naomi looked closely at the girl. 'You look . . . strange.'

'I'm not ill!' Maggie was suddenly worried.

'I didn't say you looked ill.' Naomi settled herself into a
chair and took a mouthful of cocoa. 'I think you're suffering
from a sudden bout of happiness.'

'What?'

'Think hard and then tell me honestly, Maggie, when
were you last really, genuinely happy?'

'Well, I . . . when . . .' Maggie stopped and stared into her
cocoa, reaching back in her mind. Finally she said, 'Perhaps
it was the time I won an essay competition for all the schools
in the area, and my gran and granda went with me to the
prize giving in Dundee University.' She gave Naomi a radiant
smile. 'It was fantastic, and they were so proud of me!'

'Hold old were you?'

'Thirteen.'

'And how old are you now?'

'Fifteen and a half.'

'That's a long time between bouts of happiness,' Naomi
said gently. 'I take it your grandfather fell ill not long after
you won the essay prize.'

Maggie nodded, her eyes clouding.

'Do you remember the day you found out about Andre...
cancer, and you came to the manse for tea? We had a tal...
you and I, and I said you needed to take control of your
own life and deal with whatever happened instead of letting
it make you feel guilty and responsible. Well, you've done
it. You could have fled back to Dundee when Andrew took
ill, back to your old life, but you stayed here and took control
of what was happening. I know how hard you've worked
to win Calum's trust, and by being here for him you won
Jenny's trust and her gratitude, and that's why she wanted
to have a special word with you tonight. After all, you're
more than a stepdaughter now as far as she and Andrew
are concerned; you're the daughter Jenny always wanted.'
Naomi stood up and took the full mug from Maggie. 'It's
got a skin on top, I'll make fresh.'

'It's OK.'

'Coming downstairs for supper?'

'In a little while.'

For a long time after Naomi left, Maggie sat on the bed,
arms hugging her knees. The strange feeling grew inside,
warming her, strengthening her, until it reached her face
and materialised as a broad smile.

It looked as though life in Prior's Ford was going to be
all right after all.

Read on for a sample of the next book in the
Prior's Ford series, *Scandal in Prior's Ford*,
out now from Sphere.

Life-long vendettas aren't always confined to Sicilian families, and Ivy McGowan and Doris Thatcher, the two oldest
residents in the pretty village of Prior's Ford, could have
taught the Sicilian godfathers a thing or two when it came
to nursing a grudge.

Needless to say, the grudge was over a man. Until Norman
Cockburn arrived in the village, Ivy and Doreen had been
close friends from childhood; they had played with each
other as toddlers, gone through their school years together
and were in domestic service at Linn Hall, home of the
Ralston-Kerrs, when Norman joined the team of gardeners
who tended the estate. That was the day Ivy and Doris fell
out of friendship and into love.

A cheerful young man who enjoyed feminine company,
Norman rather enjoyed their attentions. Ivy had a quick,
sometimes sharp tongue but she was also very pretty, while
Doris was quite plain but with a sweet and biddable nature.
They vied openly for his company and longed secretly for
his proposal, each feeling that snatching the prize away from
her rival would be sweet indeed. But Norman had some
living to do before settling down, and when war was declared

39 he was one of the first to enlist, leaving his sweet-
ts a passionate goodbye kiss each, but no promises.

A year later he was married. It was a shotgun wedding
ɔ the sister of a fellow soldier who had taken Norman to
his home when they were both on leave. The only war
wound Norman received came from that Dundee shotgun
. . . he survived the war and in 1945 returned to Prior's
Ford with his wife and their four-year-old son. By the time
he returned Ivy was married to a farm hand and Doris to
a joiner. Some thought that their mutual disappointment at
losing Norman might have drawn them close again, but if
anything they grew further apart, with Ivy becoming bitter
over the fact that Doris's husband could afford to buy a nice
little cottage by the river, near to where the council housing
estate was built after the war, while Ivy and her man lived
in a small and fairly uncomfortable tied farm cottage.

Norman became head gardener at Linn Hall and over
the next eighteen years, during which time he and his wife
produced another six children and the Ralston-Hall's
fortunes began to shrink, the only gardener.

Meanwhile, Ivy and Doris carried their feud to the
Women's Rural Institute, where the other members grew
tired of their determination to outdo each other in every
competition, and to the Horticultural Society, where every
year they clashed in the best flower arrangement, the tallest
sunflower, and the best fruit and vegetable entries. Oddly
enough, they both got on quite well with Norman's wife.

Widowed, and marching with clenched fists and set lips
into old age, they set up a competition to become the
village's oldest inhabitant. Ivy, the elder by three months and
ten days, had the edge, but Doris made no secret of her
hope to see Ivy off and make the oldest crown her own.

The feud finally ended in February of 2007, when Doris

was carried off by a bout of influenza that developed into pneumonia, leaving Ivy triumphant and the sole survivor of the love story, since both Norman and his wife had died in the late 1990s. Most of their offspring had moved abroad and only one daughter, Jinty, still lived in Prior's Ford. Jinty, very much her mother's daughter, had married a charmer, Tom McDonald, and given birth to seven children.

Since Doris's only child, a daughter, lived in New Zealand and was in poor health, she was unable to be present at her mother's funeral, attended by the entire village and many people from the surrounding area. Ivy set herself up as chief mourner, pointing out that she had known Doris for longer than anyone else in the church.

'And fought with her for most of that time,' someone murmured as Ivy hobbled down the aisle to take her seat in a front pew. 'Surely it's not right that she can be enemy and chief mourner?'

'If you want to challenge her go ahead,' her friend whispered. 'I'd not want to take her on. She's got a tongue like a cheese knife, that one. Pity Doris went first, she was always such a pleasant old lady.'

When Naomi Hennessey, the local minister, spoke of Doris's sweet nature, Ivy gave a sniff that echoed round the church. Naomi smiled down at her.

'It's fitting that at as we mourn Doris's passing we have with us someone who knew Doris throughout her life.' Her rich voice seemed filled as always with the warmth and bright colours of her Jamaican mother's homeland, and touched everyone present like a blessing. 'Our thoughts on this sad day encompass Ivy as well as Doris, for this must be a sad day for her . . . the end of an era.'

Ivy's head jerked up and she glared at the minister. Naomi replied with a loving smile that shamed the old woman nto turning the planned sniff into a gusty sigh. But as she led the mourners from the church, she was hard put to it to hide the satisfied smirk twitching at the corners of her mouth. It had bee a hard and long-fought battle, but from now until the day of her own death, she was safely, and undoubtedly, the village's older resident.

Doris's daughter arranged for her mother's furniture to be disposed of at an auction held in the village hall. Again, Ivy was in the forefront, running a critical eye over each lot, and making disparaging remarks.

Finally everything was sold and the proceeds sent to Doris's daughter. A 'For Sale' notice went up in the front garden of the little cottage by the river and the inhabitants of Prior's Ford settle back into their usual routines, unaware of the strange events looking ahead.

The person who bought Doris's wardrobe was very content with it. It was old, but roomy and well preserved and it looked good in its new home. The new owner put hangers in the wardrobe section and began to check the drawers. A deep drawer running the length of the wardrobe promised to be useful; kneeling down, the successful bidder reached into the back to assess the space available then frowned as the back of a hand caught on something sticking down from above.

Fingers probed and fumbled, then pulled, and there was a gasp of surprise as there was a muffled click and the shelf or whatever it was dropped down, releasing something that had been hidden there for years.

And, unfortunately for many local people, was hidden no longer.